Beneath it All

Tori Madison

Text copyright © 2014 by Tori Madison
Print Edition
All Rights Reserved

This book or any portion thereof may not be reproduced or used in any manner whatsoever without the express written consent and permission of the author except for the use of brief quotes by a reviewer in a book review.

This is a work of fiction; however, some of the experiences related directly to the main character's breast cancer were drawn from the author's own experiences. Names, characters, places, and incidents either are products of the author's imagination or are used fictitiously. Any resemblance to actual events, locales or persons, living or dead, is entirely coincidental.

The author is using a pen name; this is not a personal autobiography.

Edited by: Amanda Krause
Cover Image: Shutterstock, Inc.
Image Number: 52668643
Order Number: 17689022
Cover Design: Tori Madison

Table of Contents

Dedication	v
Chapter One – I AM BEAUTIFUL	1
Chapter Two – I AM WONDERFUL	24
Chapter Three – I AM BRAVE	42
Chapter Four – I AM COURAGEOUS	61
Chapter Five – I AM INDESTRUCTIBLE	89
Chapter Six – I AM FEARLESS	117
Chapter Seven – I AM UNAFRAID	144
Chapter Eight – I AM SPECIAL	169
Chapter Nine – I AM LOVED	192
Chapter Ten – I AM STRONG	212
Chapter Eleven – I AM CAPABLE	245
Chapter Twelve – I AM MIGHTY	267
Chapter Thirteen – I AM POWERFUL	286
Chapter Fourteen – I AM NOTHING	307
Chapter Fifteen – I AM BROKEN	330
Chapter Sixteen – I AM INVINCIBLE	355
Chapter Seventeen – I AM GOOD	372
Acknowledgments	388
About the Author	393
Contact Tori	394

Dedication

To my husband and daughters . . .
This book wouldn't have happened without you and your constant love and support. Let's not forget doing the dishes, cooking, laundry, driving the girls to dance, and disappearing for hours to give me some quiet time to write. You have stood by my side through it all and never complained. I love you all very much and couldn't have asked for
better co-survivors!

To my special angels in heaven P, J, and L . . .
You told me to "keep living the dream," and I'm trying on your behalf. I love and miss you every day!

To my breast cancer friends (BCFs) . . .
This group of amazing survivors has played an important part in my life in figuring out who I am "after" cancer. I love and adore each one of you and the impact you have made on my life and the lives of woman all over the world with your positive energy and love!

Chapter One
I AM BEAUTIFUL

"I'll get us checked in," Noah said as he held my hand in the town car that had been hired to take us to the Plaza Hotel in New York City. "Then I need to head down to the conference suites and meet with a few of the partners to discuss the breakout session I'm leading on Saturday."

"No worries, I could use a little down time actually. No need to rush on my account," I said as I snuggled into my husband's side; his dark sandy blonde locks tickled my forehead as I laid my head on his broad shoulder. It was a perfect fit.

We had just arrived in New York for a law conference Noah was to be a panelist for. He was known as the golden boy of his law firm, a bad-ass in the courtroom who was quickly becoming a highly respected attorney in Minneapolis.

"I shouldn't be too long. We need to be down

for dinner by seven o'clock with the partners and their wives. I'll need a shower before we go," he said while looking through messages on his phone with his other hand. He could multitask like no other.

Looking out the window, I took in the sights of the city as we drove along Central Park. New York was constantly moving; people were always in motion and minds were constantly going. I saw a gentleman walking briskly while adjusting his tie, which sparked my memory. "What tie are you wearing tonight? I'm not sure what dress I should wear to dinner, and I'd like to coordinate."

"I was planning to wear my red one. But why don't you just lay out your dresses on the bed, and I'll help you decide when I get back." I could hear the devilish smile in his voice, and it was confirmed when I looked up into the most intense, mischievously lit-up blue eyes.

"Well, you better hurry then. We don't want to keep the partners waiting, and I'm pretty sure it won't be a quick selection process," I replied as my heart rate sped up. Noah was all business on the outside, but I knew what lay underneath that façade. It was the mystery of who he was in college that grabbed my attention, and he was a temptation I couldn't resist.

Noah was the only child of a very prominent couple in Chicago. While he lived an exceptional childhood and never wanted for anything, expectations were always high. He had been at the top of his class, and failure was not an option. With a judge for a father and a law editor for a mother, he had been raised mostly by nannies and attended a strict Catholic school.

They were less than enthusiastic when Noah announced we were getting married shortly after graduation. "You're being irresponsible" and "you'll regret this decision," were the only acknowledgments they gave us, passed on by way of their assistants.

We pulled up in front of the Plaza and the sheer size and grandeur took my breath away. Noah stepped out of the car first, and I followed close behind. Apparently I followed a little too close, as my left breast bumped up against his elbow as I stepped out.

Ouch!

A sharp pain, followed by a slow burning sensation, startled me. Apparently my breasts were a little more sensitive today since my period was due. It was quickly forgotten as the doormen began greeting us the moment my foot hit the pavement. Noah guided me up the signature red-carpeted steps, through the revolving door, and into the lobby. I felt like royalty.

"Why don't you take a seat, and I'll go check us in?" Noah nodded toward the vast sitting area.

I sank into an oversized chair in a most unladylike fashion and blocked out everything around me other than the beauty of the lobby. Surrounded in timeless sophistication, I took notice of several large crystal chandeliers sparkling above and the marble floor below shimmering like a sheet of ice. Leaning my head back against the chair, I gazed up at the gold-framed ceiling. Everything was done to perfection.

As a child, I enjoyed art and design. My adoptive mom, Mary, was a respected artist and floral designer and had several prestigious clients. Her work was on display and featured in several local magazines, so it was safe to say design was a passion of mine after having been surrounded by it growing up.

After working two jobs while Noah was in law school, I was finally able to follow my dreams and enroll in an interior design program. I now worked as a member of the American Society of Interior Designers, I owned my own design firm, and often I traveled with Noah on business trips to look for design inspiration around the country.

"Come on, sleepyhead. Let's go check out our room; I think you'll be pleased," Noah whispered. I must have closed my eyes and was starting to drift off when he approached. Taking my hand, he helped me up and placed a soft kiss on my temple before wrapping his arm around my waist and leading me toward the elevator bank.

We followed the bellman up to the twelfth floor to one of the Rose Suites. Noah nodded for me to enter the room first; he was always the gentleman. It was beautiful with warm gold, crisp white, and soft brown colors. A crystal chandelier glistened above, inviting me in further. I was instantly lost in its beauty.

Gold curtains framed the large windows and beaux arts–inspired décor carried the classic feel of years gone by. The refined style carried throughout the room. A large king-size bed was covered in white and gold Italian linens and an ornate desk sat in front of the window overlooking Central Park. It was a designer's dream.

"Thank you," I heard Noah say to the bellman as he exited the room with what I was sure was a hefty tip. Noah never did anything small, a trait he got from his very proper and often pretentious father. He walked over and wrapped his arms tightly around my waist. "I hope you like it. The front desk offered us an upgrade."

"It's stunning. Thank you." I laid my head back against his shoulder, feeling his muscles flex as he tightened his hold. "I'm going to take a shower and relax for a bit while you're downstairs."

He gave me a kiss on the top of my head before letting me go. "Sounds like a good plan. I should get down to the conference floor, but I'll be back in a few hours. Enjoy..." Noah reached for his briefcase, gave me another kiss—this time on the lips—and left.

Once the door to our suite closed behind Noah, I grabbed my cosmetic bag and hurried into the bathroom to turn on the shower to let it warm up. This wasn't your average bathroom. The tile work was magnificent, with gold leaf designs on the floor and walls. The 24-carat gold–plated faucets were a work of art in and of themselves, not to mention the smooth marble vanity.

I placed my things on the vanity, stripped off my clothes, and stepped into the shower, letting the hot water cascade across my muscles. I grabbed the shampoo and began to work up a thick lather. I'd been feeling a bit sluggish lately, and it was nice to have a break from the office. I had been working around the clock on a major remodeling project; it had finally just wrapped up.

After rinsing my hair, I reached for the shower gel and started to wash my body when I recalled the pain I'd felt earlier. Breast self-exams were important, but regretfully, I forgot more times than I remembered. Moving my hand to my left breast, I instantly found the tender spot again. I still couldn't believe how it had caught my attention like it did.

The area felt hard, like a misshapen marble—a small but very sensitive marble. Someone once told me that if a lump was painful it wasn't cancer, so I dismissed it as such. I would call my doctor when I returned home, just to be safe. I had a history of fibroids, and I was sure it was another one. Why should I panic when it was most likely nothing?

Stepping out of the shower, I quickly dried off and wrapped myself in the fluffy robe that hung on the back of the door. I have a thing for robes, and this one looked amazing. It was a rich cream color, and when I pulled it on, I felt like I was wrapped in one of those soft newborn baby blankets.

I pulled a brush through my long brown hair and let it air dry while I studied my face in the mirror. My skin still had a touch of a golden tan from the summer sun and didn't need much makeup. I chose to apply a neutral shadow and mascara to my dark chocolate brown eyes and then swiped a layer of pink tinted gloss on my full lips and was done. Simple and elegant was my style, and, thankfully, it didn't take much to achieve it. I wasn't a woman who fussed over my looks.

Settling into one of the gold-upholstered chairs, I checked my phone and noticed that I had a missed call from my best friend, Jen. *Dammit!* Our Friday gossip sessions had been a tradition since before I got married ten years ago, and it would be a travesty to miss that conversation.

Jen and I had been best friends since junior high. We supported each other through breakups, bad grades, and, as we got older, the curve balls that life had thrown at each of us. Every brunette needs a blonde friend, and she was mine.

"What's up, love?" Jen asked in the singsong way

that always made me smile.

"I should be asking you that question," I shot back at her, "What happened to you Monday night? One minute we were celebrating a Vikings touchdown and the next you were flirting with Mr. Panty-Dropper at the end of the bar. Then you mysteriously disappeared. Did you seriously think I wouldn't notice, or better yet, know what you were doing? When are you going to get off the singles train and join the real world?"

"Never—it's too much fun. By the way, I'm still pissed that you got off it before it even left the station. 'Oh Noah' this and 'Oh Noah' that. He had you whipped from the moment you saw him," she made a gagging sound, which made me laugh.

"Yeah, yeah, yeah . . . I know, don't dish it if you can't take it. So, what do you have for me? I need some down-and-dirty gossip, so spill."

After thirty amazing minutes of naughty stories, giggles, and gasps, I noticed the time. I needed to start getting ready for dinner. Before I hung up, I briefly mentioned to her that I had bumped my breast and it was really tender.

"What the hell, Victoria! You choose to bring this up now? Please tell me you called the hotel staff and asked them to find a physician right the fuck now!" she snapped.

I took a deep breath. "I'm thirty-two years old, and it's probably just that I'm getting my period or another fibroid. You know I have a history of them, and that is most likely what it is. Don't get your panties in a bunch. I'll call when I get home on Monday."

"If you aren't going to get it checked there, I'm scheduling an appointment for you on Tuesday. This isn't something to mess around with; quit acting like it's nothing. I don't care how old you are or if your period makes your boobs mysteriously produce a lump, you're getting this shit checked out immediately. That's final and not up for discussion."

I gave into her demands and agreed to let her schedule an appointment for me. She insisted on going with me, but I knew it was her way of making sure I actually went. I was not a child, and I could go to a silly doctor's appointment by myself, so I declined her offer. Jen had mastered the art of a first-class guilt trip, and I was not in the mood to go on that excursion.

A few hours later, I was seated at dinner next to Noah and Shannon, the wife of one of Noah's partners. The décor was elegant and rich, with dark wood and deep burgundy and gold chairs and benches. "Palladio" by Silent Nick was playing through the speakers and made me smile to myself. It reminded me of the diamond commercial every time I heard it. *Diamonds . . . a girl's best friend.*

"So I'm thinking that we need to start over completely," Shannon said with a sigh of defeat. "I want to get rid of the dining room set we bought after our wedding and change the color scheme entirely."

"That room gets some amazing natural light; we could use some deep reds, browns, or burnt oranges to give it a rich feel. Let me see what I can pull together for colors. Your old pieces are very classic, but dated. I think we could still keep with the classic feel and just freshen it up a bit with a few new pieces."

"Oh, I like the sound of that. I've always wanted to do more with color. Can we schedule some time to review your ideas when we get home? You can start working on your—"

"Victoria, did you know that Tina Greene is

having a baby?" Stacey, the wife of one of Noah's partners, rudely interrupted.

"No, Stacey, I wasn't aware of that, but thank you for letting me know," I replied curtly before turning my attention back to Shannon.

"You and Tina are close in age, and it got me wondering when you and Noah are planning to start a family?" Stacey asked point blank. "You know the clock is ticking—tick, tick, tick."

Feeling my shoulders starting to tense up, I turned back toward Stacey, making sure to speak softly. I didn't want to make a scene but rather make a point instead. "Do you mind? I'm in the midst of a conversation with a friend, and my biological clock is none of your business, but thanks for your misplaced concern."

As the late twenty-something trophy wife of one of the senior partners at the firm, she was hungry for attention. She was a petite bleached-blonde woman with several physical "enhancements" and boasted the manners of a two-year-old. She dressed like a high-class call girl and frequently had men staring, and you could tell she thoroughly enjoyed it. The woman made my skin crawl, and it was no secret that I didn't like her.

Noah sensed my discomfort and promptly ended his conversation with one of his law partners before turning his attention to the issue at hand. "Stacey, while we appreciate your concern, Victoria and I are quite happy, and when the time is right, we will be thrilled." He gave my knee a squeeze, letting me know it was taken care of as far as he was concerned.

I was still a bit tense after the confrontation and was ready to leave. To my relief, Noah leaned over and whispered in my ear, "You look beat—are you ready to call it a night?"

"Yes, I am. Thank you for noticing. I was doing okay until Stacey cut in. Why do I let her get to me like that?" I shrugged in frustration.

"Just ignore her," he responded before politely excusing us for the evening and telling his partners that he would meet them for coffee in the morning.

Noah placed his hand at the small of my back while guiding me out of the restaurant. He ran a soft kiss over my temple. "I wasn't in the mood for her intrusion either. However, it does make me want to take advantage of the opportunity to practice." How did he do that? After ten years of marriage, he still made my heart race with a simple comment, and in that moment, I knew he planned to practice a lot that night.

We had a very active sex life; you could say it was part of our routine, and it was important to our marriage. It was a way for him to release the stress of the day and for us to connect. When he was working on high-profile cases, I could expect a few hours of interrupted sleep when he got home late. He'd been known to wake me up at one in the morning after working an eighteen-hour day—not that I'd ever complain.

Noah had his arms wrapped around my waist as we waited for the elevator. I eased back into his arms and rested my head back against his shoulder as he started placing kisses along my neck. "I've been dying to know what is under this dress. Is it something I want to slowly peel off of you, rip off you, or maybe, just maybe, you're bare? I've been curious all night, and I don't know if I can wait much longer." He flexed his hips into my backside and I felt his arousal thick and hard against me. I gasped as the elevator doors opened and a group of laughing people exited.

Noah guided me forward and released me. I moved back to the corner as he pushed the button to close the doors. He wasn't about to allow anyone the chance to try and catch this elevator. When he turned, he looked like a lion stalking his prey. He took two strides toward me and crashed his lips onto mine. He consumed me with his kiss, as he ran his tongue along my bottom lip before gently tugging at it with his teeth: "Open for me."

I parted my lips, giving him permission to take what was his, and he did. Our kiss deepened and heated quickly. He firmly held my arms in place at my side, and I found myself wrapping my right leg around him, pulling his body closer to mine. A soft moan escaped my throat as I started to rub against him.

The sound of a gentleman clearing his throat quickly got our attention, and Noah stepped away, buttoning his jacket in an attempt to cover his very prominent arousal. Blushing, I quickly smoothed down my dress as Noah turned toward the older man with a smirk. "Please forgive me. I can't seem to control myself when I'm confined to small spaces with my wife."

Noah escorted me out of the elevator, appearing in control, always in control, and nodded his head to the man as we passed. When the elevator door closed, I burst out laughing. "I can't believe you said that to him."

"What did you expect?" Noah quickly scooped me up over his shoulder as if he were a caveman and headed toward our room. "Can't fault a guy for being honest, and right now I need to know what's under this dress."

I gave him a swat on his firm ass, which was now clearly in my view. "How are you able to hold it together with a straight face like that? Law school definitely taught you how to act proper, when I know deep down you are anything but."

He smacked my ass in return. "We both know you enjoyed it as much as I did, and I must say you did a great job of keeping your cool until the doors closed." We arrived at our room, and the damned key card wouldn't work. What I wouldn't give for a good old-fashioned key. The blood was starting to rush to my head, and I needed him to put me down.

Finally, on the third try, the green light flickered and Noah pushed through the door like he was the Incredible Hulk and tossed me onto the bed. I was in a fit of giggles until I looked up and saw my husband untying his tie with a look of pure hunger in his eyes. Suddenly frozen in place, I watched him undress slowly. He unbuttoned his shirt one button at a time, and I swear a pot of water would have boiled faster than this... but I was not about to look away.

My husband was tall, well built, sexy as hell, and all mine. Now standing in just his boxer shorts, he leaned down, grabbing my left foot and feathering kisses on the top as he carefully removed my shoe. "The things you do to me, Victoria," he said before he repeated his actions on my other foot, never breaking eye contact.

Desire burned deeper in his eyes as I felt his hands begin to run up the inside of my legs. "You're pure temptation." My skin started to tingle as his fingers glided up higher and higher until he reached the apex of my thighs and a ragged breath left his lips.

His eyes darted down to where the skirt of my dress was now pushed up, and, before I could process what was happening, he swiftly found the zipper and proceeded to slide the dress off me before discarding it on the floor.

"Fuck, you're beautiful," he growled. The look on his face was savage as he regarded the small black lace panties I was wearing. They had threads of silver woven into them and barely covered me. He bent down and ran his fingers, and then his tongue, along the waistband. As he looked up at me with fiery eyes, I suddenly felt the warmth of his breath dance across my skin. "You're sexy as sin, and you have no idea what I want to do to you right now."

I let out a loud gasp and felt my body shiver because he had no idea what was awaiting him under my panties. Before we left for New York, I decided against my usual bikini wax and opted for the full Brazilian. Yep, he was going to freak the hell out and I was going to enjoy every second of it. I did my best to hide my expression, but he could sense that I was holding something back.

"What's that look for?" he inquired, as he circled his tongue around my naval. I felt his hot breath glide across my skin and let out a small laugh. He now had a sexy smirk on his face and took this opportunity to lightly tickle me. He knew what he was doing as I started wiggling and squealing as he continued his game.

"Stop. Stop. Stop. I give up. You win," I panted as I tried to catch my breath.

"What do I win?" he challenged.

I pushed him off of me and stood with my back to him. Looking over my shoulder, I said, "Sit down on the edge of the bed and don't move." As I heard the words leave my mouth, I panicked slightly. I had never been the one in charge. *Shit.* I was now.

He did as I asked, and I felt his eyes burning through the scrap of lace covering my ass. Bending down, I slowly slipped my panties down my thighs, looking back around my side to see his face. Pulling off the seductive act was not my specialty, but I must have been succeeding; I could see his length straining to stay contained in his boxers.

I stood up slowly and swept my long hair over one shoulder. Taking my time pivoting around, I locked my eyes on his and didn't break contact until I was completely facing him. I bit my lip in nervous anticipation of what he would think.

He dropped his gaze, his eyes moving slowly down my body, and I knew the moment his eyes reached my surprise. I noticed his muscles tensing as he swallowed harshly and shot off the bed toward me in three short strides. "Oh, fuck," he said as he dropped to his knees in front of me. "The life insurance policy is in the safe in my office, because dammit, woman, you might just kill me tonight."

He slowly nudged my thighs apart and ran his nose down my smooth, sensitive skin. A moan of appreciation slipped through his lips as his fingers found their way to my folds. "You have no idea how hot this is. I think I'm going to come just from smelling you."

Holy. Hell. The feeling of him touching me bare for the first time was incredible. All sensations had multiplied with the feel of skin against skin. I was wet and lifted my leg up over his shoulder giving him full access to explore. He didn't waste any time. His tongue quickly found my clit, and he lightly flicked my sensitive core while his fingers continued to rub my wetness around. He slowly inserted one, then two fingers, and I gasped, "Noah."

My body had always been sensitive to his touch, and every move he made was more thrilling than ever. *Who knew that a bare pussy would make such a difference? I'm never going back.* The speed of his fingers picked up, and I found myself rocking into his mouth. I was so close to my release, but I didn't want it to end.

"I love when you ride my fingers. I know you're close, I can feel your walls tightening around my fingers and I know you're ready to come. Let me taste you," he ordered before burying his face back into my sex.

He curved his fingers perfectly and increased the speed of his tongue on my clit. I couldn't hold it back much longer, and when he sucked my clit into his mouth and released it, I broke into a million pieces.

I started shaking as I screamed out his name. He guided me down to the floor and continued to softly kiss my folds as I came down from my orgasm. The satisfaction in his performance was evident from the smile he wore on his glistening lips. "So fucking hot." His lips crashed back against mine in a deep and frantic kiss. I noticed his boxers were missing and felt him hard against my hip.

"I need to feel you inside me," I told him as I spread my legs for him to settle between. Dirty talk wasn't my strength, and he knew it, but it didn't stop me from letting him know what I wanted. Noah quickly shifted his weight and pressed down on my body. The feeling of him rubbing against my core made me needy.

"You want this?" he asked, as he slowly rocked his length through my folds and kissed down my neck.

I shifted my hips up to catch his thick crown at my entrance. "I want it. NOW!"

Surprised by my declaration, he looked down at me to confirm I meant what I said. "Ask and you shall receive," he replied as he slammed into me. I tilted my hips up as his thrusts increased in speed and intensity. He had been on edge at dinner, and I knew it wouldn't take long for him to find his release.

His punishing pace escalated. "So good. So fucking good." He cursed as he thrust hard into me a few more times before finally shouting his release.

We were both out of breath as he shifted off of me and rolled onto his side. He looked even more delicious with the "well-fucked" look I had just given him. His hand glided up my body, and he started to gently knead my breast. "Your body is perfection," he said as I winced. He had made connection with the tender spot I had found earlier but forgotten to mention.

"What the hell was that?" Noah asked with a concerned look on his face. "Did I hurt you?"

"No," I responded casually. "When I bumped your arm getting out of the car, I felt a zing of discomfort in my breast. I checked it when I showered and found a little tender spot. I've already spoken with Jen, and she's calling to get me an appointment after we're home. It's most likely another fibroid anyway."

"Victoria." He sounded worried. "Why didn't you tell me earlier?"

I sighed. "Because I knew you were busy with your meetings, and I didn't want you to worry, like you are now. It's most likely another fibroid, and I'm fine. Really, I'm okay."

Noah took my face in his hands, and when I looked at him, all I saw was compassion, concern, and love. "Sweetheart, please don't ever feel like you can't talk to me. I'm always here for you." I didn't know what to say at that moment, so I leaned up to kiss him, knowing that he meant every word he said.

"Let's get off this cold, hard floor and get some sleep. Tomorrow is going to be a long day for me, and I know you'll be busy taking in the sights with Shannon." Noah helped me up and into bed, snuggling in behind me. The heat of his body soothed and relaxed me into a deep sleep.

Chapter Two

I AM WONDERFUL

Five days later . . .

I woke up to my phone ringing on the bedside table. It was Jen's "friendly reminder" of my doctor appointment for three o'clock that afternoon.

"Are you sure you don't want me to go with you?" she pressured.

"Yes, I'll be fine on my own." I heard a huff of frustration with my answer, but honestly, I couldn't have cared less. I didn't need her there holding my hand as a doctor felt me up. I was a grown woman. I let out a heavy breath after hanging up and laid back in the comfort of my warm bed.

Noah made sure to keep me busy while we were in New York. He had encouraged me to go shopping with a few of the other women one day and surprised me with a date to the theater followed by a late dinner near Rockefeller Center. The distractions were perfect, and I was grateful to my husband for planning them.

I spent the morning catching up on messages and laundry from our trip. After a quick shower, I piled my hair on top of my head in a messy bun and applied my usual light makeup. Wanting to feel happy, I threw on my favorite chevron-patterned skirt with a lightweight pink sweater set. I swiped a coat of pink gloss on my lips, grabbed my purse, and headed out the door.

Arriving early to the Medical Professionals Building, I completed my paperwork faster than expected and was able to pull out a book. I never knew if the doctor would be on time and learned to use that to my benefit to catch up on my reading. A blush had taken up residence on my cheeks during a sexy part when my name was called.

"Victoria Madison?"

Dammit. The fictional man in my life would have to wait. I stood and followed the nurse. After completing the customary pee in a cup routine, they drew blood and I was provided a lovely pink paper gown to wear, making sure the opening was in the front. I climbed up on the exam table and felt the butterflies starting to build in my stomach. *Should I be concerned? What if it really is something?*

A light tap on the door broke my train of thought, and Dr. Beth Freeman entered the room. She was a petite and attractive woman, not much older than me, with shoulder-length dark blonde hair and kind eyes. She wore a tailored camel-colored suit and a killer pair of red heels.

"Good afternoon, Victoria. It's a pleasure to meet you." She greeted me with a smile and firm handshake before taking a seat at the small desk in the corner of the room. "So, tell me what's going on."

I proceeded to tell Dr. Freeman how I discovered the tenderness in my breast and how it grabbed my attention. I also explained that I had a history of fibroids, but that my best friend and husband had encouraged me to get this one checked out since its discovery was so sudden.

"Let's take a look." She stood to wash her hands and pulled on medical gloves.

Pulling out the end of the table to support my legs, she helped me lie back. She apologized in advance that her hands were cold. Yikes, she was right—they were freezing, and my nipples immediately stiffened, which made me uncomfortable. It must have been a normal response, as it didn't seem to faze her.

She started on my right breast by walking her fingers in a circular direction around my breast until she got to the center. Then she gently pressed both of her hands together around it like she was feeling a melon for ripeness.

Satisfied with my right breast, she moved over to my left side. She began the same procedure, but slowed down as she hit the inside of my left breast. She continued her way around to the center like on my right side. When it was time for her to press her palms around it, she zeroed in on the area in question, and I noticed her eyebrow perk up and a look of discovery quickly passed over her face.

"Okay. Let me help you sit up," she stated and then walked over to her desk to write something in my chart.

"Victoria, there is definitely something abnormal in your left breast. Due to the fact that you are adopted and don't have a family medical history, I would like you to have a baseline mammogram and ultrasound done immediately."

Okay. Things were getting real. "Immediately?

As in right now?" I questioned.

"I don't mean to frighten you, but yes, the sooner, the better. Do you have anything on your schedule this afternoon?"

"No," I said quietly as I felt my heart rate intensify. "I'm free for the rest of the day."

"Great, let me make a quick call and see if they can squeeze you in." With my heart pounding, I watched as she picked up her phone and made a call. Not hearing any of the words coming out of her mouth, I sat in disbelief and tried to process what was happening. *She actually found something that concerned her.*

"Victoria?" I thought I heard someone say my name, but it didn't register.

"Victoria?" I heard it again, but this time I looked up and locked eyes with Dr. Freeman. "The breast center had a cancellation and can get you in for a mammogram and ultrasound in twenty minutes. Will that work for you?"

I cleared my throat as I tried to find my voice. "Of course." She nodded and continued her conversation to set the appointment.

"Victoria, I know this is a lot to process in a matter of minutes, but I want to be proactive and rule out anything serious at this time. The faster we can do this, the easier you will sleep at night. You're young and the fact that you're doing self-exams at all is very encouraging. Many women don't understand the importance they serve and don't realize they should do them until it's too late."

She stood and walked over to me, placing her hand on my shoulder. "I'll be happy to walk you over to the clinic." I smiled as I realized that even though she was a physician, she was, in fact, also a woman like me, and her compassion was evident. It warmed my heart to know that the words she had just spoken were said with meaning and were not just an empty offer.

"Thank you for the offer, Dr. Freeman; I truly appreciate your concern. But I know you're busy, and I don't want to leave your other patients waiting longer than they need to. I'll just go grab a cup of tea and enjoy a walk outside."

She gave my shoulder a gentle squeeze before explaining that I was her last appointment of the day and she was heading that direction anyway. Thanking her again for her concern, I reiterated that I would be fine going on my own. She nodded her acceptance of my decision, handed me the orders for the clinic, and wished me luck before exiting the room.

I quickly ripped off the gown like it was on fire and examined myself in the mirror. *How did my day turn to this?* I grabbed my bra and sweater set and put them on, bumping my breast in my hasty actions. Tears began to well in my eyes. I would not break down. I was being foolish by letting it get to my head. I straightened my sweater, grabbed a tissue to wipe away my tears, and took one last look in the mirror.

"It's nothing," I said to my reflection. "She's just being cautious. That's what doctors do—they cover their asses."

After a quick stop at Caribou Coffee for a hot mango tea, I started on my way to the next appointment when I remembered to call Noah. I had promised him I would call when I was done at the doctor's appointment. I noticed a small garden area outside of the medical building and settled onto a bench and made the call, but it went right to voice mail.

"You have reached Noah Madison. I'm unable

to take your call at this time. Please leave your name, number, and a brief message, and I'll return your call as soon as I can." *Beeeeep.*

Using the most cheerful voice I could muster, I left him a message: "Hi, it's just me. My appointment went well, and Dr. Freeman ordered me to have a baseline mammogram and ultrasound to be on the safe side. There was an opening this afternoon, so I'm heading over there now. I'll see you when you get home. I love you. Bye." I ended the call and an uneasy feeling hit me again.

The butterflies were back in full force as I stepped into the breast center clinic. The lobby was warm and comforting and didn't feel medical, which I was thankful for. I was greeted by the friendly front desk staff and offered a beverage while I waited but declined as I had already had to find the ladies' room after guzzling my tea.

Once I returned from the ladies' room, I spotted a comfy chair by the window and settled in with my book. Reading had always been my escape, and I needed it more than anything at that time. The fifteen-minute wait breezed by, as I was once again engrossed in the story.

"Victoria Madison?"

Once again, I was beckoned by a stranger with a smile. Standing, I made my way toward the woman who was waiting; her name tag said Ginny. She seemed nice; she made small talk while we walked back to a changing-room area. I was assigned a locker, and she explained that I needed to strip from the waist up and remove all jewelry. She handed me another pink robe—luckily, it was cloth this time—and instructed me to keep the opening in the front.

Ginny was waiting for me when I exited the changing area and escorted me into the mammography room. I found myself face to face with a large machine with an area that looked like a giant panini maker. She removed what looked like heating pads that were covering the plates.

"We put heating pads on them so they aren't so cold; it helps since we have to keep the room temperature cool to prevent the machine from overheating."

I got a better look as I stepped closer. *Thank God!* The surface was smooth and not ridged like a panini maker, but it was intimidating nonetheless since its job was to smoosh my boob into a pancake. "Don't worry; it isn't as bad as it looks."

Another woman, who I assumed was the mammographer, entered the room. She looked me over and gave me an odd look. "Wow, you're awfully young to be here. So many doctors send young women for mammograms when they aren't necessary."

I'm not sure if she was trying to make me feel better, but she wasn't very successful. If anything, she made me feel like I was wasting her time, which in turn had me thinking maybe this was wasting mine too. I was not looking forward to letting this disgruntled woman manhandle me.

Ginny gave me an "I'm sorry about that" look before she stepped out of the room. After explaining the procedure to me, the technician asked me to open my gown and to place my right breast on one of the plates as she directed. She positioned it a bit and told me to put my hands on the bar in front of me. I slowly felt the plates start to close and thought to myself that this wasn't the most comfortable thing, but I could do it.

After being rearranged for a few different scans, it was time to show some attention to my left breast, the "problem" breast, as I was beginning to refer to it. I placed the "problem" between the plates, but this time when they started to close together, tears instantly filled my eyes and the words "fuck, that hurts" left my mouth without restraint. I gritted my teeth together for the rest of the scans and let out the breath I was apparently holding when it was done. The spot in my breast felt like it was burning, and I was well aware of it now.

Thankfully, the woman showed a bit more understanding when she stepped back toward me; she could tell that I was hurting. I shook it off and was brought back to a private waiting area while they reviewed the results. There were a few other women waiting, and every so often a nurse would come in and tell one of them that her "boobs looked great" and she was free to leave. I kept waiting and hoping they would say my name the next time they walked in, but they didn't. My anxiety level began to creep up. For once, all I wanted to hear was my name.

"Victoria." *Finally.*

Ginny approached me. "The radiologist would like to do an ultrasound. Please follow me, and we'll get you on your way home shortly." I followed her into a dimly lit room and took a seat to wait for the sonographer to come in.

When she arrived, I was told to lie down on the reclined exam table. She offered me a warm blanket for my lower half and explained the procedure to me while she got everything set up. I opened my gown as requested, and she squirted a gel-like liquid on what looked like a microphone and placed it on my left breast by my sternum.

She moved the wand around and then stopped right over the "problem." I once again could feel the discomfort, and I stiffened. Recognizing my distress, she hit a few buttons on the machine and quickly removed the wand and wiped my breast off. "I captured a few images that I need the radiologist to review. He is expecting them, so it should only take a few minutes. Is there anything I can get you while you wait? A magazine maybe?"

"No, thank you. I'll be fine." I forced a smile, and she left the room.

I was grateful that the ultrasound wasn't as uncomfortable as the mammogram, and I was ready to be done when the door opened and in walked the sonographer, followed by a man who I assumed was the radiologist. He looked to be in his mid-fifties and was wearing a white lab coat. Glasses were perched on the tip of his nose and he was balding.

"Hello, Mrs. Madison. I'm Dr. Christopher Frank, the radiologist on duty today." He offered his hand for a quick shake and proceeded to go about his business. "I reviewed the images that were just taken and want to take another peek for myself. Can you please open your gown?"

I did as he asked and watched his face as he searched the screen. He gave nothing away, damn pokerfaced doctors. "Can you please lift your arm over your head for me?" It was a strange request, but I complied and raised my arm up and rested it back on the pillow.

He moved the wand under my arm on the left side of my breast, and it hit me. This wasn't good. My stomach began to churn as I realized what he was looking at. *Shit.* He was looking at my lymph nodes: *this was not a good thing.*

Dr. Frank cleared his throat. "Victoria, I would like to do a needle biopsy while you're here. It's a very easy procedure and will take about five minutes."

Nodding my understanding, I encouraged him to explain the procedure. The fear of the unknown coming my way was starting to make my stomach churn . . . again. I was prepared for a mammogram and an ultrasound, but a biopsy never entered my realm of thinking.

"I'll be performing an image-guided biopsy in which I'll insert a needle into the area we want to take a sample from. The sonographer will assist me by using the ultrasound machine to help me locate the exact spot to take a tissue sample. Once I've reached the area in question, I'll pull a trigger on the biopsy instrument, and it will gather tissue samples for us to send to the lab. We will give you a local anesthetic before the procedure, and you can expect some discomfort for the next day or two. Do you have any questions for me before we begin?"

Wow, he was direct and to the point. My head felt like it was going to explode. I managed to form the word *no* before he stepped out of the room and the sonographer began to prep me for the procedure.

When Dr. Frank reappeared, he gave me a comforting smile—because he probably knew I would bolt otherwise. He was a smart man.

I laid still as the local anesthetic was given and took some deep breaths. It was time to go to my happy place, which was pretty much any place but here. I closed my eyes and imagined myself sitting on a beach looking out over turquoise waves as the ultrasound wand was moved around on my breast.

"Hold it right there," Dr. Frank said calmly as

he began to insert the needle. Holy crap . . . it wasn't a small needle! I squeezed my eyes tighter and tried to continue breathing while the pressure built and a burning sensation took over.

Click. Click. Click.

I was startled by a loud series of sounds and then the discomfort disappeared. I felt the sonographer's hand press down on the area as she applied a gauze pad over the biopsy site.

"Victoria, you did very well. I was able to grab a few samples fairly easily. We'll get you some ice to pack into your bra, and you will want to take ibuprofen for the discomfort. If you have any problems with the insertion area, please call our office right away. You can expect the results within a few days. I wish you the best; it was a pleasure to meet you," Dr. Frank said before he exited the room.

When I was fully clothed again, Ginny was waiting with a bag of crushed ice. "I recommend you place this in your bra directly on the area of the biopsy. It's double bagged and shouldn't leak." I turned around and stuffed my bra with the ice pack. I remember doing this with tissue or socks as a young girl wishing I had boobs, but somehow this didn't feel quite the same.

She led me back out to the reception area, and I noticed that the office was empty. "I'm sorry we kept you so long; Dr. Freeman will call you with the results. It usually takes three to four days to get them back. In the meantime, go about your business as usual, and don't hesitate to call with questions. Best of luck," she said as she held the door for me.

"Thank you."

※

I don't know how I did it, but I arrived home safely. It was a miracle because I had been shaking from the adrenaline coursing through my body for the entire fifteen-minute drive home. My nerves were about to short circuit, and I wanted to throw up.

When I walked in, I heard "Feels Like Home" by Chantal Kreviazuk playing. The sound of her melodic voice and the piano was comforting as I walked toward the kitchen and found Noah pouring a glass of wine. The orchestra kicked in just as he turned around and saw me; a look of unease quickly washed away the smile on his face.

"Victoria, are you all right? Your face is pale, and you look like you're going to be sick." The concern in his voice was evident as he guided me toward a chair in the living room before vanishing and then reappearing with a glass of water.

He was on his knees in front of me as I took the glass from him and shakily lifted it to my mouth. I felt the cold liquid slide down my throat, and I quickly downed the entire glass, wishing it had been vodka to numb the pain. I didn't know what to say, so I stayed quiet. Noah continued to search my face and attempted to make eye contact; when he finally did, the tears began running down my face and a sob escaped my throat.

Time passed, and I found myself curled up in Noah's arms in the middle of our bed, his cheek resting on the top of my head. I looked up to find his eyes red from the tears he must have shed.

He noticed my movement, looked down at me, and simply said, "I love you." He kissed the tip of my nose, and a small, comforting smile appeared on his face.

"I love you too." I shifted myself so I could sit up and face him.

We stared at each other for a few moments before I spoke. "Noah, I don't know anything yet. I left you the message on my way to the breast clinic, and the two hours I was there seemed like an out-of-body experience. I know you want to know everything they did, but I just can't talk about it anymore. I'm mentally exhausted." I took a deep breath. "We need to believe that everything is okay, but I'd be lying if I didn't admit that I'm scared."

"You have every right to be scared. Look, I don't know what you went through today, but I know it was anything but normal, and you did it alone. I'm sorry I wasn't there with you; something came up after I got into the office, and I couldn't get away. I should have demanded I go with you, but instead, I respected your decision to go alone."

He pulled me against his chest. "I may not have been there today, but I promise to be with you going forward." I knew he felt bad about not going and hoped there wouldn't be any future appointments for him to go to.

Chapter Three

I AM BRAVE

The next morning, I woke up early and felt a little more at ease. I pulled on one of Noah's dress shirts and made my way down to the kitchen. A hot cup of coffee and yogurt with granola were waiting for me at the breakfast bar. What I didn't expect was the beautiful bouquet of flowers, and the smiling man holding them, waiting for me. Noah usually got up and left for the office by six, and it was rare to see him in the morning.

"Good morning, Sunshine." He leaned in and kissed my temple. "How are you feeling? Did you sleep well? How is the biopsy site? Do you need ice or ibuprofen?" His rapid-fire questions revealed his nerves. While I felt a little more at peace this morning, I could tell that he had been overthinking everything and didn't know what to do to help me. He looked tired.

"I'm feeling better after a good night's sleep in your arms. I felt safe." He placed the vase of flowers on the middle of the countertop and started fidgeting, unsure of what to do. "I could use some ibuprofen after I eat. My chest is a bit sore, and there is a little bit of bruising coming out . . . it's not pretty looking."

He placed the ibuprofen pills on the counter with a glass of water. I could see the anxiety in his eyes when he finally sat down; I felt the tension rolling off him. There was no sense in acting like the world had come to an end, and we needed to keep moving forward as if nothing was happening. In all honesty, nothing was happening—or at least nothing was confirmed wrong—so why should I let it beat me down?

"Do you need to go into the office today?" I asked before putting a spoonful of yogurt into my mouth.

"I had a few meetings scheduled for today, but I already called Whitney and told her to reschedule them, as well as the rest of my meetings this week. I can't focus right now."

He suddenly grabbed my legs and turned me toward him. "Victoria, what do you say to hopping on a plane and going to Chicago overnight? We weren't able to do much exploring in New York with the conference, and Chicago is the next best city to visit and it's only an hour flight. What do you think?" He seemed a bit anxious suggesting it, but I found it down-right sweet.

"Really? Just hop on a flight to Chicago?" I questioned. He made it sound so easy. We'd never done anything spur of the moment like that before. This was new, but I was actually warming to the idea of getting away. I arched an eyebrow, letting him know I was giving it some consideration.

Noah countered. "Why not? It would be a quick trip, a day or two at most, and we haven't enjoyed a getaway without work involved in a very long time. It's perfect." He gazed at me with puppy-dog eyes.

"I suppose it would work. I don't have anything major at work the next few days and an escape for just the two of us would be good. Let's do it."

He tried to control the excitement on his face, but it didn't work very well. "You're sure?"

I laughed. "Yes, I'm sure. And while we're at it . . . I'd like to visit the Bean and Navy Pier and go up to the Skydeck at the Willis Tower." Then it was my turn to flash my best puppy-dog eyes. "I think

I've finally worked up the courage to tackle my fear of heights. Would you do it with me? I might even want to step out on the Ledge."

It took him a moment to process, but when he replied, I could see that his wheels had been turning and I should prepare myself. "If I agree, I have one request."

"And that is?"

"That you hurry up and finish your breakfast. I'll go book our flight while you finish and then we need to grab a quick shower and throw a few things in a bag." He leaned down to my ear. "Hurry up, because it won't take long for me to book the flight and be prepared... it isn't going to be a fast shower."

Well damn! I looked at his sexy little smirk and thought to myself... *Two can play this game.*

Reaching for my coffee, I took a sip while holding his gaze. Then I picked up my yogurt and licked my lips before lifting the last spoonful to my mouth. With a steady hand, I pulled the spoon out from between my lips slowly and proceeded to lick it clean. The heat in Noah's eyes was rising, and I knew that I was asking for it.

Feeling brave, I saw the fruit bowl was in reach

and a nice looking banana was begging to be eaten. He followed my eyes to see what I was looking at and let out a low chuckle. "Since when do you have a banana with your breakfast?"

After the ache we were both feeling emotionally, we needed to lighten the mood, and this was the perfect distraction. I grabbed the banana and casually started to peel it. "My breakfast left me feeling unsatisfied and I needed something more . . . to satisfy my appetite." I could see humor and heat dancing in his eyes, which only encouraged me more.

"Now this I'd like to see." He smirked as he leaned against the back of his stool with his arms crossed over his chest.

Game on!

As I finished pulling the last section of the peel down, I rolled my tongue around the tip of it before lightly sucking, getting it wet and letting out a moan. "This banana is so thick and firm." I placed my tongue at the base of where it was peeled to and licked my way up to the tip and hummed my appreciation. "It's the perfect size for my mouth."

"Victoria!" Noah cautioned, but I could see the lust in his eyes, and it was betraying him. He was enjoying this as much as I was.

I made a perfect O with my lips and took the piece of fruit in my mouth and pushed it back to my throat and oh so slowly pulled it back out, never taking my eyes off my husband. "It's so long, too."

He shifted on his barstool, and I could see him adjust his pants.

"Are you okay, sweetheart?" I asked before taking the banana all the way in my mouth again and then popping my mouth off the end. "You seem a bit uncomfortable."

He let out a groan. "I suggest you finish that banana in the next ten seconds, otherwise you aren't going to finish it at all."

I ran my tongue around the tip and started licking all around the delectable fruit as I watched his patience reach its breaking point.

"Fucking banana," he cursed as he grabbed it and threw it onto the counter. He lifted me off of my stool and set me down standing on the floor. "Don't start something you can't finish."

He gave my backside a swift little swat and chased me upstairs and into the bathroom. After Noah lifted me up onto the counter, I watched as he started stripping out of his clothes like it was a race.

He turned and looked at me sitting there, trying to look all innocent.

"Oh. No. You. Don't! You're not going to sit there, acting all perfect and angelic after that performance. Get your clothes off... NOW... or I'll do it for you!" he said as he turned the shower on.

Hmm... I'll take option number two, please!

He walked over to me with a smug look, "Okay, we'll do this my way, you little tease." I gasped as he lifted me and carried me into the shower.

"Noah. What are you doing? I still have clothes on." I giggled in mock annoyance.

"Don't worry, I'll fix that." He ripped my panties off as soon as he set me down and then proceeded to tear open the dress shirt I had put on, sending the pearly buttons flying all over the tile. His eyes turned heavy when he saw the bruising on my breast where the biopsy had been done not even twenty-four hours ago. He carefully rubbed his hand on the underside of it. "Does it hurt when I touch it?"

Shaking my head no, I replied, "It's sore and I can feel a subtle burning sensation, but the warmth of your hand is comforting. I need you to touch me.

I need to feel you. Just be gentle." He leaned down and placed a tender kiss on my breast just above the biopsy site. I flinched in surprise and could see the fear in his eyes when he looked up at me.

"It's okay." I leaned forward and placed my lips on his, needing that connection. Needing to feel him and needing him to feel me. Our kiss grew more passionate but lacked the aggressiveness it usually held. He stepped back briefly, squirted shampoo in his hand and began to massage my scalp with his strong fingers. It felt so good to be pampered by my husband.

He rinsed my hair and applied conditioner before grabbing my loofah. After liberally pouring coconut body wash on it, he began to wash my body but dropped the loofah and continued washing my body with his hands. Careful not to rub too hard on my left breast, he then grabbed my right breast and started to blow on my nipple. I wanted more.

I slid my hand down his chest, feeling how hard his body was and continued the journey south to my destination. He was more than ready for me. I tightened my grasp around his hard shaft and felt him get harder with my touch. "Fuck, Victoria. Just your touch makes me harder than stone." His kiss was intense and full of need as he devoured my mouth.

When his hand found my folds and made direct contact with my clit, I breathed in sharply. He gently rubbed circles with his thumb as his fingers found my opening to test if I was ready. "Damn, you feel so good. I love how your body responds to my touch."

He shifted our position and backed up so he could sit down on the built in tile bench along the wall. I stepped toward him and climbed on top, straddling his lap with my knees resting on either side of his hips. Using my hand to position him, I slowly lowered myself onto his length and just when I thought I had slid all the way down, he leaned back against the wall tilting his hips up. That small shift pushed him in even further. We sat like that for a moment and just stared at one another.

I started to rock my hips back and forth feeling his length rubbing against the perfect spot. He grabbed my hips and started guiding me up and down slowly over him. My orgasm was building with each thrust and pull. "Victoria, I'm so close. I don't think I can hold out much longer. I want you with me. I need to feel you pulsing around my cock.

Are you almost there?" he growled. I could tell it was taking all of his strength to hold out.

"Yes, I'm with you, Noah. I need it hard." I picked up the pace and slammed myself down on him with such force I could feel the sweet pain of him as he plunged deep inside. I was gone.

"Oh. My. God. Noah." I grabbed hold of his hair and our eyes met as he slammed up in me and found his release. "Oh fuck, Victoria!" he hissed between his teeth as I felt him twitch inside of me.

We didn't move for several minutes. "I love you," Noah said as he placed one final kiss on my lips.

"I love you too," I whispered.

We finished washing, and Noah had my towel ready for me when I stepped out. He wrapped me up in it like I was a kid and placed a sweet kiss on my nose before walking out of the bathroom. "I'm going to go book our tickets." It didn't go unnoticed that his towel was slipping down as he walked away and he knew it . . . the bastard!

I finished getting ready and stepped back into our bedroom. A suitcase was open on the bed with Noah's stuff already packed. I quickly pulled a few things out of the closet and my dresser and placed them in the bag.

I slipped into a pair of jeans, my favorite sweater, and boots, and went in search of Noah, who was in his study, focused intently on his laptop. I think he felt my presence, because he quickly finished what he was doing and looked up at me. "Ready to go?" he asked with a smile as I rounded his desk. He shut his laptop and stood to catch me in his arms.

"You bet. I'm ready to go on this little adventure with you!"

The flight to Chicago was short. Noah managed to book a last minute reservation at the Drake Hotel, and it was perfect. I stood in front of a large picture window overlooking Lake Michigan from our Lake View King Suite.

The natural light from several windows filled the room, giving it a warm glow. Next to the king-sized bed, there was a sitting area with a sofa and two wing-back chairs, as well as a dining area overlooking the lake. "Maybe we should just order room service tonight? This room is incredible."

Noah walked up behind me and pulled me into his arms. "If that's what you want, then that's what we'll do. Plus, it will give us more time to explore if we don't have to come back and get ready to go out for a nice dinner."

He shifted to look at his watch. "Speaking of exploring, the clock is ticking, and we have a lot to accomplish during our short stay. The Skydeck is waiting, and we have fast passes that allow us to skip ahead of the line."

"You can do that?"

"You'd be amazed at what you can accomplish with a little extra cash and some research online while your wife is in the shower."

He backed away and smacked me on the ass. "Let's go—even with the fast pass, it will take us a few hours to get through the chaos. Luckily, it's Wednesday and the midweek, midafternoon time frame is probably one of the better options. Now, let's get a move on."

We arrived at Willis Tower and Noah was right: the line was out the door. The plan was to hit Millennium Park first thing in the morning before heading over to the Navy Pier, so we weren't in a big rush. The line for the first set of elevators took a little while, and they surprisingly took us down to the lowest level of the building instead of up.

Once we got off, our fast pass kicked into full effect, and we were able to make our way through security rather quickly before moving to the head of the line for the Chicago history video. We had the option to head straight for the bank of elevators that would take us directly up to the Skydeck, but we chose to watch the video and learned a lot about the city's history. It was a city that came back from ashes . . . literally.

The final line for the elevator ride to the one hundred and third floor moved fairly quickly, and the excitement of what we were about to do had my heart racing. We boarded the elevator for a short sixty-second ride up, and when the elevator stopped, we were welcomed by the most amazing view of the world below us.

It was a clear day, and you could see the hustle and bustle of the city below, everyone going about their day like any other day. Tour boats on the river, airplanes taking off, and the beauty of the skyline at every turn. But this wasn't just an ordinary day for me. I grabbed Noah's arm and dragged him around the corner, bringing us closer to where the Ledge was waiting. We looked out over Lake Michigan and could see parts of the Navy Pier and some large boats.

Making our way around another corner, we could easily see the John Hancock Building and several other Chicago landmarks. As we made our way down the long hall, the lines for the Ledge started coming into view.

Simply put, the Ledge is a glass box that extends about four feet out from the top floor of the Willis Tower. Once you step out into the box, you're officially standing one hundred and three stories above downtown Chicago overlooking the Chicago River. *I bet it would be fun to see the river on St. Patrick's Day when they turn it green*, I thought.

Noah and I stood in line and slowly inched our way closer. My nerves were ratcheting up with each step. I knew I wanted to do this to overcome my fear, and Noah was there to support me. *I could do this!*

I was distracted by a group of tourists from the UK that were having fun and laughing in the box next to the one we were in line for. I love the sound of a British accent, and I was so focused on them that I didn't realize that we were standing at the entrance to the room we had been in line for. It was our turn. My heart rate soared.

Noah stepped out first and turned back toward me with his hand held out, encouraging me to join him. With a deep breath, I took his hand and focused on his face as I took one step... then another... and another. The trepidation I felt melted away as I took in the beauty around me, and the chill of the room awakened me to the moment. This would be a moment I would never forget.

My nerves disappeared as I sat down. That's right. I sat down and made myself comfortable. I grabbed my phone and asked the woman next in line to snap our picture. She was more than happy to, and Noah sat down next to me after he handed it to her. He pulled me close to his side with his arms wrapped tightly around me.

The woman snapped a few pictures of us, including one with Noah kissing my check and me grinning ear to ear. She handed me my phone back as soon as I stood up. It was then that I took my first look down, and my heart plummeted. But I realized if I focused on my feet, I was fine, and I quickly took a picture of my feet with nothing but the street, 1,353 feet below, as the backdrop.

I looked up at Noah, who was beaming at me. "You're stronger than you think," he said before placing a kiss on my lips in front of everyone. It earned us a few whistles and cheers before we stepped back into the building.

"That was incredible!" I squealed like a high school girl after we made our way out of the crowd. You couldn't wipe the smile off of my face. I had conquered my fear of heights, and it was an amazing rush. My adrenaline continued to pump through me as we stopped to look back out over Chicago.

"You were amazing out there. I'm so proud of you, Victoria."

"Thank you." I turned toward him. "I couldn't have done that without you. You knew how afraid I was, and yet you got me to follow you out there just by offering your hand to me. I knew you would catch me, and the trust I saw in your eyes was all I needed."

My emotions began to take over, and I started to tear up. "I know that whatever life throws at us, you will be there guiding me, holding me, catching me when I fall." My voice was soft and the lump in my throat grew bigger.

Noah's thumb wiped the lone tear that started to fall down my cheek. "Victoria, you're the strongest woman I know, and you will conquer anything that comes your way. Today was a way for you to see that. To see that you're strong and will be able to overcome any obstacles thrown at you." He smiled as he tugged my hand and led us back to the bay of elevators to bring us back down to the ground.

"The Magnificent Mile is calling. We have a few hours before the stores close. Let's do some window shopping," I pleaded with him as we exited the building.

"Oh, really? The Mile is calling?"

"Yes, H&M, Michael Kors, and Burberry are all putting out signals for me to visit," I stated emphatically. "Plus, I want to see the Historic Chicago Water Tower, and it's all on our way back to the Drake. It's a nice evening for a walk. The bitter cold of winter is coming, and we'll be locked in our house like prisoners soon."

"We need to make a quick detour to Garrett Popcorn first." His mobile started to ring, and he looked down at the screen. "I need to grab this quick." He winked as he stepped away from me to accept the call. Seeing he needed privacy, I moved to stand by the curb and waited for the light signal to turn. He was back at my side as the light changed, and we made our way arm-in-arm the few blocks down to Garretts.

We stumbled into our hotel suite a few hours later, our arms loaded with bags. Retail therapy had never felt so good, and Noah even managed to hit a few stores for himself.

After ordering room service, we changed out of our clothes and into something more comfortable since we weren't planning to leave the room again until morning. Noah had picked up a bottle of wine on our way back to the hotel, and I poured myself a glass. I found the sound system and plugged in my iPod. After scrolling through my playlists, I selected "Lying in the Hands of God" by Dave Matthews Band and curled up on the sofa.

I heard the bathroom door open, followed by the sound of Noah's feet as he made way into the room. He made a brief stop to pour himself a glass of wine before joining me on the sofa. He pulled my legs over onto his lap while he raised his glass for a toast. "Here's to an amazing day with an amazing woman. Cheers." We both took a sip of our wine when my phone rang.

I didn't even bother to look at the caller ID.

"Hello," I answered cheerfully.

"Victoria? This is Dr. Freeman." Pause. "I'm sorry to call so late, but your results came in a short time ago and—"

I cut her off. "Wait, what? I was told it would take a few days before we got them back. I don't understand."

"Are you alone right now?"

"No, my husband Noah and I are actually in Chicago. We decided to get away for a few days to keep me occupied until the results came in. What's going on?"

"I'm sorry to tell you this, but your biopsy test showed that the lump you found is malignant." She hesitated for a brief moment. "Victoria, you have breast cancer."

Chapter Four

I AM COURAGEOUS

Victoria, you have breast cancer.
My world stopped.

I went numb and could barely comprehend what she said next. "I've made an appointment for you Friday morning to meet with a general surgeon. His name is Dr. William Lauren. I went to medical school with him, and I've the utmost confidence in his abilities. I'll e-mail you his contact information in case you need to reschedule the appointment. I have also taken the liberty of scheduling an appointment with a plastic surgeon that same afternoon. Dr. Lauren recommended him when we discussed your case. His name is Dr. Blake Forrester and he's new to the practice but has an impeccable record."

I sat in stunned silence as she continued talking. "I know you're in shock right now, and I hope you don't mind that I took the liberty of setting up these appointments for you. I wanted to provide some guidance for you and make this as easy as possible. Do you have any questions for me right now?"

What? Questions? About what?

"No, not that I can think of," I replied with no emotion or feeling. I was numb.

"Okay. Please know that you can call me anytime if you have questions or concerns. I'm so sorry to be the one to share this news with you, but the fact that we caught it early is on your side. Try to get some sleep, and we'll be in touch. Good night, Victoria."

"Good night." End.

I sat frozen, wondering what in the hell just happened. *Was this even real? What does this mean? Am I going to die?* Noah took the phone out of my hand and placed it down on the table. He scooped me up on his lap and softly caressed my hair, trying to comfort me. I didn't need to say a word. He knew.

November 9 was the day I heard those words. It was the day my life came to a screeching halt, but it was also the day it was slammed into fast forward . . . was that even possible? I've been told fighting breast cancer is a marathon, not a race. Funny, I don't remember signing up for either!

As the realization of my diagnosis sunk in later that evening, my emotions took me on a roller coaster ride. Anger, sadness, and vulnerability took over and a half hour later were replaced with determination and resolve; I was going to do anything I could to kick cancer's ass and opened my laptop to do some research.

I walked over to the sofa and sat next to Noah, who was reading. "I've been doing some research, and I'm opting for a bilateral mastectomy," I declared.

He quickly snapped his head up and looked at me. "Don't you think that's a bit drastic?"

"No, I don't. I'm thirty-two, and let's be honest—what are the chances that we will ever be able to have children after I'm done with chemo? We have at least a year of surgeries, chemotherapy, and possible radiation ahead, and my body will need time to heal." I took a deep breath. "Plus, I don't want to wake up every day worried about finding a lump in my right breast. The *what if* would drive me insane."

Noah nodded his head at me in consideration. "I

hear what you're saying, and I'm not discounting it, because ultimately it's your decision—but I really think we should get a professional opinion before you go announcing that you're having a mastectomy." He moved closer to me on the sofa and tucked me in under his arm. "Victoria, I'll stand behind whatever decision you make; I just want you to make an educated one and not jump off the deep end before we talk with the doctors." I knew he was right. I needed to understand what I was dealing with and was hopeful that Dr. Lauren would be able to give me some guidance on Friday morning.

The next twenty-four hours were a haze for both of us as we tried to ignore the elephant that was following us around Chicago. We spent time together, but also some time apart to clear our minds.

I called my parents and Jen to let them know I'd received the results. It's not the way I wanted to tell them, but they needed to know. Jen offered to call our few close friends so that I wouldn't have to repeat the story over again. I had never been more grateful for having her in my life.

Noah and I walked hand-in-hand around the Navy Pier, watching the people around us smiling and laughing. I looked out at the cracked and broken lighthouse that stood atop a rocky wall just out from the pier. It was run-down but still did its job as a beacon for ships seeking land.

We walked through Millennium Park and found our way to the Bean. The Bean is a large bean-shaped sculpture with a mirrored surface. Its curves twist and distort images, and I was brought to tears when I saw my reflection. *Distorted.* That was what would become of my body, or maybe it already had where the cancer was attacking me, only I couldn't see it. That would change in a few weeks, when I would be left with nothing but scars to look at for the rest of my life.

Our flight home was quiet; we were both lost in our own thoughts. We barely spoke to one another; however, our hands stayed intertwined the entire flight. It was the only comfort we could offer each other. We both collapsed from exhaustion when we finally arrived home. Noah slept soundly, while I woke up several times during the night with my mind racing.

By morning, I wasn't close to being rested, and it was a chore getting ready for the back-to-back appointments that Dr. Freeman had set for me. I just wanted to stay curled up in a ball and ignore the world.

Sitting in the waiting room of Dr. Lauren's office was nerve-racking, and I found myself bouncing my knee up and down, which was not something I ever did. Noah noticed my odd behavior and placed his hand on my leg and began to gently massage my tense muscles. It helped to ease my nerves.

"Victoria Madison?"

And there was my name again. I was going to have to get used to hearing it frequently now. Maybe I should change it or use a fake one at each office. That would be entertaining; however, I'm sure the physicians' billing departments and insurance companies wouldn't be too pleased. The thought did make me smile, though . . . just a little.

We were led to an exam room, and I was provided with another lovely paper gown and . . . well . . . I knew the drill. Shortly after I got settled, Dr. Lauren tapped lightly on the door, and I noticed Noah shift uncomfortably in his chair. "Good morning, Victoria. I'm Dr. Lauren," he stated as he shook my hand before turning to Noah. "And you are?"

"I'm her husband, Noah. Thank you for seeing us on such short notice," Noah said in his most proper and professional voice. He was in "attorney mode" and was going to listen to every little fact that came out of Dr. Lauren's mouth. I could see the wheels turning in his head and knew he would be cross-examining the good doctor in no time. Poor guy didn't know what was coming.

I turned my attention to the tall blonde doctor whose hazel eyes were looking sympathetically at me. "Dr. Freeman called me late in the day yesterday and explained your situation. I was happy to make room for you on my schedule since she's a dear friend."

He took a seat on the stool and flipped open my chart. "Now, let's take a look at the findings from Dr. Frank's report. I see you had quite the work up on Tuesday. Do you still have tenderness in the area?"

"Yes, it's still a bit tender, and the bruising is getting more colorful by the day. Maybe it's just in my head, but I feel a constant burning feeling in that area now," I confessed and was sure he thought I was crazy. To be honest, I did feel crazy, and since hearing those four damn words, I had felt a constant burning sensation in my breast.

"Yes, I've heard several women say that. Though

I can't say I understand it, I'm told it's a normal feeling." He looked back down at the report. "It appears that the measurement of your tumor is estimated at just over two centimeters long, and it appears to be self-contained. We don't see any 'spidering' or rough edges in the mammogram or ultrasound films. Dr. Frank also noted that he didn't see any inflammation in your nodes, which is encouraging, but we will still do a sentinel node biopsy during surgery to be safe."

"What's a sentinel node biopsy?" Noah inquired.

"It's a procedure in which we will inject a radioactive dye into the nodes under the arm of the affected breast prior to surgery. The dye travels to the sentinel node, which is the primary node, and will filter into others surrounding it, making them all a bright blue color, which allows me to locate it and the other primary nodes quickly during surgery. I'll take between three and five nodes immediately at the beginning of surgery and send them to the lab for testing. If the results come back positive, we will take more nodes until we get the all clear. There is a higher likelihood that the cancer has spread to other areas of the body if the nodes come back positive. It will allow your medical team to be proactive in planning your course of treatment."

I'm glad Noah was with me because I knew I would not be able to remember everything that was being said.

"There are two surgical options I would like to discuss with you," he said as he motioned to me to move up onto the exam table. I quickly stood and stepped up to take a seat, hearing the rustle of the paper underneath me.

He held up a diagram as he spoke. "We can do a lumpectomy, in which I'll make an incision and remove the tumor from your breast and a portion of the tissue around it. It will be sent to the lab, and they will determine if there are cancer cells in the surrounding tissue. If there is, then I'll remove more tissue until we have clear margins. You will be stitched closed and will be able to go home later that day. If we don't get clear margins or if the surrounding tissue is larger than anticipated, we will make the decision while you're in surgery to do a single mastectomy to the left breast at that time."

He switched to another diagram. "The second option is a single or bilateral mastectomy. This is a more radical surgery and will require at least a two-night stay in the hospital. The surgery generally takes close to three hours, and if you start the process of reconstruction, it will add an additional two hours. All of the breast tissue is removed, including the nipple, ducts, and areola."

I quickly interjected in surprise. "The nipple and areola? Why?"

"Because the type of cancer you have is ductal carcinoma and it's located in or on your milk ducts. Those travel to your nipple for nursing and need to be removed as well. If you decide to proceed with reconstruction, they can rebuild a nipple and tattoo the areolas for aesthetic purposes, but you will not have any feeling in them. For some woman that's an issue. Are you planning on having children?"

"Eventually, yes, but isn't that out of the question after chemo?" I questioned, feeling my emotions starting to overtake me. *Hold it together.*

"It's not impossible, but it's definitely something you should discuss with your oncologist, because chemo can affect fertility."

Noah cleared his throat. "So the chances of having children are slim?"

"I wouldn't completely rule it out, but, as I said, that is a discussion best had with your oncologist and gynecologist. There are risks involved that they will be able to explain better than I can."

He stepped over toward the desk to set the diagrams down. "A mastectomy is a very radical surgery and the recovery time is long, especially with reconstruction," he warned as he washed his hands and reached for a pair of medical gloves. "Do you mind if I take a look at your breasts?"

I shook my head no and opened the gown. Modesty was officially out the door; I was pretty sure I would be flashing them to all kinds of strangers over the coming weeks. *Sigh.*

Dr. Lauren examined my breasts, the whole grab, cup, poke, and feel routine that I had become accustomed to. He closed my gown, took off his gloves and was about to say something when Noah spoke up. "What would you recommend? In your professional opinion, what are the pros and cons?"

"Professionally, I'll say that this is a very personal decision. Every woman is different, and frankly, the decision is Victoria's. With the preliminary reports from the mammogram, ultrasound, and biopsy, your insurance would cover either option. One thing to keep in mind if you choose to do a lumpectomy: there is a very strong chance that you will have to do radiation. If you go with a mastectomy, due to the estimated size of your tumor, you most likely would avoid it."

He took his glasses off and leaned back against the counter by the sink. "Personally, if it were my wife, I would trust her instincts and support her decision. She has to live with it for the rest of her life."

"I'm having a bilateral mastectomy with reconstruction," I stated to both of them and was met with a moment of silence as two sets of eyes searched my face for confirmation of my verbal decision.

Dr. Lauren was the first to speak up. "I'm not surprised by your decision, Victoria. You're young and the fear of it coming back is more common in younger patients. There is nothing wrong with being proactive, and since you don't have any medical history, I think you're making the right decision for you."

I looked over to Noah with imploring eyes, waiting for his response.

He finally spoke up. "Thank you for your honesty, Dr. Lauren, I appreciate it. After hearing what you had to say regarding the results from Dr. Frank and watching the myriad of expressions cross my wife's face, I agree that she's making the right decision."

Noah stood up to walk toward me and placed his hand on top of mine, which were folded in my lap. "How soon can we get this scheduled?"

"I would like to get surgery scheduled as soon as possible. I see here you're scheduled to see Dr. Blake Forrester this afternoon to discuss your reconstruction, is that correct?" I nodded my head in agreement.

"Good. I think you'll like him. Once you come to an agreement on reconstruction, his office will contact mine to schedule surgery. There's no need for you to schedule another appointment with me. Have you made an appointment with an oncologist yet?"

"Umm, no, not yet. I guess I didn't even think about that," I confessed, feeling like an idiot. "I guess I need to find one."

"No worries. I've a few recommendations I can give you. I'll get their cards while you're getting dressed and will meet you in the hallway." He reached over to shake my hand and then Noah's before he left the room.

I dressed in silence and could feel Noah watching me. I could see the anguish on his face in his reflection in the mirror on the wall. He was starting to digest what was happening... really and truly happening.

When I was fully dressed, I turned toward him and our eyes met. I saw fear in his eyes, something I had never seen there before.

"Noah, it's going to be okay. We have to know that. I've chosen the most radical surgery so that it's all removed. I'm choosing to fight." I tried my best to sound confident in my words and gave him my best reassuring smile before I turned toward the door. I'm sure it wasn't very convincing, but I tried.

"Stop."

I turned back around. He placed his hands on either side of my face with his forehead against mine. "You're amazing. Simply amazing. I'm in awe of your strength because right now I'm so afraid, and I don't know how you're doing this." He leaned down and gave me a chaste kiss before placing his hand in mine to exit the room together.

Dr. Lauren was waiting for us in the hallway like he had said. "Here are two oncologists in the area that I would recommend. I suggest you call today and make an appointment for early next week with each of them. It's important to bring a list of the same questions to both doctors, as you want to be comfortable with your choice of doctor for treatment. You will be seeing him or her frequently."

"Thank you again. We both appreciate your honesty and will be in touch." I smiled, trying to keep my "I'm kicking ass and taking names" attitude going. "I guess I'll see you again on the day of surgery."

"Yes, you will. Take care of yourself, and please call if you have any more questions."

"We will. Thank you, Dr. Lauren," Noah added as he accompanied me toward the lobby.

Our hands didn't part as we left the building. It was like we were two warriors going into battle . . . only this battle was raging in my body.

"Victoria Madison?"

I cringed. *How do they do that?* It's just another normal, happy day for them, but all I wanted to do was curl up in the corner and cry.

I stood, and Noah grabbed my hand as we were escorted into another exam room with a table, two chairs, and a desk in the corner with a round spinning chair. As a kid I used to spin on them, but

I'm sure if I tried today, I would end up nauseated. It was a nice thought though.

"Are you nervous?" Noah asked me as he sat in one of the chairs.

"No, I don't think so." *Who am I kidding?!* "Honestly, I really don't know. I feel like I'm on a thrill ride at a theme park and I've no control over what happens next. I just have to trust that the ride isn't going to get stuck at the top, or worse—derail." I fought back the tears that were again threatening to spill out from my eyes.

I never thought I'd have a plastic surgeon. I'm not a vain person, and I planned to age gracefully. Yet, here I was, sitting in his office and suddenly feeling very awkward.

"It's okay, Victoria. Everything will be okay," Noah reassured me. "We are just talking with him to weigh our options. Nothing is set in stone, and if you don't want to do reconstruction, it's okay. I'll support your choices."

That did it. A few tears started gliding down my cheek just as there was a tap on the door. I quickly swiped them away and looked up as a gorgeous man walked into the room. My heart fluttered.

He was tall and lean, with thick dark hair that

was every hairstylist's dream. His eyes were a warm chocolate brown, and his skin was perfectly tanned. His suit was custom tailored, his tie was a striking cobalt blue, and his shoes... well... nice shoes were my weakness. *Gulp.*

He approached me with his hand outstretched to take mine. "Good afternoon, Victoria. I'm Dr. Blake Forrester." His firm but gentle grip caught me off guard, causing me to gasp quietly; he smiled before releasing my hand to turn toward Noah. "You must be Mr. Madison?"

"Yes, I am. Please, call me Noah." Noah shook his hand with confidence. It felt awkward, like a testosterone surge was present in the room, even though it wasn't.

Dr. Forrester sat down on the spinning chair and flipped opened my chart. He studied it for a few moments before turning back to look at me. "I received your report from Dr. Lauren's office about fifteen minutes ago and understand that you would like to move forward with a bilateral mastectomy followed by reconstruction. Is that correct?"

"Yes, that's correct. I'm not really sure what it all entails, but I know that I don't want to wake up every day wondering if today will be the day I find a lump in my other breast." The expression on his face told me that he understood my reasoning and he agreed.

"Dr. Lauren explained the mastectomy portion of the surgery to you. Did he get into the reconstruction portion of the surgery at all?"

I hesitated. *Did he?* I didn't remember. "Honestly, I'm not sure." *How was I supposed to remember everything?*

Thankfully, Noah spoke up. "He briefly mentioned that it would be started immediately after the mastectomy, but didn't elaborate much past that. I think he assumed you would explain that portion, since it's your specialty."

"Very well, when the mastectomy is completed, I'll scrub in and start the reconstruction process by placing tissue expanders under your pectoral muscles. This part of the surgery goes fairly quickly. I'll also place at least one drain on each side to alleviate the fluid build-up from the trauma."

I looked a bit perplexed, and he picked up on it right away.

"With the removal of all of your breast tissue, we will need to place the implants under your muscle to hold them in place. In order to do this comfortably, we will need to stretch the muscle out gradually to make room for the permanent implant. The mastectomy along with reconstruction causes a lot of trauma to the area, and the body naturally produces fluid to protect itself. This will cause discomfort and can lead to complications or infection, so we place a tube, just under your skin, that is attached to a bulb that will extract the fluid from your body."

A shiver passed through my body. "That's just gross."

That earned me full smile from Dr. Forrester, which made my heart skip a beat. He was too good looking for his own good. The man was charming and smart, and there was something about him that made me feel comfortable, but I couldn't put my finger on it.

"Yes, the drains are a nuisance, but they are necessary. They're generally in for one to two weeks and will be removed in the office once the fluid levels have decreased. It's a very easy procedure," he assured me.

"Understood," I replied with a note of acknowledgment and disbelief. "Now, what exactly is an expander? This is all new to me."

He reached into a drawer and pulled out what

appeared to be an industrial water balloon with a metal disk on the bottom. "This is a tissue expander." He held it flat in the palm of his hand. "It will be placed under your pectoral muscle with two hundred cc's of saline in it to start the expanding process. Once you have healed, we'll start filling the expander with saline until we get it to the size we want."

What? Wait a minute. Fill the expander? How the hell was he going to do that? The look of sheer horror was more than evident on my face.

"By the look on your face, I'm sure you are wondering how it will be filled," Dr. Forrester said, a hint of humor in his voice.

There was nothing funny about this. It sounded more like some sixteenth-century form of torture.

"Well, yes, please enlighten me, because I have a feeling that long needles are involved, and that just isn't going to fly with me!"

"You're correct; it does involve a needle." He smiled as he held up the expander and pointed to a metal disk at the top of it. "This is a port. We locate it with a magnet so that we know where to insert a needle that will fill the expander with saline and not damage the expander. The actual fill process takes about fifteen to twenty minutes in the office and can be done every week or every other week, depending on your comfort level," he explained. "You call the shots on when you want it done and how much saline you want injected. Your comfort is what's most important."

I sat there for a moment, not knowing what to say. Noah looked at me and could see I was struggling, so he jumped in: "Dr. Forrester, how long does the entire fill process typically take? Are we talking three to six months, or longer?"

"Generally, women can comfortably handle between twenty-five and fifty cc's at each fill. A few have had up to one hundred cc's, but that's rare. The tolerable amount is determined during the procedure by the patient. If they say 'stop,' we stop, and each session is different. One week you might be able to take more and the next time it might be less. However, my limit's one hundred cc's at a time. In calculating everything, it will take approximately two to four months from the first fill to get to where we are able to place the permanent implant."

"Am I awake for the fills?" *Please say no, please say no, pretty pretty please say no!*

"Yes, you're awake, but you don't need to watch.

You'll feel some pressure and mild discomfort, but it's a fairly simple procedure. Have you thought about if you want saline or silicone implants?"

Smooth change of subject, I thought, and replied, "Not really, but I think I want saline. I've heard that there isn't a problem if they leak and they're safer. All the horror stories of silicone over the years makes me hesitant."

"That's fair. We don't have to make the decision right now, but in my professional opinion, I would suggest that you consider silicone. Generally, most mastectomy patients find the silicone implants are more comfortable and less rigid."

Reaching into another drawer, he pulled out two more heavy-duty water balloons. These were full, and he handed one to me and one to Noah. He was like a magician with a magic hat, only he was pulling out fake boobs instead of rabbits.

I was holding one that appeared to be filled with gel, and he explained. "Silicone implants are now manufactured with mesh inside the capsule, and the silicone adheres to it, so if there's a rupture, the silicone stays attached to the mesh and doesn't leak out. I've been using them since they were reintroduced to the market, and I've been very pleased with their performance."

Noah looked at it with curiosity and couldn't help the smirk on his face. *Yep. Men and fake boobs. Need I say more?*

"What?" he asked sarcastically when he noticed me glaring at him. I shook my head and couldn't help but smile, trying my best to find the humor in this.

I'm picking out boobs like you would pick out melons at the grocery store. "Do I get to pick the size?"

"Yes, you do; however, I'll need to see what we are working with as the amount of skin available may limit how big you can go." He stood and opened a cabinet and pulled out my new favorite top . . . a pink paper gown. "I'm going to step out for a moment so you can slip this on. Please undress from the waist up and keep the opening in the front."

A light blush crossed my face as I took it from him before he left the room. This attractive man, who was now my doctor, asked me to strip my top off so he could see my boobs . . . in front of my husband. I felt like I was in the twilight zone or the beginning of a cheesy-ass porn movie!

Looking at Noah, it didn't seem to bother him in the least, so I quickly stripped out of my top and slid on the pink paper gown and took a seat on the exam table.

Another knock at the door, and Dr. Forrester appeared, followed by a woman. She was about my height with light brown hair and hazel eyes. She appeared to be in her mid-twenties, if I had to guess. "This is Elizabeth, my assistant. She'll be the one scheduling your surgery and appointments moving forward and will be present during all exams. She'll be a great resource for you."

I smiled politely at her, and she smiled back.

Dr. Forrester washed his hands and stepped toward me. "Let's see what we have to work with."

I opened my gown slowly and was suddenly feeling apprehensive. My boobs felt disgusting, and I hated them right now.

"Well, the good news is that you have larger breasts to begin with, looks like a full D?"

"Yes, you're correct." *Oh my god. He guessed my bra size. How embarrassing.* "And that's a good thing because?"

"Having larger breasts to begin with leaves more skin, which makes the expansion easier without the concern of stretching the skin too thin. If there isn't enough skin, we're limited by how large we can go due to the risk of the skin splitting."

Eww! All sorts of images entered my head, making me feel nauseated.

He quickly cut through my thoughts. "But you don't need to be concerned with that. We should be able to get you close to the same size you currently are, and because you have opted for a bilateral mastectomy, both breasts will be very similar in size and symmetry. My recommendation would be a full C cup. In my opinion, it would look best on your frame if you're okay with downsizing a bit."

"I'm good with downsizing," I said as I looked over at Noah, who looked a bit uneasy right now. "What do you think, Noah?"

He looked up at me and simply said, "Whatever you want to do is fine with me. This is about you, and I want you to be happy with your decision."

He looked conflicted. Noah was a boob man. No way around it. It killed me knowing this at this moment.

"I would like to downsize a bit, but don't want them to be too small. I'm used to filling out my clothes, and I don't want to go from this..." I stated and did a Vanna White move, showcasing my boobs. ". . . to looking like a school girl."

Noah and Dr. Forrester both laughed, and I heard a giggle from Elizabeth. "Happy to entertain," I said with a smirk, finally feeling more relaxed.

"No. You will not look like a school girl. I want you to feel like a confident, beautiful woman and to make you feel comfortable in your skin again," Dr. Forrester said, looking me directly in the eye. I could see that he meant each and every word.

"Are you on board with me?" I questioned Noah. I knew this decision would affect us both, even though it was my body.

"Yes, if you're comfortable with Dr. Forrester's plan, let's move forward with surgery. The sooner, the better."

"Okay. Let's get this scheduled," I said.

"Wonderful, I will need Elizabeth to take a few pictures today for my records. These will help me during the reconstruction process, and we will take them a few more times throughout the process."

He looked to Elizabeth. "When you have finished with the pictures, please contact Dr. Lauren's office immediately to get our schedules coordinated and call the hospital to schedule surgery."

"Sure thing. Excuse me, I'm going to step out to grab the camera and get the paperwork started. Dr. Forrester, please let me know when you're ready for me to come back in for pictures."

Dr. Forrester returned to his desk to look through a note in my chart. "Dr. Lauren mentioned that he would like to get this scheduled in the next week or two. With the Thanksgiving holiday coming up, it might be tight. Do you have any travel conflicts that we need to be aware of?"

"None," Noah quickly replied. "Victoria's health is of the utmost importance right now. We will take any day and time available."

"Good. Victoria, I wish we hadn't met on these terms, but I'll take good care of you and make this process as smooth as possible. I'll have Elizabeth get everything set up, and I'll see you before surgery. Until then, if you have any questions, please don't hesitate to call me directly."

Noah stood and shook Dr. Forrester's hand and thanked him for his time.

I sat there numb and in my own world until I heard a throat clear and looked up to see Dr. Forrester standing in front of me. "Victoria, I know this is a huge shock. Please know that I'm here to support you during this journey and that I'll do my very best to help you feel normal again." He placed a sympathetic hand on my shoulder. "I can tell that you're a strong and witty woman, and you will get through this. You have an amazing future ahead of you." After a gentle squeeze of my shoulder, he left the room.

A few moments later, Elizabeth was back. "Are you ready?" she asked.

"As ready as I'm going to be, I guess. Is it okay if Noah is in the room?"

"I'm okay with it if he is."

Noah stood. "I think I'll wait in the hallway to give you some privacy." He kissed me before stepping out of the room.

Over the course of ten minutes, Elizabeth took several topless mug shot pictures. Not really, but it felt like it. "Please turn this way and face the corner. Now turn this way and face the camera. Make sure your feet are pointing to the wall and are on the red line." Yep, I had officially taken topless mug shot pictures. . . . I felt like a whore.

Chapter Five

I AM INDESTRUCTIBLE

The phone rang as I was cleaning up lunch. "Hello?"

"Hi, Victoria, this is Elizabeth from Dr. Forrester's office."

"Hi. How are you?"

"I'm doing well, and you?"

"Better. Thank you for asking."

"I'm happy to hear that. The reason for my call is that we are running into a few conflicts with scheduling your surgery, and Dr. Forrester wanted me to call you immediately to see if Friday, November 25 would work for you. I know this is the day after Thanksgiving, but Dr. Lauren is available, and Dr. Forrester will free up his schedule if this works for you."

"Yeah, I think that works," I said as I scrambled over to the calendar on the desk.

Noah looked up at me with curiosity and whispered, "Is that the office regarding surgery?" I nodded. "Elizabeth, can you give me one moment, please? Noah just popped in, and I just want to check with him."

"Sure, no problem. I'm happy to hold."

I covered the phone with my hand and told Noah that they were having problems scheduling the surgery, but the day after Thanksgiving would work and that one of the doctors was making special arrangements to be there if it was okay with me. "Yes. Take it," he said without hesitation.

"Yes, we'll go ahead with surgery on the twenty-fifth."

"That's wonderful. I'll tell Dr. Forrester right away. You will need to schedule a pre-op within seven days prior to the surgery. Do you have a primary physician that you can schedule this with?" she inquired.

"Yes, I'll call my doctor and schedule one. Is there anything specific I need from her? I've never had surgery, and I don't quite know what the process is."

"If you call the office and request a pre-op appointment, they will take care of the rest. Just provide your surgery date, type of surgery, and the medical center where you will be having the procedure done. They will take care of all of the paperwork and fax it directly to the hospital's admissions department," she calmly explained. "You can expect a call from the admissions department forty-eight hours prior to surgery to complete the pre-registration process, and they will give you the time of surgery during that call. Typically, this type of surgery is scheduled early in the morning, as it's more invasive and takes about three to five hours."

"Dr. Lauren explained that I should anticipate staying overnight for at least two nights?"

"That's correct. The first thirty-six hours after surgery are when you will feel the most discomfort, and we will need to keep an eye on your incisions to avoid infection. I'll call the medical center to schedule the surgery and will mail your surgical packet this afternoon; it will explain everything in full detail. There are also a few instruction pages in there for Noah to review, as he will be your primary caregiver once you're home."

"Got it," I said as I wrote "Surgery" on the calendar. "I've got it written on my calendar and will call to schedule my pre-op immediately."

"Great, I'll get everything else lined up on our end." She paused for a moment, catching my attention. "I wish you well in surgery, Victoria, and hope you have a lovely Thanksgiving. You have so much to be thankful for, and know that you'll be in my thoughts."

"Thank you, Elizabeth. I hope you have a wonderful Thanksgiving as well. I appreciate your kindness."

※

The next two weeks went by in a blur. I met with two oncologists to discuss my treatment options. The first was an older gentleman who looked like Santa and had an accent like Arnold Schwarzenegger. While he came highly recommended, I couldn't get past the mental picture of Arnold dressed up like Santa from the movie *Jingle All the Way*.

After meeting the second recommended physician, Dr. Jill Guthrie, I knew I had found the right oncologist for me. She was genuine and didn't try to candy coat anything. Noah and I both felt comfortable with her, but the thing that I loved most was that when she was leaving, she wrapped her arm around my shoulder and said, "Everything is going to be all right, kiddo." That right there sealed the deal!

After reviewing and completing all of the pre-surgical paperwork and completing my pre-op exam, I was able to take a deep breath for a few days. I tried to avoid the urge to read about breast cancer on the Internet, but that was impossible. Noah was working longer hours to wrap up some business so he could take a few weeks off to tend to me, and I found myself reading everything I didn't want to know about breast cancer.

I researched different forms of treatment, looked at pictures of reconstruction, and found a few online support groups for younger women who had breast cancer. It was overwhelming and made me question everything. I needed to stop and find something else to do to keep my mind off of what was happening to me.

On Monday night, I had a light-bulb moment and quickly grabbed my phone to text my three best friends—Jen, Bobbie Jo, and Dana.

Bobbie Jo and I had met through a mutual friend after I had started my design firm. She was one of those people who I felt like I had known my entire life. She was full of energy and added the perfect amount of craziness to my life. Over the years, we had done some traveling together, as she was in the design business as well, and we also had gone to a few showroom events together. Wherever we went, she turned heads; she oozed confidence and had *that* look that had men staring . . . even the gay ones, who she loved flirting with, and often became close friends with. I enjoyed watching her in action. She was one in a million, and I was so happy we had become such close friends.

Then there was Dana, my college roommate. We didn't see each other as much anymore due to her travel schedule, but when we were together, it was nonstop gossip and laughter. We spent our freshman spring break flirting our way down the beach in Jamaica. We both loved Bob Marley, and so the destination choosing was easy. Planning the trip on a college-student budget, however, was not. But somehow we made it. It was my first and last college spring break, since I met Noah eight months later and skipped on the next spring break trip and all the ones after that. I lived vicariously through her on those trips, while I attempted skiing again with Noah and his friends. I definitely wasn't a snow bunny. I was a born-and-bred beach babe, and nothing would change that.

> "Hello ladies. You have all asked what you can do to help me during this time, and believe it or not, I have something you can do. Noah is working a lot, and I need an escape to get my mind off of things. I'm proposing a spa day or dinner with my besties in the next day or two. Surgery is scheduled for Friday the 25th, and I hope we can figure something in the next day or two. Sorry for the short notice."

Send.

Within minutes, they all responded with huge YES answers. In true Bobbie Jo fashion, Bobbie Jo offered to set everything up and would let us all know the details. With her running the show, I knew this would be the perfect day.

Two hours later, I received a text:

> **Bobbie Jo:** Spa day is scheduled for tomorrow! Cancel your day or call in sick because you're meeting Victoria and me at the PreserveSpa at eleven tomorrow morning. I've got us all scheduled for facials, manis/pedis, and massages, followed by hair and makeup. A late champagne lunch will be brought in and served in a private room for us. Bring your hottest cocktail dress and sexiest heels, as we will be enjoying a dinner and cocktails out before calling it a night. Time for us to all put on

our bitch bras and ass-kicking shoes in support of Victoria as she prepares to kick cancer's ass!
Jen: *OH, HELL YES!!!*
Dana: *Wouldn't miss it for the world... well... maybe for David Gandy. Just kidding... not really ;-)*

Score! This was just what I needed!

I was getting out of the bathtub late Monday afternoon to try and unwind when I heard a knock on the bathroom door. I grabbed my towel as Noah slipped into the room. "Surprise! I left the office early and picked up your favorite Italian take-out for dinner. I just need to heat it up in the oven when we are ready," he said with a sly grin as he pulled his tie loose. "I didn't expect to find you climbing out of the bath, and I'm now confident in saying that our dinner will be served much later."

I eyed him and couldn't help but smile back. Even though the bruising had disappeared, I hadn't felt very attractive or sexy with everything going on. Noah definitely could make me feel sexy, and I needed it. Over the last few weeks, my libido had gone into hiding. But the look on Noah's face as he slid off his tie, had it making a sudden appearance once more, and I wasn't going to ignore it! He had successfully flipped the sex switch back on.

He looped his tie around me in my towel and pulled me toward him. He placed a kiss on my forehead before he buried his nose in my hair and inhaled slowly. "You smell like a tropical drink and I want a taste," he murmured as he pulled me tighter against him, not at all bothered by the fact that I was getting him all wet.

I let out a sigh and quickly melted in his arms forgetting everything that was going on . . . it was just Noah and me in this moment and nothing was going to stop it!

Wrapping my arms around his waist, I felt the strong muscles of his back flex underneath my hands and started to pull his dress shirt out of his pants. The warmth of his skin against my hands only heightened my longing to feel every inch of him naked against me. What started as slow and sensual quickly changed into a hurried and urgent need to be consumed by this man . . . my husband . . . Noah.

My hands desperately found the front of his shirt, and I felt the sudden urge to attack. I clutched the front of his shirt and frantically started working the buttons open and practically tore the shirt off him when they were all undone. I looked up at Noah and watched his eyes turn dark with hunger as his hands cupped the back of my head and pulled me into a hard and impassioned kiss.

The urgency of his mouth on mine was bruising, and it only fed the fire within me. When he broke away from the kiss and stood back so I could see him, he was naked and fully erect.

"I've missed you," I said as my eyes traveled down his body. I couldn't help but run my hands over every dip and plane along the way. He stood silently, watching me.

He knew that I needed this time to get lost in him, and he wasn't about to stop me. I slowly ran my tongue down the outside of his throat and kissed along his collar bone before reaching his nipples. I lightly licked and sucked in air against one of them and felt it pucker beneath my lips. Noah inhaled sharply, and I could feel myself already throbbing between my legs. "Don't stop, Victoria."

I continued traveling down his body, taking extra time to admire each square inch of muscle on his abdomen before running my tongue down along the right side of his "V," which again earned me another sudden intake of breath, followed by a deep groan. I ran my hands along his hips down to his cock and felt it twitch in anticipation as my mouth kissed its way down his happy trail.

"Fuck, Victoria," Noah moaned as his hips jerked forward. "You're driving me fucking insane here. I want to touch you right now, but know this is about what you want. Please, tell me you want me to touch you. Please . . ." I heard the desperation in his voice.

"I want to lick and touch you. Your body is perfection and needs to be appreciated completely," I said as I thought to myself how mine was anything but. I closed my eyes as tears attempted to invade them. "Noah, I want to feel your perfection against me. I want to feel your perfection in me. I want to be destroyed by you."

"Victoria." He gripped me under my arms and lifted me up off the floor. "Open your eyes. Let me see you," he pleaded.

Opening my eyes, I expected to see pity, but I didn't. What I saw was indescribable. It was love, lust, compassion, fear, and anger. *What a fucked up combination this is,* I thought when I realized I had the same look on my face. We were in this together. Feeling this together. Coupled.

He nibbled at my lips as he rubbed his cock up against my tummy. His tongue dipped into my mouth as our kiss intensified. It was all of our emotions bleeding out in this moment together. It was heaven and it was hell. It was love and passion. It was anger and fear. It was what we both needed.

My hand grabbed his cock, and I enjoyed the feeling of him in my hand. I felt his velvety strength as he flexed his hips into my hand and I tightened it around him. His left hand came up and started massaging my right breast as he broke our kiss and sucked on my nipple. It quickly stiffened under his tongue and ached for more as my back arched, pushing it further into his mouth.

"Victoria, I don't want to do this in here," he mumbled against my breast and then blew softly on my strained nipple. I nodded my head and let go of his cock as he lifted me up in his arms and carried me into our bedroom.

I climbed up on the bed and he followed right behind me, cradling his body between my legs. With a flex of his hips, he leaned down and kissed me while he was propped up on his right elbow and continued to play with my right nipple. "Noah, please," I said as I pushed my hips up toward him. "I need to feel you inside. I need you to make me forget everything but you and me and I need it right now."

He heard my desperation and wrapped my legs around him as the head of his cock started teasing me. He continued his torture as he rubbed his cock up along my folds and hit my overly sensitized clit. My back arched. "Noah . . ." I begged as my body was screaming and wanting him to push into me. "I need you to fuck my thoughts away. I need you to help me release my anger and forget the last few weeks. I need—"

SLAM!

"Ah shit," I screamed. "Again."

SLAM! Slow draw back . . . SLAM!

"Is this what you want, Victoria? Do you want me to fuck you hard?"

SLAM!

"YES!" I screamed again as my hands grabbed at his ass, trying to push him deeper inside. He lifted my right leg and shifted sideways so that he could get a better angle.

SLAM! . . . SLAM!

"OH. MY. GOD!" I shouted as he continued his assault on my body. Like he was punishing it.

Taking out his anger on it and taking my anger with it at the same time. It wasn't romantic or passionate. It was hard and demanding. It was therapeutic in the most fucked-up way possible.

"Victoria, fuuuuuuuck..." Noah slammed into me one more time and let out a roar. I could feel his warmth fill me as I pulsated around him, feeling my own release.

"Yes. Oh my god, yes," I breathed out as my body let go. Noah continued to slowly rock back and forth inside me as I came down from my orgasm. He leaned down and trailed kisses down the right side of my neck to my breast before he slipped out of me and disappeared into the bathroom.

I laid there collecting my thoughts while Noah cleaned himself up and returned with a warm washcloth to do the same for me. Once we were both cleaned up, he climbed in bed next to me, and we quietly lay there together, sorting through our unspoken thoughts.

I mulled over what just happened in my head. It started out flirty and passionate and then quickly morphed into hot and frantic. It was quite possibly one of the most intense moments we had ever shared together in bed.

I was pleased with myself and replayed everything in my head again. It was then that I realized Noah didn't touch my left breast once. Not once. I didn't know what to think of it and suddenly my high came crashing down. Did it affect him the way it did me? Could he feel the burn that I felt constantly in my breast when he touched it? Did he look at me as damaged already?

Noah turned me toward him and smiled. Apparently he wasn't feeling the same emotions I was, and he looked . . . well . . . for lack of a better term . . . well fucked!

"Jesus, Victoria, what did you do to me? I don't think I've ever fucked you that hard. Are you okay?"

I promptly tucked my questioning thoughts away and smiled back at him. "I'm great—that was amazing and exactly what I needed."

In all honesty, it was what I needed, but I wasn't prepared for the feelings I had afterward. Noah popped up out of bed and pulled on his boxers. "Why don't you stay here and I'll go heat up our dinner and we'll eat it naked in bed?"

"Sure, that would be great." I smiled as I sat up and watched him walk out of our bedroom.

I sat naked in our bed with my thoughts waging

a war inside my head. Would this be the last time we had sex while I had breasts? Would he look at me like this again or be totally disgusted when my body was disfigured? Would he find me attractive anymore? Would he want me when I was damaged?

Hot tears started to stream down my cheeks as a soft sob left my lips. What the hell? This wasn't me. I was strong. I didn't cry. I wasn't going to let this take over my life, and I couldn't let Noah see how scared I was. Jumping off of the bed, I ran into the bathroom, quickly washed my face and tried my best to cover up the puffy and glassy-eyed look that now was present on my face. I grabbed my face lotion and cover-up and tried to hide the evidence of my mini-meltdown before Noah got back.

Once I was satisfied with how I looked, I made my way back into our bedroom at the same time Noah appeared with two plates heaped full of pasta, a loaf of bread, and a bottle of wine.

"Is everything okay?" he questioned, a troubled look on his face. He must have noticed that I had freshened up.

"Yep, couldn't be better," I said cheerfully as I jumped back onto the bed and smiled at Noah. "Shouldn't you be naked?"

He didn't seem to believe me but just smirked and shook his head at me as he placed the tray on the bed. He then proceeded to slide off his boxers and climb back in bed with me.

※

When I woke the next morning, Noah had already left for the office, so I lazed around until it was time to get ready for my girls' spa day.

Knock. Knock.

I opened my front door to find Bobbie Jo standing on the other side, holding a cup of coffee. She shoved it into my hand. "Morning, toots! Are you ready to go?" I couldn't help the smile on my face.

Bobbie Jo always knew how to settle my nerves and enjoy life. "Almost—I just need to grab my purse and my outfit for dinner. I'll be right back." I ran upstairs to grab the garment bag from my closet and was ready to go. "Let's do this," I said as I grabbed my purse and we headed out the door.

Bobbie Jo was excited to show off her new car, so she offered to drive. We listened to old-school '90s favorites and found ourselves singing at the top of our lungs, not caring if people were staring at us. I couldn't help the feeling of being young and carefree again.

We were giggling as we pulled up in front of the posh PreserveSpa, and I saw Dana and Jen waiting with huge smiles on their faces. I hopped out of the car and was quickly pulled into a mob-like hug before being ushered through the doors into the spa.

The spa was exquisite. Warm browns and earth-tone accents covered every square inch. The scent of warm exotic oils and the sounds of water trickling and soft music playing instantly relaxed me.

Bobbie Jo looked at me and the girls. "You guys take a seat, and I'll go check us in."

Jen chimed in, "Shouldn't we all check in?"

"Nope," Bobbie Jo quickly replied. "You're all here as my guests, and this is my treat." Putting her hand up to halt any argument, she continued, "We are all here for Victoria. She asked for time with us and the next few months are going to be hard on her and we'll need to keep her spirits up." She dug into her handbag, which was the size of a small child, and pulled out a little notecard for everyone. "This is the planning schedule for 'Victoria's secret adventures.' I know you appreciate the title," she said with a wink. "Each of you will be responsible for planning a girls' day where we can all forget the world and enjoy each other."

She paused a moment to gather her thoughts. "Both of you will have exclusive rights to plan whatever you want on your given day. Stay within your budget; this is NOT a competition—it's a challenge for each of us to make memorable moments for Victoria. Be creative, be adventurous, and, by all means, be crazy!"

With that, she turned on her heel and walked to the check-in desk without argument from Jen or Dana. I looked over at my dear friends, who looked dumbfounded by the hurricane known as Bobbie Jo. She had this ability to take over any situation like a drill sergeant, shout out orders and you damn well better listen.

I sat back and smiled; it was quite refreshing not to be on the receiving end of Bobbie Jo's orders for once. She was a ballbuster once an idea entered that crazy head of hers, but it was one of my favorite qualities about her. Do it big or not at all!

The next five hours were spent relaxing, being pampered and enjoying some quality girlfriend time. We laughed and cried together as only friends could. When our spa treatments were done, we were led back to our private changing rooms so we could get ready for the evening.

When I stepped out fifteen minutes later, I found all of my friends smiling with champagne flutes held up to me.

"Victoria, you're a person full of passion, you don't take life for granted, and you always find the good in the bad. You have been there for each of us when life threw us curveballs, and you have never faltered," Jen said as she stepped toward me.

"You supported me through my divorce and taught me to follow my dreams. I wouldn't be as successful as I am without you," Bobbie Jo stated as she stepped forward.

Dana handed me a champagne flute. "You're up against the biggest battle of all, and we stand here at your side, ready to go to war with you. You will *never* be alone, and we will always be there to pick you up when you feel like you can't go on." She tried to keep it together, but I could hear the emotion in her voice. "You, Victoria, are going to kick cancer's ass! Cheers!"

We all lifted our glasses with teary eyes and found our smiles as we realized that this moment would forever be cemented in our memories.

"Enough with the tears bitches—let's get this

party started," Bobbie Jo announced after she set her empty glass down.

The four of us arrived for dinner at Bar Lurcat in downtown Minneapolis. Its understated elegance and floor-to-ceiling windows overlooking Loring Park were exquisite. We were led to a table in the bar area close to the windows so we could see all of the lights shimmering in the park.

Shortly after we sat down, Matthew, our waiter, arrived to take our drink order. Bobbie Jo up and ordered a bottle of Moët & Chandon Rosé champagne. As he turned to go to the bar, I heard Dana let out a breathy whistle and noticed her watching him walk away. "Did you see that fine ass?" she asked.

Jen and I both let out a laugh, and Bobbie Jo chimed in not so quietly, "I bet you could bounce quarters off of his abs too. Man, he is a fine piece of work and I'd like to 'work' that!" We were all laughing when he returned with flutes and a chilled bottle ready to uncork.

"Shh . . ." I said under my breath and smiled up at Matthew, pretending everything was normal. I knew better.

He held out the bottle toward Bobbie Jo for her approval. "Is this to your liking?" he asked. Look out... he had walked right into that one. I felt sorry for the innocent young man.

Bobbie Jo perked right up. "Hmm... it is, but I have to admit that there is something else that would satisfy my tastes a little better."

Matthew flashed her a questioning look. "I'm sorry, miss. Would you prefer a different bottle? Perhaps a Veuve Clicquot Rosé?"

Bobbie Jo ran her tongue along her lips before gently biting down on her bottom lip, making Matthew blush. "No, the bottle of champagne is perfect. However, I wouldn't mind a little taste of you for dessert." And there you have it. The look on Matthew's face was quite priceless; he was at a complete loss as to what to say.

Jen chimed in, "You'll have to excuse our friend." She glared at Bobbie Jo. "She seems to have lost her filter somewhere between the elevator and this table. I hope you weren't offended by her comment."

Matthew timidly cleared his throat and smirked. "No, not at all. A table full of beautiful women is always a pleasure—and an adventure—to serve. I'll admit that you're the first ever to be so direct, and it caught me off guard. So, bravo on that one." He winked at Bobbie Jo and worked on removing the cork from the champagne bottle with a *pop*. He filled our flutes before excusing himself.

"To my crazy-ass friends," I declared lifting my glass.

"To crazy-ass friends," they all agreed as we clinked our glasses.

Dinner was amazing, and Matthew was such a good sport through it all. We learned that he was in his senior year of college and would be attending medical school next fall. He was working as much as he could now to save since he would be spending a lot more time studying in the coming years.

Bobbie Jo made sure to tip him extra well, and I noticed that she wrote a little note on her business card and slipped it into the black leather folder after she paid our bill.

Busted! She looked up at me with innocent eyes. "What?"

I just shook my head and giggled. "Some things never change."

"Never . . . and you can't tell me that you would

want it any other way." She gave me a quick peck on the cheek and looped her arm into mine as we left.

We had planned to hit a few clubs after dinner, but I was feeling tired from the long day. I felt like a total loser, but they knew that the next few days were going to take a lot out of me and understood.

Bobbie Jo pulled into my driveway and parked. "Victoria, I wasn't going to do this, but I can't help it." She reached over and squeezed my hand. "You and I've been through a lot together . . . good and bad. Out of all of my friends, you have been the one constant in my life. You make me smile when I don't want to. You bring me soup when I feel like crap. You text me smutty guy pictures for the shock value, which I completely approve of. You're my female other half. I would be lying if I didn't tell you that I'm scared."

I looked up at her and saw her lip quiver as she continued, "You're the sister I never had, and I can't stand to see you suffer. The thought of you having to fight this battle rips me apart. If I could fight it for you, I would—one hundred times over." I couldn't listen anymore. I pushed her hand away and leaned over to hug her. The instant her arms encircled me, we both broke into sobs.

We held each other for what felt like hours by the time our crying had finally stopped. I looked back at her. "You're not going to lose me; I'm not that easy to get rid of." I gave a lame smile and rolled my eyes. Even though I wouldn't know my prognosis until after surgery, I knew I wasn't going anywhere.

"I know. Considering the shit I've put you through, you must really like me or something. I thought for sure you'd run for the hills at some point . . . but you never did."

"Will I see on you Friday after surgery?" I asked, secretly hoping she would be there.

"You bet your ass! I'm planning to be with Noah during surgery and will do my best to keep him company when your parents start to drive him batty," she smiled. "We'll have a little party going on in the waiting room while you're working on that new set of tits."

I laughed and was reminded again of why I loved her . . . she comes up with the craziest things to say at the most inappropriate times!

"I love you, Bobbie Jo!" I said as my laughter subsided. "Thank you for being you and for taking care of my sorry ass. I know I'll pay for it someday when I'm scrubbing your dentures or helping you change your Poise pads."

"Seriously, we will be the troublemakers of senior living in about fifty years. I can guarantee that because you're going to kick cancer's ass." She was right. I was going to grow old with Noah by my side and Bobbie Jo as my trusty sidekick.

"Now get the hell out of my car. Matthew sent me a text after we left the restaurant, and he is meeting me for a cocktail in forty-five minutes."

"What the hell?" I shook my head in mock disgust. "You're seriously one in a million."

"You too, toots . . . now get a move on!" she said as she lifted her right foot and started to shove me with her killer heels.

"Okay. Geesh . . . don't break a heel; I'm sure they will be wrapped around that poor unsuspecting boy before my head even hits the pillow."

"Damn straight, they will be."

I blew her an air kiss and watched her speed away.

Thanksgiving Day had arrived, and we celebrated the holiday with my parents and a few of our close friends. While we all joked and laughed throughout dinner, you could feel a slight bit of tension in the room. While I tried to stay positive and act like nothing was wrong, a few of our friends didn't quite know how to act. It was awkward to say the least.

"Can I have everyone's attention?" Noah spoke up. "I want to say something, since you're all here and now is as good a time as any." I tried to get his attention from where I stood in the doorway to the living room, but he refused to look at me.

"Thank you for spending Thanksgiving Day with us. Victoria and I are so thankful for each of you for so many reasons. Most of all, today, I'm thankful for your support." He paused to compose himself. "Tomorrow is the first step in Victoria's battle, and being surrounded by all of you has helped to keep her spirits up. We don't know what to expect in the coming weeks, but we know that we will get through this."

Noah turned and walked toward me. Once he reached me, he took my hands in his and looked me in the eye. It was just the two of us in that moment. "Victoria, you're amazing, beautiful, smart, and caring. But most of all, you're strong. In the coming weeks, though, you will have days where you don't feel strong."

Then he turned me toward the room that was filled with my parents and friends. "Do you see all of these people?"

"Yes," I answered weakly.

"They are your strength when your tank runs out. They are the ones that will be here for you in your darkest days, and they will guide you forward when all you want to do is turn around and run away." He moved to stand in front of me. "Victoria, while this battle is in your body, we are your arsenal of strength when needed." He wrapped me tightly in his arms and let out a hefty sigh. "I love you."

I hugged him even harder to me as tears slid down my cheek. "I love you too."

As I quietly sobbed, I felt more arms start to cocoon around us. After a few minutes, I lifted my head to see everyone huddled together with us in a hug. The love I felt at that moment was indescribable and a moment I'll cherish forever . . . especially when Noah's best friend Jon chimed in, "Ready, set, new titties!" and everyone started pushing him and laughing.

Humor . . . humor would get me through!

Chapter Six
I AM FEARLESS

November 25. Surgery day. The day that the cancer would physically be removed from my body. The day that both of my breasts would be removed as well. Let the battle begin.

We arrived at the hospital at six in the morning to complete registration and get prepped for the surgery, which was scheduled for eight o'clock. It was snowing that morning and with all of the Black Friday shoppers out, it made for some unplanned traffic. During registration, we were told that Noah could stay with me the entire time up until when I needed to physically go into the operating room. That provided some comfort, but I was still nervous. Other than my wisdom teeth being removed, this was the first surgery I would have, and it wasn't one to be taken lightly.

I was dressed in my lovely baby blue gown with

a matching robe and hair net. Let's not forget the incredibly sexy white thigh-high compression stockings and slipper socks with treads on the bottom. And to add a little more to the *hot* factor... I wasn't wearing any makeup and my hair was flat as a pancake. I looked stunning! Even better was the fact that I had to walk over to the breast center for my sentinel node injection. Thank god for the robe covering my ass.

Noah opted not to be present in the room for my injection. It was rather simple but hurt like hell. They brought me back to the ultrasound room that I so enjoyed on my last visit and had me lie down like before. In walked Dr. Frank.

"Good morning, Victoria. How are you doing this morning?" he asked out of common courtesy. We both knew how I was actually doing, so I responded with, "I'm doing fine."

"Great," he said. "I'm going to have a nurse help me with the ultrasound picture so that I can place the needle in the right area for the injection. It will burn a little, but it's a quick injection."

The nurse started pressing the ultrasound wand under my arm to locate my lymph nodes.

Bingo! She found the strike zone, and Dr. Frank

quickly injected the dye.

Damn . . . I could still feel the burning sensation where the injection had been as I walked back out to the reception area to find Noah. I wondered if I was glowing from the radioactive dye, but I didn't bother to ask. He wasn't in a joking mood today, even though I needed it for my sanity.

We walked hand-in-hand back to the surgical waiting area, and they got me comfortable in a little curtained-off room with a warm blanket. Noah sat next to me with his elbows propped up on his knees and his fingers in a steeple under his bottom lip. He was deep in thought when we heard a tap on the wall just outside the curtain.

"Hello, Victoria and Noah," said a familiar voice, as the curtain slid to the side, and Dr. Forrester appeared with a smile on his face. "How are you doing today?"

"Good, I guess. Just a bit nervous, but that's to be expected, I assume." I smiled weakly at him. Noah just nodded and stayed silent.

"I'd be concerned if you weren't nervous," he said while he flipped through my chart. "I got a call from Dr. Lauren, and he's on his way, but the slick roads from the snowfall are slowing him down a bit.

We'll start the surgery as soon as he arrives and scrubs in." He placed the chart back down at the end of my bed. "I'll be the one to mark you for surgery anyway, so we'll get started. It shouldn't be too long once he gets here."

He walked over to the side of my bed and asked me to scoot to the edge, facing him with my legs hanging over the edge.

"Great, now I need you to drop the top of your gown, please," he said as he pulled out a purple Sharpie marker.

I raised my eyebrow at him. "A Sharpie marker? Really?! I thought you would have some high-tech medical marker and not a regular old Sharpie," I joked.

That brought on a laugh from the good doctor. "Still witty under pressure, I see. Believe it or not, a Sharpie is my marker of choice as it doesn't rub off easily, and I want to make sure that Dr. Lauren follows my markings for the mastectomy."

I dropped the top of my gown as he knelt down in front of me. "Okay. Please rest your hands at your side." He started to draw lines and make little markings like I was a piece of construction paper and he was a scribbling preschooler. "Can you stand up, please?"

Trying hard not to lose my cool with this gorgeous man on his knees in front of me, I stood up and left my arms at my side. A little bit of nudging, readjusting my breasts, a few more purple sharpie marks and he was done. He signed his name on the top of my right breast. I looked up, questioning: "What are you, a rock star or something? I didn't realize I was getting your autograph, too."

"Very funny. It's actually required by law that I initial my markings for surgery. It's a security and safety precaution for you and for me," he explained as he put the cap on his marker. "I'm all done. Do you have any more questions for me before surgery?"

I shook my head no, but Noah spoke up.

"Do you know if Dr. Lauren will come out once he's done with the mastectomy to let us know how things went?"

"Yes, he will come out after he's done and I've started the reconstruction. The pathology report on the sentinel node dissection will be back from the lab, and he'll share the results with you at that time." He grabbed the pen on the clipboard and scribbled something on my chart before hooking it back on the bed. "You can also expect me to come out after

I'm done with the reconstruction portion of the surgery when Victoria is in recovery."

"Okay. Thank you, Dr. Forrester." Noah stood to shake his hand. "Please take care of her in there."

"I'll do my best—Victoria is in excellent hands today." He turned to me and patted my shoulder. "As soon as Dr. Lauren arrives, we will get you back into the operating room. I promise to take great care of you." With a reassuring smile and extra squeeze to my shoulder, he left the room.

The anesthesiologist arrived next to review my chart and inquire about any known allergies to medications. Because I was adopted and this was my first major surgery, I didn't have any that I was aware of. He reassured me that I was in good hands and that his assistant would stop in prior to surgery to give me something to help me relax. *I was ready for that right about now!*

The wait for Dr. Lauren to arrive didn't take long, and he stopped by for a quick hello and to see if we had any questions. At this point, Noah and I were both in a fog and didn't need to ask any more questions; we just wanted this over. The last few weeks had been building up to this moment, and the anxiety was starting to kick in.

My sarcastic humor had vanished, and my nerves were making my insides tremble while we waited for the surgical team to arrive to cart me off. The anesthesiology assistant stopped in to introduce herself before preparing to inject something into my IV line. "I'm giving you a light sedative to take the edge off. This will help you relax a bit. You'll start to feel its effects pretty quickly."

She wasn't kidding. I felt like I was flying over Disneyland and my body took on the feeling of a bowl of pudding. I smiled over at Noah and told him just that. He just shook his head and couldn't help the small smile that crept onto his face as he leaned down over me.

He placed a soft kiss on my lips and then my temple before whispering, "I love you Victoria, and I'll be holding your hand in my heart the entire time. I'll see you after surgery."

"I love you too, and everything will be fine, I promise," I said as two other people from my surgical team arrived and started moving stuff around on my bed. I heard a loud click and was moving. "Let the ride begin . . . this is fun!" I yelled and turned to look at Noah and blew him a kiss with a smile. He stood and waved, and I noticed his eyes filling with moisture as the doors closed behind me, but I was so loopy it didn't hit me until later . . . much later.

※

I heard mumbling as I tried opening my eyes. Someone was talking to me, but I had no clue where I was.

"Victoria, can you hear me? How are you feeling? Do you feel any discomfort?"

I tried to move my arm, but it wasn't budging. Next, I tried to open my eyes, figuring that would be easier. Everything was fuzzy and dim as I squinted and tried to focus on the movement next to me; it wasn't successful, so I just shut them.

"Victoria, I'm Cara, your post-op nurse. Your surgery is over, and you're in recovery. How are you feeling?" she asked.

"The sentinel node? Was it positive?" I somehow managed to mumble, though my mouth felt thick and dry.

I think I heard her say "negative," but I wasn't sure.

"What?"

"It was negative," she whispered before sleep

took over me again.

Time passed. I'm not sure how much to be exact, but the next thing I knew I was ready to be moved out of recovery. "We're going to move you up to your room now. I've given you another dose of morphine for the transfer. Best of luck, Victoria."

Closing my eyes on the journey up to my room was easy, the lights whizzing by were making me nauseated. When I sensed that I was close to my room, I opened them when I felt the presence of Noah and my parents nearby. Noah reached out to touch my head and kissed me. "May I come in with her?" he asked as they opened the door to my room.

"We need to get her settled first and then you can come in."

Noah nodded and stepped back, making room for them to maneuver my bed into the room.

Once inside, they parked me next to another bed and started moving cords around and untucking and tugging on the edges of the blanket I was lying on.

"I need you to lie still and take a few breaths. We're going to transfer you to the bed now, and you may feel a few moments of discomfort. You need to remember to breathe out the pain," I heard one of the transfer nurses tell me. I nodded my understanding, not really knowing what to expect until . . .

Aaaaahhhhhhhggggggghhhhh! Came screaming out of my mouth, and the most horrific pain imaginable hit my chest like an elephant was stomping on me. The pain was severe and was felt by every nerve in my body, and I continued to scream. Tears instantly filled in my eyes as I screwed them shut tightly while gasping for air to fill my lungs. At that moment, I wanted to stop breathing altogether because—to be completely honest with you—breathing hurt like hell!

I didn't want to be moved ever again, but, to my displeasure, they weren't done with me, not even close!

They rolled me to my left side while rolling the blanket under me and then "gently" shifted me to my right side and removed it completely. Now when I say "gently," I mean they attempted to be gentle . . . but when your chest wall has just been scrapped out like a pumpkin for Halloween, there is nothing gentle about any type of movement. A few more screams of pain, and a much-needed hit of morphine finally made its way into my veins.

When only one nurse was left in the room, I heard the door open, and Noah appeared with a look of distress on his face. He walked up to my bed slowly and looked at me with a look of dread. "Are you okay? I've never heard you scream like that in my life, and it took your father physically restraining me not to come in here." He lifted his right hand to my face and wiped away my tears with his thumb. "I'm so sorry, baby."

"Mr. Madison, I need to finish up her vitals and get her settled a bit. I just gave her another dose of morphine, so she will likely doze on and off for a while. You're welcome to stay if you'd like or go grab something to eat with your family. You look exhausted and need to take care of yourself. Victoria is in my hands, and I'll take good care of her."

"Thank you, but I would like to sit with her for a bit and will go grab something to eat shortly," Noah said abruptly. I heard him pull a chair over to the side of my bed. "Her parents just went down to grab something with her friends, and I'll go when they return. I don't want to leave her alone right now."

The nurse nodded her head in understanding and continued to complete her paperwork and check me over while I drifted in and out of consciousness.

I awoke to whispers in my dimmed room. Opening my eyes, I found my mom and dad standing in the corner talking with Noah. My mom was keeping a close eye on me and glanced over and noticed that I started to wake up.

"Hello there, sleeping beauty," she said as she walked over to me. "How was your nap?"

My throat was still dry and sore, I assume from the ventilator tube they had inserted during surgery. "Good. Still tired," I tried to say with a smile, but failed.

My mom pulled my hand into hers and gently rubbed the top in a soothing way only a mom can. "You did an amazing job in surgery. I'm so proud of you, my brave girl."

"You sure did!" my dad chimed in, standing next to my mom. "You look stunning, by the way, who knew hospital blue was your color?" he joked. Even at the ripe young age of seventy, my dad was still the best at making me laugh. A true master of humor— thankfully I learned from the best!

I tried to giggle, but the pain stopped me dead in my tracks as I winced. A look of concern appeared on my mom's face. "Karl, don't make her laugh. Can't you be serious for a change?" she scoffed.

He gave me a wink and leaned in to my ear: "I'm

sorry, honey, but I know you needed a good laugh. I'm proud of you and know you need your rest." He moved back and kissed my head. "Mary, I think we better get going so she can get some sleep. We'll be back tomorrow when Victoria has had time to sleep off the meds."

My mother gave me another kiss and wished me sweet dreams before walking out of my room, holding my dad's hand. After all these years, they still shared a love that every girl dreams of.

Noah sat back down in the chair next to me. "You've been sleeping for about two hours. Jen and Bobbie Jo knew you needed your rest and will be back tomorrow to visit. They said to wish you hot and steamy dreams," he said with a roll of his eyes and a hint of a smile.

"Thank you. I love you, Noah," I whispered. "How are you? You look terrible."

"I look terrible?!?" he questioned in disbelief. "I didn't go through what you did, and you look amazing."

"Always the charmer, Noah Madison. Always."

"Your surgery went very well, and both doctors were pleased with your outcome. The report came back, and your nodes were clear. They removed three nodes total, but there was no sign of cancer in any of them."

"I asked my nurse in recovery, and I think she told me it was negative, but I don't totally remember. They had me doped up on some serious meds," I confessed as my eyes started to get heavy again.

"Yeah, you've been through the ringer today. From flying over Disneyland to screaming out in sheer terror. You must be exhausted."

"I'm pretty wiped out and I feel like I could sleep for days," I yawned. "Why don't you go home and get a good night's sleep. Not much is going to happen around here tonight, and I could use another dose of meds soon. Did you happen to find the elephant that has been jumping on my chest?" I attempted a joke.

"The elephant?"

"Yes, it feels like an elephant has been stomping on my chest when I move or breathe. I think I've a pretty good pain tolerance, but that feeling I had when they moved me was like nothing I could ever have imagined."

"I'll do my best to hunt down that elephant." Noah kissed my temple and stood up to leave. "You get some sleep. I'll go let the nurses know I'm leaving and give them my mobile to call if anything happens."

"Okay, sweet dreams, Noah. I love you."

"Love you too."

⌘

"Good morning, Victoria. My name is Vivienne, and I'll be your nurse today. How did you sleep?"

"As good as could be expected, considering I was poked and prodded every few hours. I think I may need a nap or two today."

"Naps are good, but I would like to get you up and walking a bit this afternoon. We don't want you staying sedentary for more than twenty-four hours, as we need to keep your blood flowing to avoid clots. Once we get you moving, we can get those pressure socks off."

Pressure socks? Oh . . . that's why my legs feel so funny; I forgot all about them. "I didn't even realize I still had them on until you said something."

"Many people don't realize it; you aren't alone." She smiled. "Do you feel like trying some juice or chicken broth this morning? We don't want to give you any solids until we see that you can tolerate liquids."

"Sure, I could go for some chicken broth and maybe a little bit of apple juice."

"Coming right up," Vivienne said as she stepped out of my room.

Looking around my room, I noticed a few flower arrangements sitting on the ledge by the window. There were gerbera daisies, roses, and lilies among the assortment, and the incredible scent of them hit my nose. *It's the simple things,* I thought to myself.

Vivienne walked in with my liquid breakfast, only it wasn't the mimosa liquid breakfast I would have preferred. She set the tray down on the rolling table and moved a few pillows carefully to prop me up. It wasn't an easy task, and when she was done, she moved the tray so I could easily reach it.

Moving my arms wasn't the most comfortable thing, but I did it slowly and bent my head to meet my spoon. Noah strolled in just as I was sipping my juice while watching the news. He looked rested and handsome as ever.

"Good morning, beautiful. How'd you sleep?" he asked as he set down a vase full of fire and ice roses on the table next to my bed.

"Better than anticipated, but I'll definitely need a nap today. I just finished some chicken broth, and the nurse told me that if it sits well in my stomach, I can have crackers or a piece of toast."

"Who knew that toast would sound so exciting?"

"Yeah, well, it's the little things, I've learned." I nodded toward the ledge by the window. "Who are all the flowers from?"

Noah walked over to the vases and pulled off the cards and brought them over to me. I looked through each of them. One arrangement was from Noah's law firm, another from my parents, and two from our friends. "They are beautiful, and it was a pleasant smell to wake up to this morning."

"I have something else for you," Noah said, as he placed a large white box tied with a pink bow on the foot of my bed. "I'm guessing it might be hard for you to open; would you like me to do it for you?"

Bobbing my head up and down in excitement, I watched him carefully remove the bow and open the box.

Noah pulled out a robe. Scratch that, he pulled out *the* robe. It was the robe I had enjoyed during our stay at the Plaza for his conference last month. I thought to myself, *Was that really only last month? Impossible.*

He put the box down on the chair and walked

over to my side and laid the robe over me like a blanket.

"Thank you—it's beautiful! How did you manage to get this?"

"The doctors told me that dressing would be difficult for a few weeks and to try and find clothing that opens in the front, so I called the Plaza and arranged to have one delivered. I figured you had loved it then, and it would hopefully be good for you to use while recovering."

"It's perfect." I tilted my face up toward him, inviting him in for a kiss. The warmth of his lips instantly comforted me, and I didn't want this simple kiss to end . . .

Knock. Knock.

"Hello? Anyone home?" I heard Jen say as she rounded the corner. "Jesus, Noah, give the girl a break. Must you molest her in her hospital bed?"

"Very funny, Jen," I said after Noah broke away from our kiss.

"Who invited you?" Noah replied sarcastically.

"I don't need an invitation; haven't you learned that yet?" she said with a wink. "How's our patient today?"

"Hanging in there, I guess. Last night was okay,

and they finally have my meds sorted out now, so I'm doing better."

"Have you eaten anything? Can I get you a bagel or a donut or your favorite chocolate croissant?"

"Easy does it, Jen," Noah cautioned. "She is still on liquids and hopes to move on to crackers and toast first. I'm sure she will be up for a croissant in a few days."

"Deal! I'll bring you a basket of pastries when you're settled at home." She walked to my bed and started fussing over me. "We need to do something about your hair."

"My hair? What's wrong with my hair?" I asked, reaching up to try to touch it, only to wince at the burning sensation it caused.

"You look like you stuck your finger in a socket, and I happen to know that you will have visitors later today and we can't have you looking like a mad scientist, now can we?" Jen said as she scrambled around the room, looking for something. "Where is her cosmetic bag, Noah?"

"It's in the bathroom where any normal person would put it," I retorted.

Before I knew it, she was attacking my head with a brush and spraying all sorts of stuff in my hair.

"This isn't a salon, and people aren't expecting me to look runway ready, you know," I said.

"I realize that, but if it were me, would you let me look like Doc from *Back to the Future*?" She paused for effect. "I didn't think so. Now, zip it and let me do my job."

I peeked over at Noah who was reading the paper in the corner. He could feel my stare and dropped the corner so I could see the smirk on his face. He gave me a quick wink and continued reading. Men!

Jen was right. I had lots of visitors that afternoon. My room was starting to look like a floral shop, and I was thrilled when Bobbie Jo arrived with a cookie bouquet for me—I was cleared for solids at lunchtime, so I knew what I wanted my bedtime snack to be! I might have to sneak it past the nurses though.

It was about three in the afternoon when Vivienne peeked in. "I see your visitors have left. Are you up for a walk?"

"Sure, why not. What are the chances I can get this catheter removed?"

"Let's see how you do walking first. If you're able to walk a few times before dinner, I'll see if we can get approval to remove it. Does that sound fair?"

"Do I've a choice?"

"Not really, but if anything, it gives you a goal to reach."

Vivienne lowered my hospital bed and helped me turn and scoot to the edge with my legs hanging down. I did the butt crawl toward the edge until my feet landed on the floor and gave a pathetic smile; I knew that was the easy part.

"Take a deep breath, Victoria, and put your weight on your heels as I help you stand. Don't rush to stand; go nice and slow."

I followed her orders and found myself standing with her assistance and minimal discomfort. A slow burning feeling was still present, but I was able to keep my balance without doubling over in pain like I had experienced the day before.

"How does standing feel?"

"It feels pretty good, all things considered. I'm ready to take a step when you are."

She gave me a nod to begin. "I want you to go slow. Keep in mind that there are grippers on your stockings, so you need to lift your feet up and not shuffle."

Taking my first step was a bit nerve-racking, but

I did it and quickly found my other foot following suit. I walked to the door and back and felt like I had run a 5K. A small victory, but I'd take any victories at this point.

"Great job. Do you want to sit back in bed? Or would you like to try sitting in a chair?"

I looked over at the tall recliner-looking chair in the corner by the window. The thought of sitting with the warmth of the sun on my face sounded lovely. "I'd love to sit in the sunshine."

We made our way over to the chair as she continued to hold my elbow and roll the IV pole with us.

Once I was settled, she stepped out and reappeared a few minutes later with a tray. She placed it on my rolling table and brought it over toward me. A piece of toast, some crackers, jello, and a glass of juice looked like a four-course meal, and I was grateful for solid food.

"Why don't you have a little snack, and we'll try another walk in a little while," she said before leaving the room.

I started with the piece of toast and enjoyed looking outside at the people going about their normal day. While the sun felt warm, I knew the chill of winter was coming and sat back to enjoy the feeling of it on my face. I was reminded of the little things that would get me through and closed my eyes.

That night, they removed my catheter, and I was finally free to walk the halls . . . with assistance, of course. And I was able to enjoy a cookie before bed, without being sneaky.

The next morning was a flurry of activity that included a much-needed shower. Normally, a shower was a relaxing thing, but this one was more like a juggling act for a first-time juggler. In addition to the surgical tape still covering my incisions, *thank god*, I had two drains to contend with and was thankful for a little trick one of the nurses taught me.

I made a beautiful necklace out of a shoelace and two safety pins, which I looped through rings on the end of the drain bulbs. It hung perfectly around my neck and kept the bulbs in one location so I could carefully wash myself without fear of snagging one of them.

While I wouldn't recommend this as a fashion

statement, I was tempted to take a picture and post it on the Internet simply for the brilliance of it.

I had settled back into my favorite chair by the window, wearing a pair of leggings and a button down shirt that belonged to Noah. It felt good to be in clothes, and I started to feel somewhat human again. There was a knock at the door and when I looked over, I saw Dr. Forrester walking in wearing scrubs and his white doctor jacket. No power suit today.

"Good morning, Victoria. I'm in between surgeries and wanted to stop by to see how you were doing." He made his way toward the ledge by the window and casually propped himself up against it. "It's good to see you dressed and sitting in the chair. I'm sure you were anxious to get out of the hospital gown. How are you feeling?"

"I'm feeling pretty good, all things considered, especially after a shower. The drains made for an interesting hurdle, but I won out." I smiled.

"Yeah, they can get in the way. I'm guessing they showed you the necklace trick?"

"They sure did, and let me tell you, it is quite a fashion statement." I laughed without wincing for the first time. "It feels good to clean up and put on clothes."

He glanced at his watch. "I don't mean to rush, but I am in between surgeries and wanted to check in and sneak a peek at your incisions, if that's okay with you."

"Sure thing." I sat forward and started scooting off the chair. The feeling of a warm hand gently grasping my elbow to help me to my feet was comforting. I smiled as he guided me over to the hospital bed and helped me lie back. "Thank you for your help."

"No problem—I'm not about to risk you slipping on my watch." He winked.

I unbuttoned my shirt as he stepped over to the sink to wash his hands before slipping on a pair of latex gloves to check on my incisions. He helped me pull down the zipper on the front of my mastectomy cami when he saw I was struggling. Wearing a cami was a new experience, and it felt strange not to have a bra on. What felt even more awkward were the built in pockets that held my drain bulbs. Disgusting!

Dr. Forrester noticed me wince when I moved a little too quickly. "It's okay," I said. "I'm getting used to the discomfort, but it still catches me off guard. I feel like there are coconuts in my chest, and it's hard to move."

He started to remove the medical tape and pulled back the gauze slowly. "I've heard several women compare them to coconuts, and I think it's an acceptable description." He studied the incisions and gently poked and prodded the area.

"The incisions look very good. I'm happy with how everything looks." He carefully zipped my cami back up. "You can go ahead and button up." He turned back toward the sink to discard his gloves and wash his hands again.

"I'd like you to stay tonight, but you can plan on going home tomorrow."

"Thank God. I'm going stir-crazy sitting here."

He chuckled. "I'm sure. Have the nurses reviewed with you how to clean the lines on the drains and empty them?"

"Yes, I've been stripping them since this morning, and it's pretty easy . . . disgusting, but easy."

"They will be out soon enough. You will be sent home with instructions on how to care for your incisions as well. I would like for you to schedule an appointment to see me at the end of the week. I'll see how the drains are looking at that time. Please keep a record of the amount of fluid that is draining and bring it with you."

"I can do that."

"Great." He reached out to shake my hand and held on a little longer than I anticipated. "You're very lucky, Victoria. You found it early, and the pathology reports are promising. I look forward to seeing you in a few days."

"Thank you, Dr. Forrester. I'll see you then."

Chapter Seven
I AM UNAFRAID

As promised, I was released from the hospital the next day. We left loaded down with meds and a novella filled with instructions and restrictions. Noah was very attentive to my needs. My comfort was his main priority, and he even scheduled my follow-up with Dr. Forrester for Friday.

Get well cards arrived in the mail, and people came and went over the next few days. Nobody would fess up, but I was positive Jen or Bobbie Jo set up a schedule of visitors to stop by with magazines, books, movies, and treats. The refrigerator was fully stocked with meals with instructions for Noah on how to reheat. Having pre-cooked meals on hand was a godsend for Noah, who tried his best to work from home a few hours a day. He wasn't sleeping much, and I could see the strain of it all on his face . . . everyone who visited could see it too.

"Hey, Noah!" Bobbie Jo yelled down the hall.

He came dashing out of his office, sounding out of breath. "What's the problem? Is everything okay?"

"Yeah, everything is fine, chill out." She smiled slyly. "I was thinking, you have been nurse, cook, pharmacist, and man Friday for your lovely woman here, and you look like shit." He glared at her. "I mean that with the deepest sincerity."

"And . . ." It wasn't a question, and he looked annoyed.

"How about you hire me to babysit Victoria for the night, and you go grab a few beers with your buddies."

"Hire you? I can only imagine what you charge per hour."

"I'm the best deal around." She smirked. "I take payment in the form of wine or ice cream. I'm sure being the big, bad lawyer you are, you can afford it!"

A loud laugh escaped Noah's mouth, and it was a welcome sound. He had been so serious the last few days, I was afraid he had turned to stone.

"Ice cream and wine will buy me a babysitter for my wife, huh?"

"Hmm . . . now that I think about it, my offer has changed."

"Of course it has." Noah rolled his eyes as he leaned back against the doorway and crossed his arms, waiting for Bobbie Jo's new offer.

Bobbie Jo took her time in responding, "Yes, it most definitely has."

I was thoroughly entertained by this point and couldn't hide the smile that lit up my face as I watched the two of them square off in "the battle of the adult babysitter."

"I'm curious as to what the going rate is for you to babysit your grown friend. This better be good," Noah sarcastically replied.

"Oh, it's good all right." She winked at me. "I'll need a bottle of red wine for me, a carton of Ben & Jerry's finest for your wife, and two bars of Godiva dark chocolate with sea salt, one for each of us. That is my final offer, Counselor."

Noah put his hand up to his chin, appearing to consider her request. "You drive a hard bargain." He paused for effect; Bobbie Jo was getting antsy. "I accept your offer," he said as he walked over and pulled her up from the sofa and into a hug.

I heard him whisper "thank you" into her ear as she patted him on the back. "You need a break, Noah. I worry about you, and you need to get out of here for a few hours."

He released her and walked over to me and leaned down to kiss me. "Are you okay if I leave for a bit?" Concern was apparent in his voice, but I could see that he really did need a break when I looked into his weary eyes.

"Yes, I'll be just fine. It would be good for you to get out of here for a bit. I'm in good hands, and I'll probably go to sleep early again." I tilted my face upward, inviting him to give me a kiss on the mouth. "Call one of the guys and head to a bar to watch the Thursday night game. My appointment with Dr. Forrester isn't until one-thirty tomorrow, so you can stay out late and sleep in."

"Thank you, baby," he said to me as he stood and looked over to Bobbie Jo. "This means a lot. Please take good care of her while I'm gone."

"Promise."

I woke up early on Friday morning to an empty bed and the smell of coffee. After pulling on my robe, I strolled down to the kitchen to find Noah sitting at the breakfast bar, reading the paper. He was in his pajama pants and a white T-shirt and looked relaxed for a change.

"Good morning. How did you sleep last night? You must have been tired; Bobbie Jo texted me shortly after you passed out at eight. She's still asleep in the guest room."

"Really? She stayed the night?"

"Yeah, she said she was pretty tired and was going to make use of the guest room since she didn't know when to expect me and wasn't about to leave you alone." He took a sip of his coffee and nodded toward the counter where there was a tropical fruit salad in a bowl and a flaky chocolate croissant. "I thought you might enjoy a special breakfast treat. Come join me."

"When did you go to the store?"

"I couldn't sleep, so I went for a walk and stopped at the bakery. I know they are your favorite, and I wanted to do something special so I could see your smile."

He was right; it did bring a smile to my face. "Thank you. It was very thoughtful."

I grabbed the croissant and bowl of fruit and sat next to Noah to enjoy my breakfast. It didn't take long for Bobbie Jo to make her way out of bed and suck down a pot of coffee before heading to a meeting.

The shower was warming up as I started undressing. I still couldn't look at myself in the mirror; I wasn't quite ready to see what I looked like, so Noah continued to help me with my bandages. Once they were off, I hopped under the hot water and let it cascade across my back. It felt amazing. I had gotten pretty good at lifting my hands high enough to wash my hair without help and was feeling more independent while bathing. Drying off was getting easier, but it was nice to have Noah's assistance when I stepped out. Once I was dry, he reapplied the dressing, and I was able to finish getting ready.

I had just slipped on my shoes when Noah appeared in the doorway to let me know that we should get going for my doctor's appointment. "Do you need any help?"

"Nope. All good. Let's go," I said with a smile as I leaned up and gave him a quick kiss. I had a little spring in my step today and was hopeful about getting the drains out, well one of them at least.

The drive to the medical professionals' building was quick, and Noah dropped me at the door before he parked. As I stood in the lobby, I heard a familiar but unwelcome voice: Stacey.

"Victoria Madison? Is that you?" I heard, but I pretended I didn't hear her. The only problem was that she was walking right toward me, and there was no escape. Shit!

"Hi, Stacey," I responded as I tried to sidestep her and make my way toward the building directory. My attempt to avoid her failed as she followed me.

"I just visited my dermatologist for a little boost. It's never too early to start reversing the aging process," she mocked, as she looked me up and down. "I heard you had a boob job or something like that." She waved her hand in the air like it was no big deal.

"Yeah, something like that," I scoffed, trying again to move away from her. "It was nice seeing you, but I need to get going. Noah should be walking in any minute, and we have an appointment."

"Oh, really?!" she said, looking around for him. "Are you seeing a fertility specialist? I had heard Noah was eager to start a family and figured you were having troubles in that department. Good for you for realizing you need help."

I stared vacantly at her, not knowing what to say. Considering I was recovering from a mastectomy, there was no way we would be trying to get pregnant. Was she really that dense? I was about to ask her that very question when I saw Noah approaching and thought it best to bite my tongue.

"Stacey," he nodded to acknowledge her as he slipped his arm around my waist.

"Hi, Noah," she purred, looking him up and down like a drooling dog. "It's good to see you again. It's been too long."

Looking as uncomfortable as me, Noah guided me toward the bank of elevators and glared back at Stacey.

"What's her deal?" I asked.

"I haven't the faintest idea. I'm sorry she makes you so uncomfortable. Let's forget we even saw her."

"Agreed."

"Everything looks great, Victoria. According to your notes, the drainage from your right side has been minimal for the last day or two. Correct?"

"Yes. I've only stripped the tube once a day and, even then, there hasn't been much."

"The left side still has measurable drainage, so I'm not comfortable removing that one quite yet, but we can remove the right one today if you'd like," Dr. Forrester said has he scribbled something in my chart. "Shall we?"

"Definitely!" the excitement in my voice was clear, and he stood up to wash his hands and grabbed his gloves. There was a tray already set up with a few medical instruments, and he moved it toward me on the exam table.

"Do I need to leave for this?" Noah asked, a slight unease in his voice.

"No, you can stay if you're comfortable with it. But I don't want you passing out," Dr. Forrester hesitated. "It's a quick process: I just need to snip the two stiches, and the tube will slide right out. The incision is very small, and I'll just clean the area and place a Steri-Strip over it. Are you good? Or would you like to leave before I start?"

"I'm good, go ahead."

Dr. Forrester turned his attention back to me. "You will feel a slight tug followed by a little pressure, but it's very quick."

I took a deep breath and nodded, giving him the go-ahead. "It will take a day or two to completely close, so you need to keep the area clean and dry." He spoke while he worked. "I'm pretty confident that the other drain will slow in the next day or two. Call the office when you notice this decrease, and we'll get you in." He paused a moment. "All done."

"What?" I looked down and noticed the tube was out, and he was wiping up a slimy string of blood from my side. He cleaned and covered the area. "Wow. I didn't even feel it."

"I'm not surprised—the nerves are still recovering from surgical trauma." He removed his gloves. "Truthfully, you might not get a lot of feeling back in the breast area at all, which is normal."

"Good to know."

"Do you have any more questions?"

"Not at the moment," I said, turning toward Noah to see if he had any.

"When will the fill process start?" Noah asked.

"The earliest I'll start filling the expanders is four weeks post-op. I want to make sure the area is healed and the swelling has completely disappeared. However, we will have to see how chemo treatment goes, as some patients choose to put reconstruction on hold until chemo is done. It's a lot of stress on the body . . . and the mind."

"I see," Noah said brusquely.

I looked over at him, wondering what the hell he

meant by "I see." He almost sounded irritated, and that wasn't sitting well with me. Ever since we had arrived in the office, he had been acting strange and something was off. I was pretty sure Dr. Forrester noticed it as well.

"Well, if you have no further questions, you're good to go. I still want you to avoid lifting things until the last drain is removed. Call the office when you're ready for it to come out. In the meantime, keep doing what you're doing; everything is healing up nicely."

"I'll be in touch, thank you again," I replied. He helped me step down off the table.

I slid my arms out of the gown after he left the room and confronted Noah. "Is everything okay? You seem angry."

"Yes, I'm angry," he barked. "I feel like he didn't tell us everything. I mean, it would have been nice to know that you wouldn't have any feeling in your chest and that the reconstruction was going to take longer than he made it sound." He calmed his voice after I gave him a stern look. "I just want this over. I can't stand it anymore."

Shocked by his statement, I was now the one who was angry. "You can't stand it anymore? Are you kidding me?" I seethed. "It has been one week, Noah, one goddamn week, and *you're* angry? I cannot believe you said that."

Feeling like I had been hit in the gut, I turned my back on him and started to pull my shirt on. I felt his hands reach out to help me, but I moved away. "I can do this without your help."

He stepped in front of me. "I'm sorry. That was insensitive of me, and I didn't mean to take my frustrations out on you. I've nothing to complain about; I'm not the one going through it. But I can't stand by and keep my mouth shut when I feel like we weren't told everything." He let out a heavy sigh.

"You need to step back, Noah. I cannot have you doing this. I can't." I paused to gather my thoughts before continuing. "The next several months are going to be full of unknowns. Do you honestly believe that we will be prepared for everything thrown our way?"

He looked away as I continued: "No way. I'm not giving myself false hope that everything will go smoothly because I've no idea what to expect. I've never dealt with this, and I'm just going through the motions of what the professionals are telling me I need to do. I have to have faith in their judgment and their guidance. I..." My emotions were starting to get the best of me, but I pressed on. "I just need to keep getting up every day thankful that I'm alive, thankful that I found the lump when I did, and thankful that I have a team of doctors who are helping me battle this beast."

I reached out and grabbed Noah's hand. "I need you to believe in me. I need you to trust my doctors. I need you to have faith that I'll be okay. It isn't going to be easy for either of us, but blowing a gasket isn't going to make it better. If you need more breaks and need more help, tell me. Every day I get a little stronger, and I'm able to do a little more. A month from now, it will be even better. We need to measure progress week by week. Look at where I was a week ago and where I am now. That *is* progress. We need to see the little things and pay attention. Can you do that?"

Noah looked up at me, and I could see the tension in his face as his eyes met mine. Looking defeated, he replied, "I'll try my best."

While his comment wasn't what I expected, I tried my best to understand that he was hurting too. "Thank you. That's all I ask."

The next few days passed, and I was getting stronger and able to do more things on my own. The final drain was removed, which helped me feel more like myself and not so broken.

My appointment with Dr. Guthrie, my oncologist, was scheduled for two o'clock, and Noah had gone into the office for a few hours. Soaking in a bath still wasn't an option after surgery, but a hot shower would help to relieve some of the tension in my shoulders.

I turned on the shower to let the water warm up while I brushed my teeth. As I undressed, I realized that Noah wasn't home to help me with the bandages. He was still helping me even though the bandages only consisted of a gauze pad and tape. The incisions weren't weeping anymore, but I kept the gauze on to protect the incisions from rubbing up against my camis.

Reaching down with my left hand, I held the skin taut by the outside of my left ribcage and reached across my chest with my right arm and carefully lifted the corner of the tape. Slowly pulling it off, I let it drop onto the bathroom counter before repeating the process on my right side. As the last bandage landed on the counter, I opened my eyes and slowly looked down at them lying there. Two large white pads with tape still attached; they weren't flat, but slightly curved from the warmth of them hugging my chest.

Taking a deep breath, I raised my head and looked at the bottom of the mirror, daring myself to raise my eyes to look at what was left of me. I carefully moved my arms up around my chest in a gentle hug, but it wasn't a hug to comfort myself, it was a hug of protection. My hands settled in place and curiosity took over as they started to move around. The skin under my fingers was soft and squishy, but I could feel ridges along the line of where my incisions were. They were rough and hard, a sharp contrast from the rest of my chest.

Drawing my eyes upward in the mirror, I found my stomach and moved up past my arms that were crossed over my chest until I met eyes staring back at me in the mirror. These eyes were familiar but held something I had never seen before—fear. Fear of what was hiding underneath. Fear of what I would see. Fear of what cancer had done to me. Fear. Plain and simple.

I kept staring back into the eyes in the mirror as I slowly started to drop my arms down to my sides. Focused on slowing down my breathing, I tried to calm myself. When I felt strong enough, I let my eyes travel down past my mouth to my neck and along my collar bone. Yellow and green discoloring started to come into view as my gaze dropped farther down until I saw two long lumpy and twisted-looking scars where my breasts once were. I no longer had areolas or nipples. If I ever questioned what a medical experiment was, I now knew. I looked and felt like one.

Sucking in a harsh breath, I slowly moved my hands back up so I could watch them lightly run along the horrifically long scars that were now two weeks old. Watching my fingers move across this foreign part of my body, my eyes instantly filled with tears and my vision became blurry as I stood there, realizing for the first time how very broken I still was.

Suddenly feeling the hot tears landing on the backs of my hands, I snapped my head up quickly and looked at the face in the mirror again. The face of a woman I didn't recognize appeared with tears streaming down her face and grief heavy in her dark chocolate brown eyes. I quickly turned and stepped into the shower, letting the hot water drown my face, hoping it would wash away the tears that would not stop falling.

I'm not sure how long I was in the shower, but when I emerged, the tears had stopped and anger was in its place. The extreme switch of emotions was unfamiliar and unwelcome. I dried as quickly as I could without looking back into the mirror and stormed into our bedroom to dress.

"There you are," Noah said with a sound of concern. He looked down at his watch. "I expected to find you in the kitchen ready to go since your appointment is in forty-five minutes." He moved closer to me. "Is everything okay? What happened?"

"Nothing. I'm fine," I clipped back. I wasn't about to share my weak moments with anyone. They were mine, and nobody else would ever see them. Ever. "I was in the shower and just lost track of time." I turned and walked into the closet to attempt to find something to wear, but my options were sparse. I stood in my closet, staring at the tops that wouldn't fit me anymore.

Feeling defeated, I grabbed a baggy dress shirt of Noah's and paired it with leggings... again. My wardrobe was pathetic. I walked back into our bedroom to find Noah sitting on the edge of the bed, watching me.

"I'm ready to go."

"Are you sure?" he questioned with a raised eyebrow.

"Yes, I'm dressed and ready to go. Why are you looking at me like that?"

He smiled as he stood and walked over to me, turning me toward the mirror above our dresser. "I love the au naturel look you have going here, but I'm surprised you're going out in public with wet hair and no makeup."

I looked into the mirror on our dresser and saw that my face was naked of makeup and my hair was in a messy wet heap. I couldn't help the giggle that escaped me, and I was again reminded of the extreme mood swings I was having. "I think I've officially lost my mind." I continued to giggle, and Noah joined me. It felt good to laugh again.

"Let me help you," he said as he led me back into the bathroom.

"Thank you. I can't believe I did this, and I'm finding it quite funny." I shook my head while I continued laughing. "Give me a second. I'll just swipe some gloss on my lips and put some mascara on. Maybe that will distract people from noticing the wet-dog look of my hair!"

Noah grabbed my hairbrush and was careful as he made my mop of hair look neat. Well, as neat as a guy who wasn't a stylist could. He was a keeper!

We arrived at Dr. Guthrie's office with ten minutes to spare and took a seat in the waiting room. In the lobby, there was a small kitchen-like area with coffee, tea, and hot chocolate, as well as a bowl of various hard candies. There was a hat rack with an assortment of baseball caps, crocheted hats, and scarves set off in the corner with a placard at the top explaining that the hats were donated for cancer patients and to take one. My hair was still long, and I wasn't ready to start picking out hats yet.

"Victoria Madison?"

You guessed it—there was my name again, but I was surprisingly getting used to it. Noah was right behind me as we walked down a short hallway to a large room that had chairs set along one wall and curtains pulled as dividers. I noticed that some chairs were occupied with patients and others sat empty. I turned back as we were led to one of three exam rooms on the other side of the room.

There was a light tap on the door, and Dr. Guthrie stepped in. "Good afternoon, Victoria. You're looking good after surgery. Are you feeling well?" she asked with a comforting smile.

"I'm feeling much better since Dr. Forrester removed the final drain a few days ago. What a difference that has made, but it's still an adjustment with the expanders. They're different than I had expected, not that I knew what to expect."

"The expanders are rough from what I've been told. They can be a nuisance, but they are necessary to stretch the muscle and skin. Keep in mind that they're temporary, all of this is temporary." She turned to face Noah. "How are you doing with all of this? I'm sure being her nurse has been a major adjustment."

"Yeah, it has been interesting, but we are making it work and taking it one day at a time. It's definitely more than either of us expected," Noah said honestly, without hesitation.

"I'm sure it is. All you can do is to take it one day at a time." She looked down at my chart and cleared her throat. "I've reviewed your pathology report, and everything looks encouraging. Your lymph nodes tested negative, which means that the likelihood of the cancer having spread is extremely low. The tumor size was 2.3 centimeters and had clear margins; there was no 'spidering' of the cells. That means that the tumor itself was self-contained and that it was surrounded by normal tissue. You're classified as Stage IIA, since the tumor size is between two and five centimeters and the cancer had not spread into the nodes."

"That's good, right?" I asked, trying to sound upbeat and looking over at Noah, who was processing everything Dr. Guthrie had just hit us with.

"Yes, it's positive. However, we also need to take into consideration the fact that your tumor tested 'triple negative,' which will change how we are able to treat this."

"I don't understand what that means. I did some preliminary research, but I stopped after surgery because, honestly, the more I read, the more it scares me."

Noah cut in, "Can you please explain?"

"Definitely. I'm sorry if you're overwhelmed with all of the technical terms. When Victoria's tumor was sent to pathology, they ran several tests on it, and a receptor test is one of them; it determines if the cells contain specific proteins. Three specific receptors are targeted: HER2/neu, estrogen, and progesterone. If any of these three receptors test positive, then we have more treatment options available. If they test negative, then we have fewer options. Victoria's tumor tested negative for all three receptors."

"Does that mean that my chances of beating this are slim?" I whispered, trying to process what she just said. The words "fewer options" was not sitting well with me.

"No, not at all," she assured me. "While only fifteen to twenty percent of breast cancer in the United States is triple negative, it doesn't mean that it's untreatable; we just need to pursue other options for treatment. You're extremely lucky that you found the tumor when you did, Victoria." She paused for effect. "Triple negative is less likely to be found and tends to grow faster. It's very aggressive, but since you caught it early and the surgical results were positive, there is no reason to believe that we are unable to treat it."

Dr. Guthrie sounded like Charlie Brown's school teacher. All I heard was a bunch of noise except for "grows faster" and "very aggressive." The tears began to well in my eyes as I mentally chanted:

I will not cry. I will not cry. I will not cry. Dammit. It didn't work.

"Sweetheart, it will be okay," Noah reassured me as he reached out to take my hand in his. He carefully raised it to his lips and kissed it softly. "Don't let your thoughts run away on you right now. Dr. Guthrie just needed to explain all of the pathology results so that we better understand the treatment plan."

I looked up into his eyes, searching for something, but I wasn't sure what I was searching for. Noah's eyes expressed that he believed in me, that he knew I was strong and he knew I would survive. It was the same look he gave me on the Skydeck. I turned back toward Dr. Guthrie. "So, you have a plan?"

"I do. What I'm proposing is a sixteen week cycle of three different drugs that will be given every other week—eight treatments total. The first eight weeks will be a combination of doxorubicin and cyclophosphamide, followed by paclitaxel. This combination and schedule will be aggressive, and I feel positive about the results." She moved to grab a few brochures from the cabinet before continuing.

"Because your tumor was fewer than five centimeters and you had a mastectomy, you don't need to undergo radiation, in my opinion. You're just over two weeks out from surgery, and I would prefer to start treatment four to six weeks post-op so that your body is a little bit stronger. I'll be sending the two of you home with some information on the type of treatment I'm suggesting. I would like you to discuss the options and come back next week with a decision. I'll answer any questions and concerns you have at that time. You don't have to decide anything today."

I sat numb, trying to absorb the information that was just heaved at me. Words were being spoken, but I couldn't understand them. Suddenly, Dr. Guthrie reached over to pat my hand before saying good-bye. The room was quiet, and I felt Noah's hand tighten in mine as he tugged me up and out of my seat into his waiting arms. A soft hush left his lips as they grazed across my forehead. "It will be okay. We'll talk about everything in a few days. Right now I want to get you home to rest and then tomorrow we're going out. You've had enough doom and gloom, and, if you're up for it, I would like to take you to dinner. What do you say?"

"That sounds nice" was all I could manage, and he understood I was still processing what was going on. He opened the door to the hallway and quickly led me out of the office and toward home.

Chapter Eight
I AM SPECIAL

Noah was good on his word and took me to dinner and the theater. It was a nice distraction and got my mind off of the decision to move forward with chemo. I could refuse to do it if I wanted and felt that they removed all the cancer during surgery, but what if they didn't? I was struggling with what to do because chemo would definitely change things.

We had walked from the restaurant to the theater holding hands and reminiscing about when we lived in our apartment with a yard. Back then, our dreams felt like they could really happen and we were free to do anything we wanted. Over time, we grew up, and somehow those dreams dropped off our radar as Noah built his clientele and I started my design firm. Maybe being diagnosed with breast cancer was a wake-up call for both of us—a warning that we couldn't let our dreams disappear and that we needed to start following them again.

It didn't take much for me to decide to take a leave from my design firm. I notified my clients of my medical leave and that I didn't know when I would be returning to work at this point in time. I had contacted a few designers I had worked with on previous projects, and, thankfully, they were more than happy to take over my client load until I was ready to return . . . if I returned.

I spent the next few days in my office cleaning up my files and organizing design boards I had completed. The work was a nice distraction, but it didn't stop my mind from spinning out of control about my appointment with Dr. Guthrie in two days.

The phone rang, interrupting my thoughts. Looking at my caller ID, I saw Jen's face pop up with a smile.

"Hello, pretty lady. Are you free for lunch? I'm in the area."

"Are you buying?" I asked with a bit of sarcasm in my voice.

"Of course! Did you think I wouldn't? Get your mopey ass out of your chair and let me in—it's fucking cold out here."

"What?! You're here already?" I made my way out of my office to the front of the building, and, sure enough, Jen was standing there with her face mashed up against the window, trying to make me laugh. She succeeded!

"Hey, sorry—you should have knocked."

"I did. But you didn't answer."

"Sorry, I must not have heard you."

"No shit. You were too busy with the voices in your head telling you what you should do, but then questing yourself and listening to what Noah's wants instead." She shook her head in dismay. "I know how you work."

"Yeah. Yeah. Whatever," I said, shaking my head. "Let me finish up this file, and we can head out for lunch. Where do you want to go?"

"I was thinking we could grab a quick sandwich at the Good Earth and do some window shopping at the Galleria. Remember, Christmas is in a few weeks."

"I haven't even thought about Christmas, let alone bought anything. I'll be right back." I walked back into my office and realized the file I had been working on was pretty much complete, so I just shut it and put it aside. My phone rang as I was reaching for my jacket and purse. I hollered out to Jen, "Hold on, I need to grab this."

"No problem, you have plenty of magazines to keep me entertained."

I smiled as I grabbed my phone. "Victoria Madison Designs."

A deep, charming voice spoke up. "Victoria Madison, please."

"This is Victoria. How may I help you?"

There was a slight pause. "This is Dr. Forrester. I heard you were back in the office, and I wanted to check in to see how you were doing. I hope I'm not interrupting you."

"Oh. Hi," I responded, surprised that he was calling me instead of his nurse, Elizabeth. "I'm doing well. I suppose you're calling to find out if I have a plan for reconstruction. Sorry for the delay. I'm still trying to determine my chemotherapy schedule and didn't think to call your office."

"No, no. No rush at all. I just wanted to make sure everything was okay since you hadn't scheduled your six-week post-op appointment with Elizabeth after your last visit."

"I totally forgot. I'm trying to clean out my office, with my medical leave, and there is too much on my plate."

"That's okay. I was just concerned about you and wanted to make sure you were doing okay with everything."

I could feel the blush rising on my face for some odd reason. "I'm good, really. I'm just heading out to lunch with a friend. I'll be sure to call Elizabeth when I return to set up that appointment."

"I'll let her know you'll call later this afternoon. I'm glad you're doing well." He paused again like he had more to say, but he didn't expand. "Well, anyway, have a nice lunch, Victoria. Bye."

After he hung up, I stood there holding my phone and feeling a bit confused by Dr. Forrester's phone call. He seemed genuinely concerned, but it felt like I was missing something.

Tucking my phone into my purse, I walked out to the lobby to find Jen totally engrossed in *Architectural Digest*. My curiosity took over when I noticed she was holding it upside down. She quickly put it down, trying not to look guilty of something when she heard me approach. "Ready to go?"

"Yep, ready!" I glared at her suspiciously. She turned her back on me and proceeded out the door.

After a quick lunch at the Good Earth, we decided to walk around the Galleria, an upscale shopping mall. "So, how are things going with your treatment plan? I know you're stressing about it and that you and Noah are having the big talk tonight."

We continued walking like this was a normal conversation to be having while window shopping. "Yeah, we are going to discuss everything tonight. I would skip doing treatment altogether because I feel like they removed all of the cancer during surgery, but the triple negative results have me concerned." The images in one of the store displays of a young couple playing in the snow grabbed my attention and I stopped to look at it. "This type of cancer is more aggressive, and I would feel like I was giving up if I didn't at least try to do something to help my chances."

"You aren't giving up. That's ridiculous." Jen pulled me away from the window and over to a bench. "Sit!" she commanded. "We have been friends since before either of us lost our virginity. We've supported each other through break-ups and make-ups. If there is one thing I know, it's that you have never been one to give up. You don't like confrontation and you have a deep driving passion for what is right. You're fierce, and let's be honest . . . you aren't going to let this take you down. That is *not* your style."

"Thanks. I needed to hear that." I had done a good job of keeping my tears away during her little speech, but I knew they weren't far away. "I know what I need to know, but I'm worried about the impact it will have on Noah and our relationship. He has seemed so stressed lately, and I know it's because of me. I don't want to be a burden on him, and I know that there is a good chance chemo will kick my ass and it isn't fair for him to be my caregiver."

"Wait a minute! What the hell?" Jen cursed under her breath. "Let me get this straight—you're worried about being a burden on Noah?"

"Yes."

"That is the stupidest thing I've ever heard. Dammit, woman, you have breast cancer and are fighting for your life and you're worried about your husband, who agreed, for better or worse, in sickness and in health, to be there for you? That is just fucked up. You can't be serious!"

"He just hasn't been the same since surgery, and I feel like he thinks I'm diseased and unattractive.

Don't get me wrong—he is still caring and loving with his words, but I can tell that he is avoiding me physically, and we both know that isn't normal for him. He comes home and either goes right into the office or to bed, saying he is busy or tired from working extra hours. It's almost like a woman making the excuse of having her period or a migraine to get out of having sex." I sighed heavily, finally able to verbalize my insecurities.

"I can understand your feeling that way, but did you ever stop to think that maybe he is afraid to touch you because he doesn't want to hurt you? I know it's hard to see his viewpoint, and I can't believe I'm taking his side on this, but what your body has gone through in the last few weeks is kind of a big deal. You still walk around like the Hunchback of Notre Dame protecting your chest and you don't even realize it."

What? I looked down and noticed how my shoulders were curved forward and my chest tucked in, as if I were protecting it. I quickly relaxed my shoulders and tried to stick my chest out, only there was nothing to stick out. Just a flat chest hidden under my jacket. A lone tear made its way down my cheek, and Jen brushed it away.

"Victoria, I know you're hurt and feel alone. It's okay to hurt, but you need to realize that you're not alone. I'm here for you, for better or worse, in sickness and in health, just not legally. I know you don't swing that way . . . but I'm here!"

I couldn't contain the snort that came out. "I don't swing that way, huh?! How is it that my friends find the most inopportune times to make sarcastic comments that make holding back a laugh virtually impossible?"

"It's part of my charm. What can I say? I love to make you snort."

"I say you owe me a piece of Godiva chocolate cheesecake from the Cheesecake Factory now!"

"Deal—if you put those damn tears away and let me be here for you. I want to sit with you during chemo to make you laugh, and I want to go with you to see your Dr. McHottie plastic surgeon who personally called you today."

Gasp! "You heard my call? You sneaky bitch!" I snickered, not able to conceal the smile on my face. "And to think I wasn't going to bust you for looking so engrossed in reading *Architectural Digest* . . . upside down."

"Shut it—let's go stuff our faces with cheesecake." She stood and started walking away from me.

We passed Tiffany & Co. as we were making our way to the parking lot. Jen quickly detoured into the store. We ogled at the diamond rings that cost more than I'd ever make in my lifetime before we found our way back to the cases that were within our budgets.

Immediately my eyes were drawn to a delicate double heart tag pendant. It had the classic Tiffany's inscribed sterling heart as well as a pink enamel heart behind it on a silver chain. Jen instantly caught the attention of one of the sales associates and requested to see it.

She clasped it around my neck, and I looked in the mirror. Understated elegance best described it. There was so much meaning in this classic yet simple necklace. Hearts are the symbol of love, pink is the color of breast cancer, and two hearts symbolized that I wasn't alone. It was perfect!

"We'll take it." Jen presented her credit card to the associate. "Make it two—I'll take one as well." She winked at the guy and he smiled before disappearing to process her payment.

She turned to me before I could argue and covered my mouth. "Think of it as an upgrade from the best friend hearts we had as kids, only now they aren't broken in half and they won't turn our skin green. They are two perfect hearts, one for you and one for me!"

The tears reappeared, damn her, but they were happy this time. "Thank you Jen. I have no words . . ."

"Anything for you, toots! Always and forever." She winked. "Now, quit your crying, and let's go indulge in that piece of cheesecake."

After a quick stop back in the office to clean up the last of my files, I pulled into the garage at six-thirty and Noah still wasn't home. I decided to change into something comfortable, but first I headed into the kitchen to preheat the oven for dinner. I was still flying high after lunch and shopping with Jen, and I didn't want it to end. It had been awhile since I had prepared a nice dinner for Noah and I wanted to surprise him.

Slipping into one of Noah's dress shirts again gave me comfort. But I decided to forgo the standard leggings since his shirts were technically long enough to be considered a short dress and it was only going to be the two of us tonight. The new necklace sparkled when I looked in the mirror, and it made me smile.

I pulled out the lasagna that a neighbor had brought over and poured myself a glass of wine. I wasn't sure when Noah would be home, so I started gathering the fixings for a salad. "Strong Enough" by Sheryl Crow started playing, and I couldn't help but sing along while slicing a few tomatoes and fresh mozzarella.

I felt an arm wrap around me from behind, and Noah placed a soft kiss on my cheek before he backed away. "Don't mind me... you can keep singing. I'm going to go grab a quick shower, and I'll be back down in ten minutes."

"You don't have to shower on my account. I've smelled you after the gym, and you don't smell that bad," I said as I turned to lean in for a kiss, but he moved toward the door.

"I'd feel better if I did, and you might appreciate it later," he said with a wiggle of his eyebrows before he headed upstairs to shower, and my jaw hit the floor.

I silently cheered, *Noah is back!*, as I placed the lasagna in the oven and drizzled olive oil on the plate of tomatoes and mozzarella. I pulled out a few candles and lit them. This day was getting better by the minute; even though I knew "the talk" was coming. Neither of us was looking forward to it, but now there was a glimmer of hope of something more tonight.

By the time Noah appeared back in the kitchen, I was pouring myself another glass of wine. The music had changed to "Bitch" by Meredith Brooks, and I couldn't help dancing as I worked in the kitchen. I turned to grab a towel and noticed Noah leaning against the counter in a pair of running pants and no shirt. Damn. That's hot. He is totally back!

"I love watching you when you cook. It's like my own private dinner show," he said as he moved toward me, stopping to pour himself a glass of wine along the way. He wrapped his arm around my waist and began moving with me to the music. We continued to dance through a few more songs, and I felt at peace . . . safe and secure in Noah's arms.

Out of nowhere, Noah spoke. "I've been doing some research, and I spoke with one of my clients today who is an oncologist. I told him the treatment plan Dr. Guthrie laid out, and he agrees with her recommendations."

"I see." I felt my heart rate rising and stopped swaying to the music. "And what does that mean?"

"It means that I'm comfortable with the plan she has laid out and that I think you should do it, if you want to, that is." He paused and looked down at me. "Is that what you want?"

Wow. I hadn't expected this conversation to be so sudden and direct. I felt like I was witnessing him in a court case. It was so cut and dry for Noah, no emotion, just facts. But then again, did I really expect anything else? This is how he handled big decisions.

"I guess it's what I want." I cleared my throat and stepped away from him to reach for my glass of wine. My mouth suddenly felt dry. "I've mulled it over in my head so many times that I'm dizzy."

I took another large gulp of my wine, hoping it would give me courage. That's right, I was seeking liquid courage. But I wasn't sure why. Maybe it was because I would be admitting that I had cancer and that I was, in fact, afraid of dying. Reality was a bitch and her slap hurt like hell.

Noah broke my thoughts. "What's making you hesitate? Talk to me."

"I'm scared."

"That's understandable, and I'm scared too. But I think you need to look at the big picture and step back to look at what it says on paper."

"I did, and it said that a 2.3-centimeter cancerous tumor was removed from my body. It was removed from my body dammit! Why the hell would I want to let someone poison me 'just in case,' if it was removed? Honestly, Noah. Why?" I screamed as anger took over. Hadn't I been through enough, physically and emotionally, already?

Noah stepped toward me and attempted to comfort me, but I stepped away. "I feel trapped in a body that has a vendetta against me, and I can't escape it. My thoughts wake me in the middle of the night and won't shut off. There isn't a time in the day where cancer isn't on my mind. It was removed from me, and by agreeing to chemotherapy, I'll be adding to the stress by dragging my body down physically more than it already is. I'm afraid of what it will do to me. I'm afraid of what it will do to us. I'm afraid of dying. I'm just so goddamn afraid," I sobbed uncontrollably.

Noah caught me as my legs gave out, and we sunk to the floor. I curled up on his lap and buried my face in the crook of his neck. He rubbed my back lightly and laid his cheek against the top of my head. Silence was what I needed. No words could heal the pain I was feeling and he knew that.

The tears stopped, and I spoke softly: "I'm going to try it."

"Are you sure?"

"Yes. I'm not going to let cancer beat me down anymore. If this will help me make sure it doesn't come back, then I'm willing to try."

"I think you're making the right decision." He kissed the top of my head.

"I'm glad you agree. The deciding factor for me was the triple negative markers; they scared the hell out of me."

"Me too. Now let's get off of this damn floor and check on dinner." Noah moved from under me and stood, reaching his hand out to help me up. Once standing, he tilted my chin up and placed a kiss on my mouth. "I love you, Victoria," he murmured against my lips.

"I love you too."

Noah leaned in to deepen the kiss. The sudden surge of heat between my legs overwhelmed me, and our kiss became frantic. Noah's tongue slid powerfully against mine, like it was a battle and he was going to be the victor.

He backed me up against the counter and shifted so that his right leg was between my legs, and I felt his erection stiff against my hip as he rubbed up against me. I couldn't hold back the moan that had been building in my throat. Noah's hand started to make its way from my side, down my tummy, and finally settling between my legs. Instinctively, my hips started grinding down on his fingers as I could feel the moisture start to pool in my panties.

Beep. Beep. Beep. Damn.

All grinding came to a sudden stop as the oven announced that dinner was done.

"Cock blocked by the lasagna," Noah laughed as he pulled away and adjusted himself. I looked down at the evidence and had to admit: that must be pretty damn painful, as we hadn't had sex in over three weeks. Poor guy.

"You know I can take care of you quickly while the lasagna sits. It would be cruel for me to make you sit through dinner like that." I smirked as I nodded to the very prominent bulge in his pants. He removed the lasagna from the oven, and when he turned back to me, I felt like his prey.

"You realize that you cannot take that offer back, don't you?" he said as he stalked back toward me. My panties were now as slick as a slip-n-slide, and I squirmed. Damn, this felt good.

"I intend to let you relieve my discomfort soon, but first I think I need to finish what I started," he said as he slipped his hand into my panties and immediately pressed his thumb to my clit. Two fingers slid through my folds before they plunged deep up inside of me. "Oh fuck," we said in unison.

"It would be a waste to only let my hands enjoy this." He stepped back, and within seconds, my panties were on the floor, and I was lying on the cold granite countertop with my legs spread and Noah's face closing in on the goal.

Score.

As soon as his mouth made contact with me, the coldness from the counter instantly disappeared and all of my attention was on one tiny part of my body. A part that I had forgotten about until Noah found it. It didn't take long for my body to respond, and I raced toward an orgasm that I so desperately needed. I screamed his name after one more flick of his tongue and my body released for the first time in weeks.

He started to kiss his way up my body and stopped just above my belly button as his hands moved up my back to help me sit up. His mouth found mine instantly and the taste of me on his lips drove me crazy. It had been too long. "Thank you," I whispered against his mouth. "I've missed you."

I didn't give him a chance to respond as I slid my tongue deep in his mouth and felt his erection firm against me. I carefully scooted forward. "Please help me off the counter."

Not saying a word, Noah helped me down and made sure my legs wouldn't give out, as I was still trembling from my orgasm. I indicated for him to hop up where I was. "I don't think I can drop down to the floor or get back up easily—if you were up higher, it would help."

How sad was that? While my chest was healing nicely, I still had restrictions, and moving around was still uncomfortable when my pectoral muscles were involved. I had to interrupt our moment with a physical restriction . . . was I eighty years old now?

Noah could see the wheels turning in my head and frowned. He quickly discarded his pants and boxers and hopped up on the counter as he pulled me between his legs. I placed my hands on his thighs and rested my forehead against his chest for a brief moment before his hands cradled my cheeks and he tilted my head up to look at him. "Don't," he said as he slowly shook his head. "Just feel this moment—forget about everything else. Just focus on this moment."

He leaned down and kissed me hard. There was no question in this kiss; it was intense and he was in charge. My hands worked their way up his thighs feeling every inch of muscle until they came to rest on his throbbing cock.

He was hard and ready. I slid my hand up his length, feeling his skin glide smoothly upward in my grasp. A drop of wetness was on the tip, teasing me and tempting me.

I broke our kiss and moved back a little so that I could lean down to taste. Keeping my right hand in place on his cock, I placed my left hand around his sack and gave it a light squeeze, which was answered with a groan from Noah. "Wrap those sexy plump lips around me."

He really didn't have to ask, but his demand made me want to take control, so I continued to lick around the tip and down his shaft. This position was perfect as my arms were tucked perfectly against my body and I could still control him without any discomfort; I wanted to stay here for a while. The scent of his fresh showered skin and sex took over the smell of the cooling lasagna, and the only thing I was hungry for was him.

"Victoria," he begged, and I gave in and wrapped my mouth around him. I slowly sank down, taking his cock as far back into my throat as I could. I stilled for a moment before sucking my way back up his shaft and twirling my tongue at the top. I made sure to give a little extra pressure at the sensitive spot at the tip, and he jumped.

"God, you're so damn good at that. Your lips and tongue"—he hesitated as I drove my mouth back down on him with force and picked up the pace—"fucking perfection." I continued to devour him, wanting to bring him closer to the edge. Applying a little more pressure around his sack, I focused my tongue on the tip of his cock and flicked it a few more times over the magical spot before he finally went over the edge and gritted out words I couldn't even understand.

His body was stiff and twitching as I swallowed what he had to give. I loosened my grip on him as I carefully licked him clean and placed a feather-light kiss at the tip, which earned me one more little twitch. With a smile on my face, I stood up and looked at a naked and highly satisfied man sitting on my kitchen counter.

"Well, I've got to say the first course of dinner was impeccable," he said with a sexy smirk. "Should we move on to the second and third courses now, or skip right to dessert?"

"I may need some nourishment if I'm going to have enough energy to enjoy my dessert."

"Smart choice," Noah said as he hopped off of the counter, reached for his boxers, and pulled them on.

"Stop," I said, and he looked at me in surprise. "Just the boxers. Nothing else."

He quirked a brow. "Any more requests?"

"Not at the moment, but that could change."

"That is to be expected—you *are* a woman," he said with heavy sarcasm as he slapped my ass on his way to the stove. "Grab the bottle of wine; I've got the salad and lasagna." He winked. "You better hurry before I change my mind about the second and third courses."

Shaking my head, I said, "Men."

As we sat down for dinner, I realized that it felt like old times, when our lives weren't ruled by appointments and the unknown. We discussed my plans for handing over my clients to a few colleagues, and Noah filled me in on a new case he was handling. He seemed pretty happy about it, but informed me that he may have to do some traveling. Leaving me alone concerned him, but he promised to arrange for someone to stay with me when he was gone.

The thought of him being gone normally didn't bother me, but I was in a fragile state right now and I wasn't sure about it.

"What is that?" Noah interrupted my thoughts as he nodded toward my hand.

I looked down and realized that I was playing with the two heart charms on my necklace. "Jen stopped by my office today to take me to lunch followed by some window shopping. We ended up at Tiffany's, and I was walking around and this necklace caught my eye. I tried it on and Jen whipped out her credit card and I've yet to take it off." I smiled as I found comfort from it between my fingers.

"It's beautiful," he said as he leaned forward and placed his hand over mine, "and I'm glad to see the smile on your face from it."

"Me too."

Chapter Nine

I AM LOVED

I woke Friday morning to a note on my bedside table from Noah.

Good morning,

I had to run into the office to sign a few documents this morning, but I will be home in time to go with you to the appointment with Dr. Guthrie.

Love, Noah

I looked over at the clock and saw that I had three hours to burn before we needed to leave. Coffee was on my brain, and I swung through the kitchen to grab a cup before heading into the study to read for a bit. I loved sitting in the study; it's where Noah worked when he was home, and it had the perfect leather reading chair sitting by the fireplace. I flipped on the fireplace and made myself comfortable.

Bobbie Jo had taken it upon herself to stock up my eReader library, and my to-be-read list was out of control. Looking through the bevy of books, I settled on one with a fighter on the cover. I figured I was in a battle of my own, so maybe I could relate to the character? Clicking on the book, I started reading and quickly got lost in the words. I didn't realize the time until I heard my phone ring.

"Hello?"

"Hey, it's me," I heard Noah say. He sounded out of breath.

"Are you okay? You sound like you're running somewhere."

"Yes, I'm fine. I just had something blow up in my face, and I'm running to the courthouse. I won't be home in time to take you to the doctor, but I should be able to meet you there. Is there any way you could find someone to drive you?"

"Yeah, sure, I'll call Bobbie Jo and see if she can take me, otherwise I can drive myself. Don't worry, I'll work it out and meet you there."

"I would prefer if you could get a ride. Driving to your office was one thing, but maneuvering the medical building parking lot is another with all of the terrible drivers. Be careful. I'll meet you there. I've got to run. Bye." Click.

I shrugged as I hit Bobbie Jo's number.

I could hear her laughter as she answered. "What's up sizzle tits?"

"Sizzle tits?" She sure knew how to answer the phone and drag a smile out of me when I needed it. God I loved my friends!

"Come on. You know they are going to be sizzling when Dr. McHottie gets done copping a feel and making them pretty!"

"What is with you and Jen naming my surgeon Dr. McHottie?" I questioned, trying to sound ticked off, which I most likely failed at.

"What kind of friends would we be if we didn't check out your medical team before you let them touch you? We let our fingers do the walking online and did a little research. And ... well ... Dr. Forrester's picture just happened to pop up. You can't honestly tell me that you don't think he's hotter than hell?! Even I know that blindness is not one of the side effects from breast cancer. Fess up!"

I couldn't control the laughter that took over as I pictured the two of them online staring at Dr. Forrester. It wouldn't surprise me if Bobbie Jo had gotten off thinking about him, but I couldn't honestly admit to being attracted to my doctor. Could I? "Yeah, he's cute, I guess."

"Liar." She deadpanned. "Now what can I do for you?"

"I have an appointment with Dr. Guthrie today and Noah just called to tell me he won't have enough time to come home and get me, and he doesn't want me driving myself there. Any chance you could drive me in at one thirty?"

"No problem—I'm happy to be your chauffeur! Is he still planning to meet you, or should I plan to stay with you?"

"He had to run to the courthouse, but he said he would meet me there. I suppose it wouldn't hurt if you stayed with me until he got there. I'm happy to pay for your gas and parking."

"Don't be ridiculous! This is what I'm here for, and I expect you to call me when you need help. And remember, if I can't help, you know Jen is available as well. You're stuck with us, babe. I'll see you in an hour. Now, go get ready. I have something urgent I need to take care of before I leave." I heard some rustling in the background, and she let out a giggle.

I rolled my eyes. "I'll see you soon, Bobbie Jo and . . . tell Matthew to spank you on my behalf." I heard a hitch in her breath as I ended the call.

An hour later I was dressed and reading when I heard the front door click open and the sound of high heels hit the floor. "You ready to go, smartass?"

I bookmarked my page and looked up to see Bobbie Jo with a satisfied smirk on her face. "Good to see you too. You look thoroughly—"

"Spanked!" she interrupted. "Matthew overheard your comment, and I'm not sure if I should be pissed or thank you."

"You're welcome," I winked as I moved past her toward the door. "Let's get going; I want to get this over with."

———

We sat in the waiting room, and I glanced at the clock on the wall. My appointment was in five minutes and I had yet to see or hear from Noah. Bobbie Jo sat next to me. "It's okay—I'm sure he is just stuck in traffic. You know how downtown Minneapolis is during the holidays: it's a parking lot."

I nodded in acknowledgment, as my nerves were

on high alert. I was not looking forward to this appointment, and I was worried when my name was called and he still wasn't there.

"Come on, toots, I'm going back with you," Bobbie Jo said, offering her hand to me, and we walked back into the office. The nurse brought us back to an exam room, explained that Dr. Guthrie would be in shortly, and excused herself from the room.

As the door shut behind her, Bobbie Jo turned toward me. "Victoria, I'm sure he's on his way and just got tied up."

"You're right. He promised me after my first appointment that he would be sure to be at every appointment going forward. I'm sure there is a good explanation."

There was a tap on the door and my heart soared, only to come crashing down when Dr. Guthrie walked in. "Good afternoon, Victoria. I see you have someone new with you today." She turned toward Bobbie Jo and introduced herself with a smile before settling down in her chair. "So, how are you doing?"

"I'm okay. The last week has been a roller coaster, but I feel like I'm where I should be and I'm confident in my decision to move forward with chemotherapy," I blurted out. Why beat around the bush and prolong my decision.

Dr. Guthrie looked relieved. "I agree completely with your decision, and I'm proud of you for making it. I wasn't sure—"

The door flew open, and there stood Noah, looking like he had been mugged. His hair was a mess, his tie was askew, and he was panting. "Are you okay?" I asked as I rushed up to him.

"Sorry I'm late." He took a breath and acknowledged Bobbie Jo. "Thank you for staying with her."

"You bet. I'm going to slip out so the three of you can talk. Do you want me to wait for you, Victoria?"

"No, you go on ahead, and I'll call you tonight. Thank you again, Bobbie Jo." She stood and gave me a hug before slipping out the door.

"Are you sure you're okay?" I asked Noah again.

"Yes, I'm fine. Just took longer than I expected at the courthouse, and it took forever to make my way out of downtown. I couldn't find a parking spot when I got here, so I parked in the hospital lot and ran across the street dodging cars. I'm sorry." He smoothed out his hair and did his best to tidy up his appearance before taking the chair Bobbie Jo had just vacated. "What have I missed?"

"You haven't missed much," Dr. Guthrie stated after Noah had settled down. "Victoria just finished telling me that she has decided to move forward with chemotherapy. I'm assuming you were part of the decision?"

"Yes, we did some research and both agreed that she should move forward with treatment."

"That is what I figured. I was about to tell Victoria that I wasn't sure if she was going to go ahead with it. I saw hesitation on her face last week, but I'm glad you both took the time to talk about it and come to a decision you're both okay with." She said the last part while looking at me for confirmation.

"Yes, I'm good with my decision. So what do we do next?"

Dr. Guthrie explained the treatment plan she had laid out before signing orders for a chest x-ray and blood work to be done before my first treatment. She wanted to run some baseline tests so that she could refer to them during the treatment cycle if needed.

Her explanation of what to expect after my first treatment was helpful, but not very reassuring. I could anticipate being extremely fatigued for the first week and would gradually get my strength back. Nausea, as well as issues with certain foods, was to be expected as my taste would be altered due to the meds they would have me on. I was relieved to hear that my hair wouldn't fall out right away—most likely a few weeks later.

"Please stop at the front desk on your way out to get your first treatment scheduled. They will also take care of scheduling your appointments with imaging and the lab." She closed my file, and we all stood, as it was time to leave. "Everything is going to be okay, kiddo. You're doing the right thing."

"I hope so. I'm nervous and relieved. I just want this over," I confessed.

She leaned in to give me a hug. "I know you do. Hang in there. I'll see you next week."

Noah grabbed my hand as we walked to the scheduling desk. "I'm sorry for being late, baby. It won't happen again."

"I know you're sorry and it was out of your control. I'm just happy you're okay; I was really worried about you."

He pulled me to his side and put his arm around me. "I promise to never make you worry again. You have enough on your plate." He placed a kiss on my head as we rounded the corner to the scheduling desk.

The weekend was uneventful, and I found myself sitting in the study on Monday, looking at the calendar for the week ahead. Tuesday was my post-op appointment with Dr. Forrester, followed by x-rays and labs on Wednesday, and my first chemo treatment on Friday. I had also scheduled an appointment with my stylist for a haircut on Thursday.

Dr. Guthrie explained that my hair wouldn't start falling out until after my second round of chemo, but I wanted to do this on my terms. My hair was currently past my shoulders, and I was planning to make a drastic change and go for a short pixie cut. I figured this way, when it started falling out, it wouldn't be as dramatic. I was looking through short hairstyles when my phone rang and I saw it was my parents on the caller ID.

"Hello?"

"Hello, stranger. Your mother is concerned since we haven't heard from you this weekend. Is everything okay?"

"Sorry, Dad. Yes, everything is okay. I guess time just got away from me and I forgot to call." I sighed in exasperation. I can never win. "I'm just going over my schedule for the week ahead, and it's full of tests and doctors' appointments, plus I start chemo on Friday. I guess I'm focused on that right now."

"That's what your mother told me after your quick call on Friday evening. How are you feeling about it? Are you ready?"

I slumped down in the chair and gave the canned speech I had already used over a dozen times to friends. "I'm good and I know it's the right decision. It won't be easy, but I'm up for the fight and will beat this."

"That's my girl—go get 'em! Mom and I were talking, and we're still planning to head down to Gulf Shores for the winter after the New Year."

"Wow, I totally forgot you were heading there again this year. I know how much you and Mom enjoy the escape."

"Yeah, we do. The older we get, the harder Minnesota winter is on us. Plus we've made so many friends down there over the years, and it feels like home." He hesitated for a moment before getting down to the real reason for his call. "Your mom doesn't want to go this year. She is worried about you and doesn't want you to feel like we're abandoning you by going south for a few months. I was hoping you could call her tonight and give her some peace of mind."

"Really?" I asked. "That's surprising—she loves it down there."

"She really does, and it would be good for her right now. She obsessively searches the Internet about breast cancer and refuses to go out to lunch with friends anymore. We're both worried about you, but she is taking it to an extreme, and she needs a distraction right now. The benefit of Gulf Shores is we will have limited Internet, lots of friends for her to visit with, and activities to keep her busy outside."

"Sure, I understand. I'll call her tonight."

"Thank you, sweetheart. It means a lot to me. I know this isn't easy for you, and I'm sorry to ask this of you. I'm just really concerned about her, and I know we can't do much from afar and the escape would help her." He rambled on, trying to make an excuse for asking me to help him.

"Dad, I understand, and I'll call her tonight and

tell her to go. I don't need the two of you suffocating me by being overly concerned. I'm a grown woman, and I can handle this," I snapped. I immediately felt guilty for lashing out at my poor father who had done nothing but love and protect me my entire life.

"I'm sorry, Dad. I didn't mean for that to sound the way it did," I said with a shaky voice as a soft cry escaped my throat.

"Victoria, you don't have to be sorry. I know you're under a lot of pressure right now, and I didn't mean to upset you. . . I shouldn't have asked this of you," he said. The regret in his voice was evident.

"I'm terrified, Dad, completely and utterly terrified. I don't know who I am anymore. One minute I'm happy and the next I'm annoyed and tearing the heads off the people I love. What is that?"

"It's called being human. You're under an extreme amount of stress right now and have every reason to be terrified and lose your temper. I would be worried if you didn't. I raised a strong little girl who never sat and cried when she fell down; she would brush herself off and stand back up and try again. She got even more determined as she grew up and would never give up. I don't see her ever giving up. I see her conquering things she never imagined, and I'm extremely proud of her." His voice cracked at that last part, and my heart split in two.

I swallowed the lump in my throat and pulled myself together. "I love you, Daddy. Thank you for being my hero and my rock since the day you and Mom signed the papers making me yours. I'm truly blessed that I found my way to you. I won't let you down, and I'll continue to be that strong little girl you raised. Thank you for giving me strength when I needed it. Go ahead and start packing. I'll call Mom tonight."

"I love you, baby girl, and thank you for putting up with your old man. You're such an amazing woman, and we are so proud of you! I'll make sure Mom answers when you call later. Bye."

"Bye, Dad." I ended the call and started sobbing again. This was becoming a daily occurrence, and it freaked me out. I got up and ran for the bathroom.

I stripped out of my clothes and stepped into the shower without letting it warm up. The cold water was a welcome shock to my system. The tears continued as I shivered and wrapped my arms around myself before sinking down along the tile wall to the shower floor.

The shower had become my private refuge from the world around me. I didn't have to be strong. I could curl up in a ball and cry without judgment or pity. It was my personal hell.

The water was running hot when I heard someone yelling my name. "Victoria! Where the hell are you?"

I heard the bathroom door swing open, followed by the shower door, and looked up to find Jen's concerned eyes on me. She grabbed a towel before she stepped into the shower fully clothed and turned off the water.

"Victoria, what's wrong? Are you okay?" she asked as she wrapped me up in the towel and helped me get up and moved over onto the shower bench. I sat there with nothing to say. I wasn't okay and I wasn't sure what was going on. I had just snapped at my dad and felt completely out of control for the first time in my life. I couldn't control anything, and that scared the shit out of me.

Jen crouched down in front of me. "Look at me." I obeyed and looked into her blue eyes that were full of worry. "What's going on? You missed our lunch date, and that's not like you."

"Who am I?" I asked point blank.

"What?"

"Who am I? Honestly, Jen. Tell me who I am, because right now I have no fucking clue, and it scares the hell out of me."

"Oh honey, stop." She took my hands in hers. "You're Victoria Madison. The girl I met in junior high because of a boy. The girl who spent the summer with me at the pool. The girl who let me numb her ears with a frozen can of juice concentrate before double piercing her ears. The girl who made me laugh until I spit my drink out and the girl who knew when I needed a hug the most. And most recently the first girl I've ever stood in the shower with ... thank god I'm clothed, or it might look suspicious." She winked and smiled, encouraging me to get up. "Let's get you dried off and dressed. We will continue this conversation in the family room. I'm starving and picked up pizza and beer."

"What is it with you and Bobbie Jo?"

"What do you mean?" she asked, totally confused.

"The two of you have this insane way of making me smile during the shittiest times."

"It's our job as your best friends." She nudged my shoulder to move me out of the shower. "I learned from the best—you. You never let me enjoy my pity parties and you constantly crashed them. I felt like being a party crasher today."

"Sorry to say, but it doesn't appear that you will get to motorboat me right now. Maybe in a few months you could come back?" I giggled as I stepped out of the shower.

"There's my girl! Pulling movie scenes like a champion, even though it was *Wedding Crashers*, the motorboat comment was classic." She smacked my ass. "Get dried off and dressed. I'm going to heat up the pizza and toss in a chick flick—any requests?"

"*The Sweetest Thing*. I could use a dose of Cameron, Christina, Selma, and a tinfoil chicken." I smiled. "Did you know that singing helps open your throat if something gets stuck?!"

"And the smartass is back as well. Now hurry the hell up! I'm hungry!" Jen barked as she walked out of the bathroom.

I looked at my haggard self in the mirror. The mood swings were out of control, and I was seriously starting to question my sanity. Bobbie Jo and Jen had already earned their halos for putting up with me.

Jen and I stuffed our faces and drank beer while watching the movie. I forgot how much I loved it; it reminded me of the road trip we took after high school graduation. Granted, it wasn't as crazy because we were only eighteen, but it was a girl road trip nonetheless.

"Do you remember the weekend we drove up to your grandparents' cabin the summer I came back from college?"

"How could I forget? Remember when we lost our anchor and floated across the bay to Camp Courage? We woke up to kids trying to dive bomb us off their dock."

I snorted. "We swam so fast back to the dock that I'm pretty sure we might have won a medal in the Olympics."

"We definitely hauled ass. That was a fun trip. Can you imagine if we went now? We'd get in so much trouble. We were fairly tame back then."

"What did you expect? We were young."

"It was our first trip without a chaperone, and we should have torn it up at the resort next door," she said with a wiggle of her eyebrows. "We could have totally landed a boy or two easily."

"Yes, but I had just started dating Noah. *You* could have landed a boy or two." I took a long sip of my beer, regretting mentioning that.

"Correct, but you didn't have a ring on your finger, and we could have had a little fun flirting. We were young, and you know I wouldn't have let you do anything you'd regret. I've always had your back and best intentions in mind."

"I know. You have been a tried and true friend through everything. I love you, Jen."

"Love you too, sweets, but don't you dare cry again! I'm done with tears for the day." She polished off her beer and started cleaning up the pizza box and empty bottles. "I've got some errands to run before going home. Do you want me to stay until Noah gets home?"

"No, I'm good. You go ahead. He's been working long hours lately with a new case." I shrugged. "He said he might have to do some traveling over the next few months. Normally I would go with him, but with being in the midst of treatment, it probably wouldn't be a good idea. Any chance you'd be willing to go to a few treatments with me?"

"Of course, send me the dates and I'm all yours!"

"Thanks, Jen. I don't know what I'd do without you." We hugged before she left, and when the door clicked shut, it was silent. I dropped back down on the sofa and started surfing the movie channels for another movie and picked *You've Got Mail*. After making a bowl of popcorn and grabbing my favorite blanket, I settled in and waited for Noah.

Several hours later, I awoke to strong arms carrying me from the sofa to our bed. I'm not sure what time it was, but it was dark and I noticed that Noah was still in his suit as he laid me in our bed. He placed a kiss on my temple. "Go back to sleep, sweetheart. I'm home and you can sleep peacefully."

He quietly stepped into the closet and took off his suit before slipping into the bathroom and starting the shower. It must have been another long day.

Chapter Ten

I AM STRONG

I felt surprisingly relaxed while flipping through a stack of magazines as I sat in Dr. Forrester's waiting room. Noah had come with me to the appointment, but he had just received a phone call when Elizabeth called my name. He nodded for me to go ahead without him.

I followed Elizabeth into the room and chatted for a few minutes before assuming my position on the exam table with my pink gown open in the front. I grabbed the new issue of *Real Simple* magazine I had snagged on my way back to the room. I was absorbed in an article and barely heard the knock on the door when Dr. Forrester appeared with a warm smile.

"Good afternoon. How are you doing today?" he asked as he sat down and studied my chart.

"Better."

His head was still down. "That is good to hear. The drain areas are feeling good? No swelling or discomfort?"

"Not really, but they are starting to itch."

"Are you still using bacitracin on your incisions?" He was still focused on my chart and hadn't looked up yet.

"Yes, I am. They are softening up, but it still feels lumpy in spots."

"That's normal," he said when he finally looked back up at me then looked around. "Did you drive yourself today?"

"No, Noah is out in the waiting area. He got a call when Elizabeth called me back and nodded for me to go ahead without him." I felt the strange need to explain more because he was giving me a peculiar look. "He was assigned a new case a few weeks ago and has been working a lot."

I tried not to appear affected, but it was getting harder. I was used to him being gone and traveling, but it felt different lately. I contributed it to the fact that I felt so damaged, broken, and needy.

"Do you want to wait for him?"

"No, that's okay. Not much for him to do anyway."

"Well, then, let me call Elizabeth in, and we'll take a peek." Dr. Forrester exited the room and came back a few moments later with Elizabeth trailing behind. She was always present for exams, I'm assuming because he was a male physician and needed to cover his ass in case some psycho tried to sue him for harassment.

He stepped over to the sink to wash his hands. "Let's see how things are healing up, shall we?"

"I guess." He helped me lie back on the table, and I opened my gown and let out a deep sigh.

Dr. Forrester's hands were cool as he studied his work. He pressed his hand along the top of my chest where the expanders were and seemed pleased with whatever he was feeling for. Moving his hands along both incision lines, he stopped a few times and felt the area more intently. He gave me a gentle smile. "Everything looks great and is healing very nicely. Can you lift your arms up over your head for me?"

I stretched my arms above my head as far as I could comfortably. He nodded. "You can put them back down. How did that feel?"

"It feels tight, but better than it did a week ago. The expanders aren't very forgiving. I'm pretty sure this is what it feels like to have a coconut shoved under your skin."

He laughed. "Humor is a good thing to have. This is an emotional journey, and your attitude will make all the difference." He closed my gown and helped me back up. After washing his hands again, he leaned against the counter.

"Elizabeth, I'd like some post-surgical pictures taken today. While you're getting set up, I'm going to review a few things with Victoria."

"Sure thing," she said as she stepped out of the room.

"Everything is looking great, and I'm really happy with how you're healing physically. I know you will be starting chemo this week, and I'm assuming you would like to postpone moving ahead with the expander fills?"

"I'm not sure. Frankly, I would like to get the reconstruction done as soon as I can. I'm anxious to feel like a woman again"—I hesitated—"and I know Noah is anxious too." I looked down at my hands, trying not to let him see the discomfort in my eyes.

He let out a deep sigh. "Victoria, please look at me."

I lifted my eyes to meet his. "I don't want you to bite off too much at one time. Chemo can be very difficult for some patients, and if you push yourself too hard, you will do more harm than good. Noah needs to understand that this is your body and your health on the line. I don't want you, or any patient of mine, jeopardizing their health because they want to make someone else happy. This is about you. Not him. I want to see that smile on your face again. It's been missing the last two times I've seen you. You're a beautiful woman, and you need to put yourself first this time."

I swallowed slowly and tried to absorb what he had just said. "Thank you" was all I could manage. I wasn't prepared for a man, let alone my physician, to genuinely care about what I was going through physically and emotionally. He understood, somewhat, what I was going through, and his encouraging words gave me a boost I needed.

He stood to leave. "Elizabeth will be right in to get a new set of photos. Please think about what I've said before making your decision. I'll be in touch."

My photo shoot with Elizabeth was quick; I knew the drill of where to stand and what to do. I changed back into my clothes and headed out to the waiting room. Confused, I looked around for Noah.

I heard a voice call out in my direction: "Dr.

Forrester is meeting with the gentleman you arrived with in his office. They should be out shortly," the woman at the reception desk said before answering an incoming call.

"The gentleman I arrived with"? That sounded odd, but I figured I didn't know her from Eve and I'm sure she had made a mistake at one point by calling someone a spouse when they weren't. After all, how many times do people congratulate women on being pregnant when they aren't? Smart move on her part.

A short time later, Noah walked into the lobby looking like the professional he was, but something was off. I couldn't put my finger on it, but he didn't seem like himself. "Everything okay?" I asked.

His eyes met mine and I saw a flash of something different, but it quickly disappeared. "Yes, everything is fine. Shall we get going?" He held out my jacket for me.

As we made our way toward the elevator, the awkward silence continued and I couldn't handle it anymore. "Dr. Forrester said he was very happy with my recovery so far and wanted to talk with me about next steps with chemo starting on Friday."

"Yes. That's what we talked about. What are

your plans?"

"I'm not sure. I think we should talk about it together, don't you?"

"It's your body, not mine," he snapped. "You need to do what you feel you're capable of doing."

"Really? This isn't a business decision, Noah—this is life. My *life*. And I would appreciate you treating me like a person. No! Better yet, I want you to treat me like your wife, the one who you agreed to love for better or worse, in sickness and in health. Is that too much to ask?" I exclaimed before turning to take the steps. Alone. Noah didn't follow.

I contemplated what to say as I slowly made my way down to the lobby. What was going through Noah's head? And what had Dr. Forrester said to him? They were obviously talking about me, and I felt betrayed.

When I made it out of the stairwell, Noah was leaning against the opposite wall.

"I'm sorry," he said as he moved toward me. "I didn't mean for you to feel that way. You have every right to say what you did."

"I can't do this anymore, Noah. I can't argue with you like this. This isn't us."

"You're right. We will talk about everything

tonight over dinner and figure out a plan. Does that work for you?"

"Yes. Thank you."

"Do you mind if I stop by the office on our way home to pick up a few files?"

"No, not at all. It would be nice to see something other than our house for a change."

We arrived at Noah's office to smiles and "how are you doing?" questions from a few of his partners. His secretary, Whitney, welcomed me with a tender hug. Noah stepped into his office and started collecting a few files.

His phone rang, and Whitney picked it up. "Noah Madison's office," she answered. "Yes, just one moment, please."

"Noah, you have a call regarding the Baxter account. Do you want me to send it to voice mail, or do you have time?"

"I should really take that call. Why don't you take a break and go grab a cup of coffee with Victoria? I'm sure the two of you have a few things to catch up on," he called out from his office.

Whitney looked over at me looking for approval, and I nodded in agreement. "Coffee sounds heavenly right now."

"Sure thing, Noah. We'll be back in thirty minutes," Whitney said as she grabbed her purse and looped her arm in mine like old girlfriends. "Let's go get caffeinated and gossip."

We made our way to my favorite coffee shop and found a cozy spot by the fireplace. Whitney had been Noah's secretary for the last two years, and we had grown to be friends. She was someone I could always depend on.

"Have you noticed Noah being on edge lately?" I asked her, trying not to fidget in my chair.

"Not more than usual," she answered while blowing on her tea before taking a sip. "He seems to be running around more than he used to, but I know that is due to all of your medical appointments."

"I haven't had that many appointments, but he has made it a point to come to most of them when he can. I know the new case he is working on has been stressful with the extra hours and upcoming travel schedule. Has he given you my chemo schedule to put on his calendar?"

Whitney hesitated for a moment. "No, he hasn't given me the schedule. He said he would take care of blocking your medical appointments on his calendar. I saw the one today and then another on Friday, but I didn't see anything else. Why don't you send them to me, and I'll make sure they are on there."

I pulled my phone out of my purse and forwarded the e-mail I had sent Noah with my appointment schedule. "Just sent it. These appointments are longer, and I'm sure he won't be able to make them all, but it would be nice to have him there for a few."

"I'll do my best to manage his schedule so he can be there with you. I know it isn't going to be easy. Maybe I could sit with you sometime?"

"I would like that very much." I smiled and noticed Noah approaching us. "Hey there, that was fast. Has it been a half hour already?"

"I'm sorry to interrupt, but something has come up with the Baxter case, and I need to stay in the office a bit longer. I'm not sure how long it will take, so in fairness to you, I would like to head home for dinner and come back later."

"Sure." I stood from my chair and picked up my empty cup.

"Do you need me to stay late too?" Whitney asked Noah as she rose to leave.

"That won't be necessary tonight. I e-mailed you a list of a few files I need pulled from the archives. If you could have those on my desk for when I return, I should be all set. I'll see you tomorrow morning before the partners' meeting."

I gave Whitney a hug. "Thanks for the quick chat and coffee; let's plan to do this again soon. That is, if your boss will let you sneak away."

"Her boss is in earshot," Noah said with a hint of amusement, which was refreshing.

"I'm well aware and expecting his approval," I said, looking up at him and batting my eyelashes.

He slipped his hand to my waist and started leading me toward the door. "Time off approved. Now let's get you home."

During dinner we discussed my chemo schedule and decided it would be best to get two treatments under my belt before deciding to move forward with reconstruction. I had heard that the first treatment was the worst because there was no way to know how your body would react, so the second treatment was usually better because they could prescribe the right drug combination to combat the side effects. If

I was doing well after two treatments, I would decide to move forward and start the expander fill.

"What did Dr. Forrester call you into his office in private for?" I asked with slight hesitation, unsure of what the answer might be.

"He wanted to discuss your recovery and, more importantly, the plan for your reconstruction. He wanted to make sure I was on board with your choices and was supportive of the plan we had discussed previously. I told him I was. That was it." He moved to clear the dishes from the table.

"Okay, I just wanted to make sure everything was fine. You weren't yourself after we left."

"I know, and I'm sorry for how I acted." He placed the dishes in the sink and turned back toward me. "I should really head back to the office now before it gets too late. Forgive me for eating and running?"

"Of course, I know you have a lot on your plate at work. I'm just going to take a quick bath since I've been cleared to 'submerge' once again, and then I'll curl up with a new book."

I leaned in for a kiss and was startled when Noah pulled me close to him. My expanders hit against his chest, and I gasped, causing him to step back abruptly.

"Don't," I pleaded. "Don't step away. I want to be in your arms; I just wasn't prepared for the feeling."

Noah stepped forward again steadily, letting me lean into him. He gently wrapped his arms around my waist as I looked up to search his eyes for approval before my lips met his. They were soft and welcoming. Just what I needed, a simple connection to him that gave me comfort. I felt safe and cherished in his solid arms;, I always had. I knew things were distanced between us lately and hoped that the road ahead would eventually even out. I just didn't know when. So I would hold on to these little moments to keep me moving forward.

※

I went to the hospital Wednesday morning for my chest x-ray and a visit to the vampires, technically called lab technicians, for my blood draws. Needles were now going to be a frequent annoyance in my life, but I was deathly afraid of them. It was a huge triumph when I finally discovered that if I didn't look at them inserting the needle into me, I was fine.

My sarcastic and witty personality helped to get

me through, although I knew several people probably thought I was completely out of my mind. I didn't care; I was going to do whatever I damn well pleased to get through each day.

Thursday found me in the salon, staring back into the mirror at my stylist, Ann, who was standing behind me with a shocked expression. "You want to go that short right off the bat?"

"Yep. I figure I have about three weeks before it all falls out and instead of wasting your time with coming in and doing it in stages, I might as well go big or go home." I gave her an unsure but convincing smile.

"Are you sure?"

"Yes, cut it." I made sure to look her directly in the eye.

She took a deep breath and put the cape around my neck. "Okay. Let's do this. Can I get you a glass of wine to calm your nerves?"

"Do you have anything stronger?" I joked, and she gave me a troubled look. "Deep breath, I'm only joking. I'd love a bottle of water if you have it."

"Sure thing, I'll be right back."

An hour later, I left the salon with hair shorter than Noah's, a complimentary makeup application, and a smile on my face. I was feeling sassy and good about myself for the first time in several weeks. Something told me that Noah was going to hate it. But, within a matter of weeks, it was going to fall out, and I would look like a cue ball. He needed to get used to a different look.

I decided to stop by his office since I was in the area and wanted to kidnap Whitney for that coffee date her boss had approved earlier in the week. Making my way into the building, I headed toward his office and ran into Whitney.

The look of surprise on her face was priceless. "First off, what are you doing here? And secondly, what happened to your hair?"

"I was in the area after my salon visit and decided to stop up and see if I could kidnap you for coffee after I popped in to say hi to Noah. Is he around?"

"No. He said he was going out to meet you," she said, pulling up his calendar. I peeked over her shoulder.

"That's odd. He knew about my salon appointment today but never mentioned meeting after it."

I tried to recall if he mentioned anything that morning before he left for the office. But nothing came to mind. "We discussed our plans over breakfast and he knew that I was nervous about chemo tomorrow. Maybe he is working on a surprise to keep my mind off of things tonight or tomorrow?"

"You're probably right. He goes above and beyond to make sure you're happy," she said as she locked her computer. "When the boss is away... his wife and I get a pass to go have coffee. Let's go!"

We hadn't really paid attention to how long we were gone until we arrived back at the office and Noah hollered from his office: "Where have you been?"

I heard him making his way out of his office. "I just got back from my long lunch with... Victoria—what are you doing here?" He seemed surprised to see me.

"Hi. I decided to stop by the office after my haircut to surprise you and see if Whitney was available to sneak away for a cup of coffee."

"It's certainly a surprise," he said as he walked toward me to place a customary kiss on my cheek in the workplace. "Your hair is... cute." He wasn't really sure what to say, and I could see the disappointment in his eyes as my long hair was now gone.

He always tried to hide his disappointment, but

I had become familiar with this look as I had been seeing it more frequently.

"Thanks. I know it's really short, but this way it won't be as big of a shock when it falls out."

Whitney scurried by me. "I think its super cute, Victoria. Thanks again for coffee."

"You bet—let's do it again soon. Well, depending on how I'm feeling, I guess. I've heard that things don't taste the same during chemo, so I should avoid my favorite foods or I might end up hating them later."

I moved to leave, feeling like I had intruded on their day. "I should get going and let you both get back to work."

"Sorry I wasn't here earlier; I had to step out for an appointment, but I'm happy I did get to see you." Noah sounded sincere in his words, but he shifted on his feet uncomfortably. "Do you want me to pick up dinner tonight on my way home?"

"That would be great. Surprise me. I'm considering it 'the last meal,' though, so make it good." I winked before I turned to say one last good-bye to Whitney.

Traffic was starting to back up, so I decided to drive around the lakes instead, which gave me time to call Bobbie Jo.

She picked up on the second ring. "What's up, hooker?"

"Oh, you know, business is slow since the boobies have disappeared. Apparently men like them. Who knew?"

"Damn girl, even with all of the shit you've been through, you still have a sense of humor. How do you do that?"

"Let's just say I've gone into survival mode. I think I would lose my damn mind if I didn't try to find something to laugh about. I'm on an emotional roller coaster... up one moment and down the next. I'm getting motion sickness already and chemo starts tomorrow. I'm afraid I'm doomed."

"Drugs. Take the drugs." Bobbie Jo giggled. "You know they give good ones too. Have you asked about medicinal marijuana? I'd totally like to try that one."

"Why am I not surprised?" I responded before trying the steer the conversation to my reason for calling. "I'm kind of freaked out for tomorrow and was wondering if you would stop over this weekend for a visit. I don't want to come off as needy, but I'm not sure what to expect or how Noah will be with the unexpected. I'm sorry to ask this of you, but I'm scared."

"Oh honey, don't be sorry for asking. You know I would do anything for you and Noah. When do you want me to come over? Do you want me there tomorrow night after chemo or on Saturday?"

"I don't know. I shouldn't have called. I didn't really think this through and should have. I'm just unsure of what to do and what we need."

"Where are you?"

"I just left Noah's office, and I'm on my way home. Why?"

"I'm just leaving the office. Are you still downtown?"

"No, I'm taking the scenic route and driving around Lake of the Isles right now."

"What time will Noah be home?"

"He said he'd be home with dinner, which will probably be around six."

"Good, that gives us plenty of time. I'm stopping to pick up some treats, and I'll meet you at your house in a half hour. This conversation cannot happen over the phone."

"But—"

"Shut it, Victoria. I'm on my way." Click.

Well, shit. That didn't go how I planned. Actually, my mistake was not planning the conversation at all. I let my emotions take over and my mouth started running out of control.

"What the hell?" I said out loud to myself.

I managed to make it home in good time and ran upstairs to change into something more comfortable. There was a knock on the door as I started sorting through the mail.

"Why do you always knock?" I asked as I opened the door. "You know I leave the door unlocked when I'm expecting you."

"Because my mom taught me manners," she said as she gave me a quick peck on the cheek before beelining toward the kitchen. She set down an assortment of FunkyChunky containers, shrugged her coat off, and tossed it over the back of one of the breakfast bar stools and sat down.

I grabbed the container of ooey-gooey chocolate-drizzled caramel corn and pretzels and sat down next to her. "I didn't mean to sound so desperate when I called. I don't know what I was thinking."

"I know. It's okay to be scared and ask for help

when you don't know what you're asking for. Part of being a friend is anticipating your needs when you don't know what they are. You can count on me to be there for you and Noah. You both have my number and I'll be 'on call' this weekend for anything you need. I'm a phone call and a fifteen-minute drive away."

She grabbed my hand and squeezed tight. "I love you to pieces, and I know our friendship is based on sarcasm, humor, and shenanigans, but right now we need to focus on keeping you and Noah sane. Come hell or high water, I'll be here for you, and you can count on that."

"I love you," I said, lightly bumping into her shoulder and smiling.

"Love you too. Now enough of this sappy crap—are you going to share that shit with me or not?"

I was curled up on the sofa in a lightweight sweater dress when Noah arrived home with two grocery bags just before seven o'clock. He looked rather frazzled.

"Hey, sorry I'm late," he said as he kissed my

cheek and went to set the bags on the counter. "My afternoon got out of hand, and by the time I called to order dinner, it would have taken an extra half hour, so I decided to stop at the store and make you dinner instead. I hope you don't mind."

"Not at all... a home-cooked meal actually sounds better. What are we having?" I asked as I peeked into one of the grocery bags and started pulling things out. Romaine lettuce, several varieties of fresh vegetables, French bread, baby red potatoes, and a package of filet mignon beef. "Good choice."

"I'm glad you agree," he said as he slipped off his suit coat. "I'm going to head upstairs to change and then start the grill. Do you mind washing the romaine and veggies?"

There was a pause.

"Earth to Victoria. Are you there?"

"Huh? What? Oh sorry. I guess I drifted off." I turned toward him with a few veggies in hand and gestured to them. "This reminds me of when you made partner. Do you remember that night?"

"Yes, I remember it well." He smiled. "I called to tell you the good news and tried to get a reservation at Kincaid's but couldn't on such short notice. You ran to the store and splurged on the best cut of beef you could get, and we made our own five-star dinner and enjoyed it on the floor drinking wine," he said with a wistful look on his face, as if remembering the happy times that seemed to have disappeared from our life recently.

I stepped toward him and wrapped my arms around his waist. "I miss the simplicity of life back when we didn't have so much pressure. Granted, we would scramble to pay bills, but we always found creative ways to have fun."

"That we did." He placed a kiss on my lips before stepping back. "Let me go change. We'll have dinner, and then I think we should enjoy dessert in bed. You have two options: 'Better than Sex' chocolate cake with vanilla ice cream . . . or sex."

"I choose option three: sex with cake. I think that might be my new favorite dessert . . . and hold the vanilla," I said with a wink. "I'm not in the mood for vanilla tonight."

Noah's eyes instantly blazed fire, and I could see a twitch in his pants. "You. Are. Evil," he said matter-of-factly. "How do you expect me to cook and sit through dinner now?"

"I expect you to just be you. You know—a gentleman in the streets and a freak between the sheets."

He shook his head at me. "Evil, I say . . . pure evil. Start prepping dinner; I need a cold shower and then I'll be back down to start the grill."

He gave my ass a good slap before disappearing upstairs to change and well . . . I would guess relieve the "issue" I caused in his pants.

I poured myself a glass of wine and started prepping dinner. It was too quiet and my mind started racing about tomorrow. Scrolling through my playlist, I landed on "Unwritten" by Natasha Bedingfield. Before long, I was singing at the top of my lungs between sips of wine, and damn, it felt good. Then the music changed.

Noah was back and had on a pair of sleep pants and a white T-shirt. God, he looked incredible with his wet hair and lazy look. As much as I loved his suits, I loved his relaxed look even more because it was so rare. Ukulele strums started playing and the smooth voice of Chris Rene started singing "Trouble." The beat quickly picked up, and I think it was fair to say it was a subtle hint.

"Are you suggesting that I'm trouble?" I asked innocently, swaying my hips to the music.

"It's not a suggestion—it's a fact. While the shower helped, it did not solve the problem that you created," he whispered against my neck. "But right now I'm hungry, and it would be wise for you to eat a good dinner; you'll be burning a lot of calories tonight."

"Promises. Promises," I teased back since I was feeling that first glass of wine already. Since I hadn't been drinking the last few weeks, my tolerance was slipping.

Tonight, I was going to be the unknowing gazelle dancing its way into the lion's den looking like his last feast. Which was pretty much true. Who was going to want to have any kind of a physical relationship with a bald and boobless woman? *Nobody.* Tonight was going to be memorable.

Dinner was beyond amazing. Noah had set the dining room table with candles and a bouquet of fresh flowers I hadn't seen, but then again, I only looked in one of the grocery bags. The lights were dim and The Piano Guys played in the background. He served our dinner using our wedding china and pulled out all the stops to make this a romantic night to forget the madness swirling around us. It was perfection.

Noah cleared the table, and I started washing the dishes by hand. It felt good to be able to do daily chores again such as dishes and dusting. Yeah, I said that. It felt good to do chores. I left the heavy stuff for Noah since I still had a post-surgical weight restriction on lifting. We worked well together, and I was starting to feel a bit more like I was doing my share around the house.

Noah reached around me to grab a towel and started to dry the dishes. He would casually brush up against my hip or his hand lightly grazed against my side when he would move to put them away. While it felt innocent, I knew it was anything but.

As stuffed as I was, I wasn't going to let the fat feeling I had from dinner get in the way of what Noah had planned for dessert. I was going to let my libido and heart run the night, not my brain. *It was time to shut that shit off!*

Once the kitchen was clean, Noah steered me into the living room where a fire was flickering. He lay back on the sofa and I quickly found my spot, lying carefully on top of him and listening to the calming sound of his heartbeat.

I sighed deeply and closed my eyes as his thumb gently glided across the small of my back. We were both content lying together; the only sound other than the beating of our hearts was the crackle of the fire roaring to life.

I soon realized it wasn't the only thing roaring to life as I felt Noah growing hard between us and his heartbeat became more pronounced. He kissed the top of my head, and I lifted my face up to look at him. His eyes were dark and all consuming. They swallowed me up and there was no escape. To be honest, I didn't want to.

With his help, I slowly slid back up his body, and he assaulted my mouth with a force I had never experienced. His tongue was demanding and his mouth took what it wanted.

He was careful as he rolled us so that I was now on my back and he was hovering over me. I couldn't explain the look in his eyes. They were full of lust, passion, and something I couldn't put my finger on. But whatever was driving him was making me wet and he knew it.

His mouth crashed back against mine as I lifted my hips to try and find the friction I was craving, but I couldn't find it. He broke the kiss, stood up from the sofa, and walked away without a word. *What the hell?*

"Noah, did I do something wrong?" I called out after him as I sat up, utterly confused.

No answer.

"Noah?" I called out a little louder as I stood up and moved out of the living room to find him. I walked by one of the bathrooms on my way to the kitchen, but he wasn't in there, and when I made it to the kitchen, I found an envelope propped up on the counter with my name on it.

I slowly lifted it and felt my heart pounding in my chest as I slipped my finger under the seal to open it. I pulled out a cream-colored notecard.

Victoria,
You're in trouble.
Noah

A heavy beat suddenly filled my ears, and a woman's deep scratchy voice started singing, "Baby did a bad, bad thing." I turned to follow the music. It led me upstairs, and I saw a soft flickering light coming from our cracked bedroom door.

I slowly opened the door and found candles lit all around our room. Our bed was stripped of everything but the fitted sheet, and a chocolate cake sat on it, waiting to be devoured. It wasn't the only thing that would be devoured tonight.

A strong arm wrapped around me from behind,

and I felt a hard erection grind against my ass. It was perfectly cradled between my cheeks; the only barrier was my dress and panties. Noah was naked.

The heat of his breath against my neck attacked me next, and he started kissing a trail up to my ear, finally sucking and biting on the lobe. My knees began to go weak as the music changed to a hypnotic mind-game song.

Welcome to the lion's den, I thought to myself. *There was no escape.*

Noah nudged me forward toward the bed. Once we were at the foot of it, he reached for the hem of my dress and carefully lifted it up and off my body before tossing it to the floor. Soft kisses worked their way down my spine and then disappeared.

I was then assaulted with the wetness of his tongue as it ran a line across the small of my back along my panty line. His fingers ran up the outside of my legs and I heard the rip of my panties, which were now massacred as they fell to the floor. His tongue continued its journey as it ran down the crease of my ass and then kissed over to my right cheek, which he bit softly.

I heard a moan escape, but wasn't sure if it was from him or me.

He stood quickly and rubbed his length along the wet trail he had left on my ass. I was ready to explode from the foreplay alone, and we were just getting started. He reached around me and ran a finger through the chocolate frosting and brought it up to his lips. I could hear him sucking and licking the chocolate off of his finger and tried to calm the orgasm that was building.

The frosting became his finger paint, and soon my body was covered in chocolate frosting. I was a human feast and Noah was going all in. He licked the chocolate from my neck down my back and ass before he turned me around to lick my belly button.

I tried not to notice the lack of attention to my deformed chest, but I couldn't blame him and I wasn't about to ruin our night. Noah was acting differently. He didn't speak at all and focused on worshiping me.

His tongue trailed down and began licking at my chocolate-covered clit. That was all it took. I screamed out his name as my body trembled, and Noah firmed his grip on my legs to keep me standing while he continued his assault. Another orgasm quickly followed, as he made sure not to leave any frosting behind.

Moving to lay me down on the bed, he leaned over to kiss me and the mixture of chocolate frosting and the glaze of my orgasm consumed my senses. It was intoxicating. He was still standing as he lifted my legs up and over his shoulder. He gripped his length with his right hand and rubbed it through my wet folds. I looked down to see his swollen crown glistening as it slid up against my clit.

"Fuck," I whispered as I dropped my head back down to the bed.

Noah took that exact moment to slam into me hard and fast. He was frantic and each time he slammed into me he let out a pained grunt. It was like he was trying to fuck the cancer out of me. It was a punishing force that pushed me to another orgasm and ultimately pushed him over the edge with a loud shout.

I felt him twitch as he pumped himself into me and he stayed there until every last drop was out. He pulled out slowly and scooped me up from the bed to carry me into the bathroom.

He set me down on the cold counter and I let out a yelp. He smiled at me briefly before he turned to start the bath and poured in my favorite coconut bubble bath from the Body Shop. He helped me into the tub before leaving the bathroom.

When he returned, he climbed in behind me and began to wash me gently with a washcloth. He was uncharacteristically attentive, and I loved every second of it, even though he had yet to say anything.

After he washed all of the remaining chocolate frosting off of me, we sat in silence, me with my back to his front and his arms wrapped around my tummy.

He noticed that I was starting to shiver. "Let's get you out and dried off," he said as he rose up and out of the tub to wrap a towel around his waist before he grabbed a towel for me. "Come on, sweetheart."

I placed my hand in his as he helped me step out onto the soft rug. He dried me off, taking care not to be rough as he ran the towel over my chest. Placing a kiss on my forehead, he stepped away and dried himself off quickly before stepping out again.

He reappeared a few moments later with my robe. "Put this on and meet me down by the fire when you're ready." The bathroom door closed, and he was gone.

I made my way down to the living room and found him sitting on the sofa, tapping away on his phone. I noticed two new glasses of wine and a frosted chocolate cake placed on the coffee table.

"You frosted the cake again?"

He looked up in surprise and put his phone down. "I didn't hear you come down the stairs."

He scooted over and patted the spot next to him. "No, I bought two cakes. I figured we might ruin one and wanted you to be able to enjoy your cake and eat it too."

"God, I love you, Noah," I said as I leaned down and placed a kiss on his lips before making myself comfortable next to him. I picked up the cake and moved it to my lap and dug in with one of the forks that were waiting.

"Mmm . . . this is amazing," I muttered with my mouth full of chocolate cake. "However, they failed on the marketing. There is no way this is better than sex with you," I said before I continued to stuff my face full of cake, making sure to share a few bites with Noah.

Chapter Eleven
I AM CAPABLE

Today was the day—the day I was knowingly allowing someone to flood my veins with poison. It seemed barbaric, but it's what was recommended, and I wasn't going to go down without a fight. I was still holding on to the good mood from the amazing night with Noah. Scratch that, "amazing" wasn't the right word. It was fan-fucking-tabulous!

I spent the morning soaking in another bubble bath and fielding calls from my parents and friends, all wishing me "good luck." It felt odd. What the hell did luck have to do with it?

I pulled on a pair of yoga pants and a T-shirt and considered bringing a jacket. I wasn't sure if I would be cold during treatment, but I figured dressing in layers would be smart. Dr. Guthrie and I discussed the pros and cons of having a port put in place for my chemotherapy treatments, and to be honest, the whole thing freaked me out.

The procedure consisted of having a port with a catheter surgically placed just below my collar bone. The catheter would be inserted most likely into my jugular vein, and chemo drugs would be administered using the port, which would also be used for my weekly blood draws. While having a port seemed like the easy and logical way to go, there was a risk of infection, which could potentially delay my treatment plan.

My philosophy was if I had options available to me, I would do the research and make the best decision for me. I was aware of the risks with having the treatment directly administered through the veins in my arms, but I wasn't about to undergo another surgical procedure that wasn't a necessity.

There would be no port for this girl, and I didn't care what anyone said. This was my battle to fight. It was my body that would be going through hell, and I wasn't about to let anyone tell me what to do.

Thankfully, Dr. Guthrie respected my choice. I'm pretty sure that's part of the reason why she was named one of the Twin Cities' premier oncologists. I lucked out in the physician department for sure.

I heard the door open. "Victoria, I'm home," Noah called out from downstairs.

"I'll be right down—just finishing getting dressed."

"I need to change too," he said as he walked into our bedroom. He had planned to go with me to my first treatment, and I'm sure he didn't want to sit for hours in the clinic wearing a suit. He stepped out of the walk-in closet wearing a pair of jeans and a sweater. He reached for the tablet on his bedside table.

"I loaded up a few movies and thought we could watch one," he said nervously as he walked toward the door and waited for me.

I had just finished putting on a pair of pearl earrings and looked up at him. "That sounds great, thank you. They also mentioned that I should bring a few snacks and they recommended hard candy to suck on—apparently chemo will cause a metallic taste in my mouth."

I moved past Noah, who was standing in the doorway, and made my way down to the kitchen to pack a small bag with a granola bar, some pretzels, and some Jolly Ranchers.

He walked up behind me, and I turned to ask if

he wanted me to pack anything for him but stopped when I saw his face. He was pale and looked like he was on the verge of throwing up. "Are you okay?"

"Yeah, I'm just a little freaked out. I don't know what to do, and I'm not prepared for what tonight might bring. I feel like things are going to change once we walk out that door, and I'm not even sure what that means."

"I'm not prepared either. I'm trying not to freak out, because honestly, it will only make things worse. They will send me home with the meds I'll need for the nausea, and all we can do is follow their advice. Everyone reacts differently to treatment. All we can do is hope for the best," I said as I moved closer to him and wrapped my arms around his waist.

"Bobbie Jo, Dana, and Jen all said to call if you need help with anything. They can run to the store or pharmacy or just come and sit with me if needed. You're my husband, not my babysitter, and I don't expect you to know what to do. We are learning this together." I squeezed him tighter. "Are you with me?"

"How are you so damn strong?"

"I'm not. I'm a good actress and I deserve a goddamn Oscar. Because honestly, I'm scared as hell and don't want to do this. A part of me wants to ignore what is happening and run the other way, but I can't. I just can't."

I let out a heavy sigh before continuing: "I need to give this a shot. I committed to doing it, it was an educated choice I made, and I don't go back on my word. I'll give it all I've got, and when I've got nothing left to give, I know that you and the people I love will give me the strength I need to keep going. Right now I'm strong because I know everyone else is weak with worry. I need to go in with a positive attitude and a smile on my face."

I noticed that his eyes were slightly glossy looking before he turned toward the door to the garage. I grabbed my snack bag, a bottle of water, and my jacket and headed toward the door and whispered to myself, "Let's do this."

We arrived at the clinic with ten minutes to spare before my appointment. I decided to make use of the little kitchen area and made myself a cup of hot chocolate while Noah opted for coffee. We had no idea what the next twenty-four to forty-eight hours would be like, and I was sure that he was prepared to be up all night.

"Victoria Madison."

Noah and I stood and approached the woman.

"My name is Margaret, and I'll be your primary nurse. It's nice to meet you," she said as she led us into a treatment room with a hospital bed, a recliner-like chair, and two regular chairs. "Have a seat wherever you will be most comfortable."

I looked at my options and opted for the recliner, and Noah slid into one of the standard chairs.

She flipped open my chart. "Your labs look great, so we can go ahead with today's scheduled treatment. It will be a combination of the two drugs in the treatment packet Dr. Guthrie gave you. The first drug, doxorubicin, will be administered by me personally through a push injection rather than an IV drip. I'll be injecting two large syringes of it slowly into your veins so I can monitor you for an allergic reaction. It's red in color and has earned the name the Red Devil, but it is the most effective in treating breast cancer. Do you have any questions so far?"

I shook my head. "I don't think so."

"After the push infusion is complete, I'll start an

IV drip of cyclophosphamide. This drug breaks down the DNA in the cancer cells. It also affects normal cells and is the drug that will cause your hair to fall out. However, you shouldn't see any major hair loss until after your second treatment. I would like to get you a dose of Zofran before we start; it's the most effective anti-nausea medicine we use, and if we can get started on a dose right now, then we will be ahead of the game. How does that sound?"

"Sounds good to me—the more stocked up my system is against getting sick, the better I feel about doing this. I'd like to avoid spending my night praying to the porcelain god. There is nothing appealing about that."

Margaret let out a laugh. "Agreed. Dr. R. will send you home with a few prescriptions, including more Zofran, Compazine, and Decadron for nausea. She also wants you to stop into the infusion lab at the hospital for a Neulasta injection tomorrow. It will help to stimulate the growth of new and healthy white blood cells in your bone marrow. It will help build your immune system back up and fight infection. We encourage you to drink lots of fluids the first forty-eight hours to flush your system as quickly as possible. I'm going to go prepare your 'cocktail,' and we'll start when I return."

"By 'cocktail,' you mean a beverage, correct?" I attempted to joke with a hopeful smile, knowing that was not what she meant.

"I wish it was, but sadly I only have my nursing license and not a bartender license," she said with a smile before stepping out of the room.

"You ready to do this?" Noah asked, trying to sound encouraging, even though I knew deep down he was just as freaked out as I was.

"As ready as I'm going to be," I said nervously, trying to stay calm. "What are our movie choices?"

"How about *50 First Dates*? A little Sandler and Barrymore to pass the time?"

"Excellent choice. Get it queued up, and let's forget why we are here."

"You got it." He started the movie on his tablet just as Margaret walked back into the room with a tray. It consisted of an IV needle and tubing, the two red vials of the so-called Red Devil, a large IV bag and two smaller vials of what I'm assuming were anti-nausea meds. She set the tray down on a cart and rolled it over next to my chair.

She pulled a rolling chair over next to me. "Let's see what we have to work with. Can you roll up your sleeves for me or take off your jacket?"

"What would be easier?"

"It would be easier if you could take off your jacket. If you're chilled, I can get you a warm blanket." I nodded my head in agreement and started removing my jacket as she went to get a blanket.

"Here you go," she said as she laid the blanket out over me and resumed her spot facing me. She tied a large band tourniquet around my right arm and started tapping down my arm to find a viable vein to attack. "Perfect."

She reached for an alcohol swab and gently wiped the area clean before gripping the IV needle. I turned to look at Noah who was glued to the screen of his tablet to avoid looking. Smart man.

"You might feel slight stinging, but it should go away fairly quickly once the needle is in place. Take a deep breath . . . here goes."

I took a deep breath and slowly let it out while focusing on the movie. I felt a pinch and then a slow burn followed by a cold feeling in my vein. She released the tourniquet, and I relaxed.

"You did great. I ran a quick flush and gave you a dose of Zofran to help keep the nausea at bay. I'm going to start the first vial of doxorubicin. If you start feeling hot, dizzy, or have difficulty breathing, we will stop the infusion immediately. Okay?"

"Yes. I'll let you know." I tried my best to stay calm. It wasn't very comforting to hear a medical professional tell you they will stop poisoning you immediately if you start feeling hot, dizzy, or have difficulty breathing. Isn't that how people typically feel at a doctor's office?

My discomfort in the situation was easily spotted by Noah, and he reached for my left hand and gave it a squeeze. I looked up at his concerned face, and he gave me a wink and a small smile before he mouthed, "I love you."

I mouthed "Ditto" back at him, and he squeezed my hand one more time and turned his attention back to the movie, as did I.

"We're done with the first part, and you did a great job," Margaret said with a reassuring smile. "I'm going to get the cyclophosphamide going. It will take around two hours. Can I get you anything before I step out?"

"No, thank you. I brought a few snacks, and I should be okay."

She reached over to the hospital bed and pulled

over a remote. "If you need anything, just push the 'nurse' button, and I'll be right in. I've got two other patients right now, so it might take a minute or two to respond if I'm in with them."

"I will." With that, she left the room, and Noah and I watched the movie, sharing a few laughs and the bag of pretzels I brought.

The time passed quickly, and she was back in my room removing my IV and placing a cotton ball and Band-Aid over the area. She handed a few prescription sheets to Noah. "These are the prescriptions I told you about earlier. I suggest you get them filled on your way home so you have them ready when needed. If you can stay ahead of the nausea, it makes all the difference. Once it hits, it can hit hard, and it's difficult to play 'catch up' with the drugs."

"Other than being a little light-headed, I'm actually feeling pretty good. I don't feel nauseated at all."

"Let's keep it that way," Noah said as he tucked the slips of paper into his jacket pocket. "I'll drop them off at the pharmacy on our drive home. We'll get you settled and have some dinner, and then I'll go pick them up."

"Just don't forget to pick them up. You want to be sure to stay on top of it," Margaret warned.

"Yes, ma'am," I said as I stood up slowly. Noah placed his hand under my arm to help steady me. I guess he was prepared for me to drop.

"Don't forget to stop into the lab for your Neulasta injection tomorrow. It might make you a little achy, but a warm bath can usually help with the discomfort, and it goes away within a day or two. Don't hesitate to call the office immediately if you have concerns. The nurse line is open twenty-four hours to answer any questions and can put you in contact with Dr. Guthrie if needed. If you have no further questions, you're free to leave."

"I don't have any. Do you, Noah?" I asked as I headed toward the door. If I didn't have to stay here any longer, I wasn't going to. I'd spent enough time in this drab and monochromatic room; I was eager to get home. Taking my cue, he shook his head no and thanked Margaret.

We arrived home to heavenly smells coming from the kitchen and Bobbie Jo wearing an apron. "Welcome home, sizzle tits! How ya doing?"

Noah got me settled at the breakfast bar. "Not too bad actually. I feel a little light-headed, almost like I'm a little buzzed."

He took the seat to my right. "What are you doing here? I thought you were going to drop off dinner. I didn't expect to see you."

"I wasn't about to drop off food and not see how she was doing. So I picked up a rotisserie chicken, mashed potatoes, fresh bread, and Gatorade at the store."

She made note of the inquisitive look on my face after the Gatorade remark. "I heard that Gatorade will help keep you hydrated, and if it were me, I'd get bored with water quickly. I hope you like Ice Blue."

"Sure, sounds good. I'm hungry... is dinner ready?"

She reached into the oven, which was set on warming, and pulled out three plates and set them down one at a time on the breakfast bar. "Do you mind if I stay?"

"As long as Victoria is okay with it. It would be nice to have some extra company," Noah responded before taking a forkful of mashed potatoes.

"We would love to have you stay for dinner," I answered back inviting her to sit to my left.

"Jen wanted to be here, but she was called in for

an emergency at work. She is planning to stop over tomorrow if needed."

"Great," Noah said before he sat upright and cussed, "Oh shit!"

"What?" I said, looking at him questioningly.

"We forgot to drop of your prescriptions on the drive home. I don't want to be too late in getting the meds," he said as he quickly stood up. "I'll heat up my dinner when I get back. It shouldn't take too long. Can you stay with her, Bobbie Jo?"

"Yes, go ahead and do what you need to do. Victoria is in good hands."

Noah kissed me on the back of the head as he rushed to the door and was gone. Bobbie Jo and I finished dinner, and she cleaned up the kitchen while I sat and sipped Gatorade.

"I'm not feeling the best; I think I'm going to go sit in the living room. Come join me when you're done," I said as I stood and had to catch myself on the edge of the countertop. "Whoa."

Bobbie Jo rushed to my side. "Are you okay?" She took my arm and helped me to the leather chair in the living room. "Can I get you anything? Do you feel like you're going to be sick?"

"No, I'm just dizzy and my stomach is a little

queasy. I'm sure I'll be fine if I close my eyes for a bit. They said they loaded me up on anti-nausea meds, so I'm sure this is normal," I said as my stomach started to churn, and I closed my eyes as tight as I could, trying my best to block it out.

My body continued to revolt against me. No mercy. I shot out of the chair and ran for the bathroom as fast as I could. I sank to the floor as my body began to tremble from adrenaline and the fear of what was coming next.

I wasn't able to hold back and proceeded to see my dinner in reverse. I pinched my eyes shut and reached for the handle to flush. Bobbie Jo sat next to me rubbing my back, not saying a word.

I spent the next five hours throwing up until there was nothing left but bile and dry heaves. I felt like I was having an out-of-body experience.

At some point Noah took over rubbing my back, and they changed me out of my clothes and slid one of his T-shirts onto me. I was now curled up in the fetal position on a towel spread out on the bathroom floor.

"Sweetheart," Noah whispered. "You haven't thrown up for over an hour, and this can't be comfortable. It's three o'clock in the morning, and you need to get some sleep. I need to move you to the bed."

I grunted my acknowledgment, and he carefully scooped me and carried me into the bedroom. He laid me down, placing the top sheet over me. "Do you want a blanket?"

My attempt to answer failed; my throat was so raw from all of the acid that had traveled through it that I just shook my head no and frowned. Noah could see my struggle and didn't ask anything more. He just placed a kiss on my head and left me to pass out.

I slept sporadically, waking up every few hours. Noah never did come to bed, but I noticed him sitting in the chair in the corner watching over me.

I woke the next morning in a fog. My mouth was dry and tasted like sewage. I tried to sit up, but my body felt like it was weighted down with sand bags and my head was buzzing. It wasn't worth the effort to get up, and luckily, I heard Noah's feet on the floor. He made his way from the chair and sat down on the edge of the bed. I found comfort in his touch as he gently placed his hand on my jaw and his thumb slowly rubbed my cheek.

"How are you feeling?" he asked in a whisper.

"Like road kill," I rasped out, and that was no joke.

"You really need some fluids. Do you want to sip some water or Gatorade through a straw? How about some crushed ice cubes? I'm worried about you getting dehydrated; you haven't had anything to drink since eight thirty last night."

I could sense his distress over me not having any fluids after vomiting all night. "Ice, please."

A few hours later, I was sitting up in bed, which was a small miracle. I had managed to avoid throwing up, but trying to get anything solid in me to eat was nearly impossible. Everything tasted like I was licking a hammer. Honestly, that was the best way to describe the metallic flat taste that wouldn't go away.

I was starting to get restless lying around and knew we still needed to go to the hospital to get my white cell booster shot. I wanted to get it over with.

"Can we go get my shot over with?" I asked while turning to set my feet down on the floor.

"Are you sure you want to go right now? Shouldn't you move around the house a little bit first?"

"I want to go now and get it over with," I said as I gingerly started to shuffle my feet toward the bathroom. There was no way I was going to attempt a shower, but I needed to brush my teeth, wash my face, and put on some deodorant. I looked at myself when I was done and was thankful that I had cut my hair so I didn't have to contend with it even though it was sticking out in every direction.

When I stepped back into our room, Noah had my clothes laid out on the bed for me and asked if I wanted some help. I told him no, but when he saw me struggling to get my leg into the leg of my pants he stepped in immediately.

He pulled me into a hug after I was dressed. "I'm sorry you're going through this." He paused and I felt like he wanted to say something more profound but couldn't. He gave me one more gentle squeeze and led me out of our bedroom.

Noah pulled up in front of the hospital, got out of the car, and walked around to open my door. As I stood, a young girl appeared with a wheelchair and asked if we needed help.

"Yes, thank you," Noah said to the girl. "I'm going to go park in the ramp, can you wait for me in the lobby?"

"Yes, sir. I'll wait with her until you arrive." She smiled down at me before pushing me through the front doors. We found a nice place to sit by the front window and the heat of the sunshine felt amazing.

"Ma'am, can I get you anything while you wait? Coffee, tea, or some water?"

"Thank you, but no. I'm good right now," I answered with the best smile I could muster up, but the look on her face told me that she was worried about me. She couldn't have been more than fourteen or fifteen years old, and I noticed the name Emma was on her name tag.

"Emma, I had my first chemo session yesterday, and I'm here for a shot to help boost my immune system. I'm feeling crummy, and that's why I look this way. I've been told that I'll be fine in a few days when it's out of my system."

She nodded her head, telling me she understood, but didn't say any more.

"Hey," Noah said as he jogged toward us. "How are you doing?"

"I'm good. Emma here was a great babysitter." She smiled back at me this time, and I could tell that she felt a bit more at ease.

"I'm happy to show you to the infusion lab, if you'd like?" she asked looking at Noah, who had a soft smile on his face. It was nice to see that the simple kindness from a young girl could ease the stress of the last eighteen hours.

"That would be nice. Lead the way," Noah said, holding his arm out and signaling her to go ahead.

When we arrived at the infusion lab desk, we were checked in and brought back to a small private room and told a nurse would be in shortly. There were two reclining treatment chairs, so we each sat down in silence and stared up at the ceiling.

"You okay?" I asked as I looked over at Noah.

"Yeah, I'm fine. Didn't get much sleep last night, but I'm not going to complain. You had it far worse than me."

"It definitely wasn't my favorite way to spend a Friday night. Most times you have a lot of fun on a Friday night before you throw up, like it's a package deal. There was nothing fun about last night."

"You can say that again. Have you had any water since we left?"

"No, I left my bottle in the car," I confessed as the nurse walked in the room studying my chart.

"Good afternoon. You must be Victoria?"

I nodded. "Yes."

"Great, how are you feeling today?"

"Not the greatest. I spent most of the night throwing up until there was nothing left but bile."

"Have you been drinking fluids to stay hydrated?" she inquired.

"I've been trying my best," I answered sheepishly, because honestly, I was afraid to put anything in my mouth after the violence of last night. "I'm just so wiped out." Tears started to well in my eyes, and Noah sat up on the edge of his chair and reached over to hold my hand.

"She has been having a hard time with drinking because her throat is so raw. I've given her crushed ice, and she has been sipping Gatorade and water through a straw. She has maybe had two cups of fluid today, and she hasn't attempted food."

"Okay. I'm concerned about dehydration," she said as she stood up and stepped over to wash her hands at the sink in the room. "I'll get your injection ready, and then I'm going to ask you to stay for at least one bag of fluids. I want to avoid further dehydration issues down the road, and you're right on the cusp of potentially becoming dehydrated. I'm not willing to take that risk, and it will help you feel better."

I nodded in agreement, feeling completely defeated. This whole experience had done nothing but beat me down mentally and physically. It felt like I was leaning over the edge of hell and the only thing that was keeping me from falling in was a fine thread that was starting to fray. It was only a matter of time until the thread broke and I would free fall.

Chapter Twelve
I AM MIGHTY

It had been six days since my three-hour stay at the hospital for an IV bag of fluids and my shot. I was feeling a bit better and had begun to eat a little bit here and there. Gatorade was my friend. I froze it into ice cubes to suck on and also found out that I loved frozen banana slices and frozen grapes. Anything frozen was my preference.

Curling up with a book with "She Will Be Loved" by Maroon 5 quietly playing in the background finally gave me some peace.

I heard the click of a key in the door, and Noah made his way inside not so quietly. I felt a shift in my relaxed state and grew anxious.

"Did you have dinner yet?" he slurred, sauntering past me and into the kitchen.

"Yeah, I had some of my mom's chicken noodle soup. She had Dad bring over a few containers of it.

I guess she wants to make eating easy for me." I laughed before I noticed he was standing in the kitchen, pounding the glass of water with his eyes closed. "Are you okay?"

"I've been better. We went out to dinner with a few clients, and I had a few too many cocktails. I'm not used to drinking like that anymore, and I don't know how I lost track of the number of drinks I had. I think I need to head up to bed if you're doing okay."

He looked pitiful as he tried to seem concerned about me. He was most definitely drunk. "Did you drive yourself home?"

"No. I got a ride. I'll sort out how to get my car tomorrow."

"Good. Go up to bed . . . I'll be up shortly." I eyed him as he started pulling at his tie while trying to make his way toward the stairs.

He was struggling, and I heard him cuss when he couldn't get the knot out of his tie. "God dammit."

Noah hadn't been drunk in years; he always seemed to stay in control when it came to business dinners. There was no way this night was going to be kind to him. Unlike my situation, in which I did not have the choice of making myself sick or not, he had chosen to drink too much, and chances were high that he would be throwing up tonight. In fact, I'd bet on it.

Men were dumb, and my husband was at the top of the heap tonight.

Something startled me awake. I looked over at the clock and noticed it was just after eleven. I turned off all of the lights, made sure the door was locked, and made my way upstairs.

The bathroom light was on but the door was only partially closed, casting a shadow over the room. I saw Noah sprawled out on the bed in his boxers; he was moving around a bit and babbling unintelligible words as I went into the bathroom to brush my teeth and put on my pajamas. Turning off the bathroom light, I tiptoed to the bed and climbed in.

Lately, I'd been having a hard time falling asleep; my brain seemed to be on a constant buzz. It was doing some serious mind traveling while my body needed to sleep.

I counted backward from one hundred. *Fail.* Still awake. I went through each letter of the alphabet, thinking of something I was grateful for that started with each letter. Still awake.

I felt the bed shift as Noah cuddled next to me, throwing his leg up over my body. He let out a sigh of contentment and started to softly snore. Sleep was a lost cause now.

My mind travel continued, and Noah started getting fidgety again. *Wait. What's that?* I paused my train of thought and focused. He was starting to grow hard against my hip.

Did grown men still have wet dreams? I wondered as he started thrusting against me, getting harder with each stroke against my hip. I wasn't sure what to do.

Should I wake him? Should I give him a hand? He sped up and started mumbling again. His grip tightened around me, and his breathing was erratic. I could tell he was close to release and lay as still as possible to not surprise him.

"Stacey!" he shouted as he startled himself awake while coming against my hip.

His frantic eyes looked around the room and settled on me. I stared back wide-eyed and speechless as my mouth hung open in shock.

"Oh shit. What the hell?" he questioned as he

looked down at the mess he'd just made and dashed out of bed. I heard him curse again as he stumbled into the bathroom. He closed the door and started the shower.

What. The. Fuck, I thought, as I lay with the warm, wet spot on my hip that felt more like a cold bucket of water. I knew people talked in their sleep and said random things. Most of the time, they don't even remember talking.

Confusion and anger were at war in my brain now, and as much as I wanted to feel settled, I didn't. I was conflicted with my feelings and wanted to cry.

How had her name even come up? It's not like we spent much time with her and her "sugar daddy" husband. He was one of Noah's partners at the firm. Noah must have been at dinner with him, and she was a topic of conversation. That made complete sense. *Right? Yes.*

"That's the answer," I mumbled to no one in particular, as I convinced myself that it was true. I got out of bed, careful not to get my side of the bed all wet and sticky, and went into the closet to put on a fresh pair of pajamas.

The feeling of being cheated on was real, but I

knew it was only a dream. However, it didn't make me feel any better. Anger had taken the forefront of my mind as I stepped back into the bedroom.

The bathroom door was still closed, but the water had stopped running. I looked over at the bed and decided to go back downstairs to make myself a cup of tea.

My head hurt from my brain racing at Mach speed, and my heart was still thundering as I sat down on the sofa. Escaping into a book usually did the trick to calm me down. I silently prayed that it would not fail me now.

It didn't take long for my mind to get sucked into the story on the pages; my eyes began to get heavy and struggled to stay open. I gave in to the sleep that had been so elusive and didn't move a muscle until the next morning when I smelled coffee and heard noise coming from the kitchen. Surprisingly the smell and taste of coffee was still okay in my chemo-induced world.

I quietly strolled into the kitchen and found Noah busy making pancakes, which were one of the things I figured out that I really liked eating this week. The secret was a little extra Watkins vanilla added to the batter.

"Good morning," I whispered as I reached for a coffee cup in the cabinet.

"Good morning," he turned away from what he was doing to look at me. "I'm so sorry about last night. I can't believe I let myself drink like that. It was irresponsible, and I apologize."

"It happens," I answered as I poured my coffee and went to sit at the kitchen table instead of the breakfast bar. While I couldn't be mad at him for what he said in his sleep, I felt betrayed. It hurt and I couldn't talk with him about it right now, so I opened my book back to where, I assumed, I had left off before falling asleep the night before.

He continued to make breakfast in awkward silence. I wondered if he knew what he had said while he rubbed himself against me and came in his sleep, or perhaps he really did feel guilty about coming home drunk. I couldn't tell, but I knew that something was off.

As much as I tried to focus on reading, I couldn't. "Did you sleep well after your shower?"

"Yeah. I hope I didn't wake you when it happened. It has been years since I've had a wet dream." He sounded embarrassed as he placed a plate of pancakes on the table. The fact that he was so honest made me think he really was out of it and didn't remember calling out Stacey's name when he climaxed. *Should I say something or just ignore it?* I didn't want to make this anymore uncomfortable than it already was.

"Thank you for breakfast; it smells great."

"You're welcome. I feel terrible about what happened last night and wanted to make peace this morning. I promise that won't happen again." He seemed sincere in his apology, and I decided, at that moment, that I needed to move on and forget what happened. It was just a dream, and my overactive mind was getting the best of me.

"So what do you have planned for today?" I asked as I took my first bite of pancakes. They were perfect and melted in my mouth. I quickly took another bite.

"I have to catch up on a few cases, but I'm not in the right frame of mind to work right now. I still have a headache to remind me that I'm a dumbass."

"Yeah. Last night was not one of your brighter moments."

We spent the rest of the day being lazy and hadn't changed out of our pajamas.

"What would you say to going out for dinner

tonight?" he called out to me from the office.

"Where do you want to go?" I got up and walked toward the office. When I got to the door, I peeked in to see he was leaning back in his chair and pinching the bridge of his nose. "Everything okay?" I asked.

He opened his eyes and looked up at me. "Yeah. Just been working on a few things and I need a break, and I remembered that I don't have my car. We could grab a quick dinner and stop to pick it up on our way home."

"Sure. That sounds good. Give me fifteen minutes, and I'll be ready to go."

"Great," he said as he started organizing the papers that were strewn all over his desk.

We stopped at one of my favorite old-fashioned malt shops, and I sucked down a large banana malt like it was my last meal. It was amazing; the burger, not so much. This not being able to eat certain things was going to be a challenge for sure. I did manage a few French fries, but the banana malt was a winner. Noah even ordered two more to go.

"We'll put them in the freezer for later," he said when he saw the surprise on my face. "If we find something that works, we're stocking up."

"That must be why you get paid the big bucks, Counselor," I teased as I elbowed him in the side. It felt good to joke a bit. Life had been so serious lately, and it sucked. We drove a short distance to where Noah's car was parked.

"I need to run a quick errand on my way home. Is there anything you need at the grocery store?" he asked as I sat down and adjusted the driver seat of my car.

"Why don't you get some more grapes and bananas? They seem to be winners right now—and a few bottles of blue Gatorade. Friday is my next chemo, so we should be prepared."

"Got it. Drive carefully and don't forget to bring the malts in and put them in the freezer. Text me when you get home so I know you're safe, please."

"I will. Where else are you stopping?"

"Christmas is in two weeks, so should you really be asking?"

"Oh my god! How did I forget about Christmas?" I exclaimed.

"You've had a little bit going on lately. Not to worry, though; I've done most of the shopping already so you can just focus on feeling better." He leaned in to give me a kiss. "I've got it under control."

"Thank you. I'm sorry that our life has been nothing but madness lately. Jen and I did a little bit of shopping a few weeks ago, so I have a few things for you at least. I'm so out of it," I confessed as I felt the weight of the world push down on me a little harder.

I closed the door and watched Noah walk to his car. He paused and grabbed a slip of paper out from under the wiper. Most likely an advertisement since people loved to hit the popular restaurant lots and put a flyer on your car. Noah crumpled it and tossed it on the passenger seat before he got in. He nodded to me once he started his car, and I headed home.

Noah arrived home several hours later with his arms loaded down with bags. I got up to help him unload the groceries as he brought the other bags up to one of the extra bedrooms.

When he came back down to the kitchen, he was already changed into his sleep pants and a T-shirt.

"Are you feeling okay?" I asked while motioning my head at what he was wearing.

"Yeah, I'm just tired. Last night has caught up to me, and I think I'm going to turn in. I've got a busy week, and I need to be on my game." He wrapped me in a hug, and I automatically nestled my head into the crook of his neck. It was my favorite place to be.

We stood like this for a few minutes before he released me. "Good night. I love you," he said before placing a kiss on my lips and leaving.

"Good night," I called after him as he walked away.

I turned to my faithful teapot and put it to boil. I settled into a seat at the breakfast bar and flipped mindlessly through the free monthly magazine from the grocery store. I'm not sure what I was even looking for; I was just going through the motions of what would have been normal. Normal. *What was normal anymore?*

The first part of the week went by with little fanfare, which was a welcome change. I received a text from Jen on Thursday morning asking to meet for lunch. She knew that tomorrow would be my next chemo session, and I wouldn't feel like eating much for a few days.

We arrived at the restaurant in the upscale 50th & France shopping area. Jen and I spent a lot of time in the area during our teen years, and I still loved it. It felt like home. We were shown to our table, and when we arrived, two seats were already occupied.

"What the hell are you doing here?" I asked Bobbie Jo and Dana in surprise. A smile so big it hurt stretched across my face.

"Jen said she wanted to surprise you for her Victoria's Victors' Day, and here we are," Dana squealed. "It thankfully worked that we were both able to take the afternoon off."

Bobbie Jo cut her off. "We are going to stuff our faces, spend lots of money shopping, and take in a matinée at the movie theater if you're up for it."

"Sounds like the perfect distraction. Thank you, ladies." I sat down and was handed a menu.

Between all of the stories and giggles, it was a wonder we even ate our food. It felt good to laugh with my girlfriends. I missed them.

"We need to do this more," I declared. "I feel like I've been living on another planet lately, and I miss my girls."

"All you have to do is ask," Jen said while Bobbie Jo and Dana both nodded since their mouths were full. "Call or text and we're there."

"I'm sorry I haven't been around more." Dana tried to hide the fact that she was feeling guilty. "I've been traveling so much for work, and I'm barely home. I'm happy today worked out."

"Stop it! Don't feel bad. I know how busy you are, and I know you're always a call or text away."

"I'll try to get over more often when I'm in town. I promise." Dana leaned in to give me a side hug.

"Okay, ladies, enough of the sappy shit," Bobbie Jo interrupted. God, her bluntness always made me smile. "Let's go tear up some stores."

We spent the next two hours popping in and out of various stores, claiming we were helping the economy. I was able to buy a few more Christmas presents, and I felt settled for the first time in a few weeks. I was happy.

We headed toward the theater for the matinée. Something caught my eye as we were standing in line to buy our tickets. I noticed a woman being seated at a table by the window at a restaurant across the street. Something about her seemed familiar. I squinted to get a better look as she sat down and flipped her hair over her shoulder revealing her face. She didn't see me, but I knew who it was, and it gave me a shiver. Stacey.

I was just about to say something to Jen when my phone buzzed, and I looked down to find a text from Noah.

> *I hope you're having a fun day with the girls. Jen texted me to let me know that she was planning a girls' day. I'm going to be working late but should be home by 7:30 so we can have a late dinner.*
> *I love you, Noah.*

We stepped up to buy our tickets to the movie, and I typed a quick message back telling him that I was looking forward to dinner.

I had a hard time focusing on the movie. My brain was preoccupied with what happened with Noah in bed last night and now with seeing *her*, my stomach was a mess. It wasn't the same uneasy feeling I had experienced from chemo; this was different. I'd take the chemo stomach over this one, quite honestly.

As we exited the movie theater, my eyes quickly scanned across the street to the restaurant. Stacey was just getting up, and I caught a glimpse of a man's hand on her lower back as she leaned up for a kiss. I couldn't make out his face since it was now dark outside and the lights in the restaurant were dim. But one thing I knew in my gut was that it wasn't her husband. My stomach rolled as I watched them walk away.

"Jen, we need to go. Right now. I'm not feeling well." I feigned as I tried to stay calm and not freak out completely. "I need to get home." My mind was getting away from me, and the ideas going through my head needed to stop.

"You don't look well at all. Do you need to go to the hospital?" She put her hand to my forehead. "You're cold and clammy and all the blood has drained from your face."

"No. I'll be fine. I just really need to get home. The sooner, the better," I said pathetically.

"You sure you don't need to go to the hospital?"

"Yes. I'm sure," I said as I gave quick hugs to Dana and Bobbie Jo before Jen and I headed toward her car.

I rushed out of the car as soon as Jen stopped in the driveway; my feet hit the sidewalk hard as I dashed toward the front door. The door began to open as I shoved my key in the lock, and I was met by brilliant blue eyes.

Noah stood barefoot in front of me, wearing a pair of jeans with an untucked dress shirt, a glass of wine in his hand. His hair was slightly damp from a shower he must have taken, and he looked relaxed.

"Welcome home, sweetheart. How was your girls' day?" he asked as he gave a wave out to Jen as she pulled out of the driveway.

"Good," I responded as my mind started racing again. *Was he really home waiting for me all this time? Were the drugs making me hallucinate? Or was I simply losing my fucking mind?*

I moved past him and ran upstairs as fast as I could and went straight for the closet, closing the door behind me. I sank down on the bench and buried my face in my hands as the tears began to fall. I heard a light tap on the door.

"Victoria, can I come in? Are you okay?" Noah asked through the door.

I tried hard to settle my breath before answering. "Give me a few minutes."

"Okay."

I took a little extra time to gather my thoughts before changing into something more comfortable. When I finally looked at myself in the long mirror, I gasped when I saw how sickly I looked. Pinching my cheeks to bring some color to my face was no use, and Noah already knew I was wrecked. There was no use worrying about it at this point.

He was sitting on the edge of the bed with his head in his hands when I opened the door. The tortured look in his eyes was undeniable. Tension rolled off him in waves. He looked hurt.

"I'm sorry," I whispered, not moving from the doorway to the closet. "I'm not feeling like myself today, and it probably wasn't wise for me to go out."

It was a total bullshit line, but I was in no mood for a total breakdown, and if I told him what I thought I had seen just a short time ago, it would only piss him off. I was walking a fine line with Noah's emotions right now and it felt like it was starting to fray like a thin piece of thread.

"What's going on?" he demanded.

"Nothing. I'm letting little things get to me. I'll work it out." I stepped toward him and put my arms around him. He laid his head against my flat chest and when I winced, he started to pull back. "Please don't. It's fine. You just caught me off guard."

He pulled me closer between his legs and looked up at me. "I love you, Victoria. I'm worried about you. It's my job as your husband. Please understand that."

"I do understand. I'm sorry—this is something I

need to sort out on my own." I felt like a petulant child and stepped out of his hold. "I'm hungry. Did you still want to have dinner?"

"Sure. What would you like?"

"A cheese pizza sounds good."

"Cheese pizza it is," Noah said as he stood up and grabbed my hand to halt my movement toward the door. "It'll be okay. You *will* get through this. Just take it one day at a time. I know it's easier said than done, but try your best."

"I am."

I had nothing more to say. The constant battle with my overactive brain was starting to make me feel foolish. It was like the angel and devil had moved from their respective shoulders and started to cohabitate in my head. It wasn't pretty.

Chapter Thirteen

I AM POWERFUL

Friday afternoon arrived, and I felt like I was walking the plank as I made my way back to a treatment room with Noah at my side.

Margaret flipped open my chart. "I heard you had a rough go for a few days after the first treatment. How are you feeling now?"

"Better now, but we need to do something different. I cannot go through that again. It was miserable."

"Dr. Guthrie is going to stop in before we start your second treatment. She has a few ideas that might help, and she wanted to discuss them with you. Let me get your blood pressure and heart rate in the meantime."

She went about her business recording my stats before stepping out to get Dr. Guthrie.

A few minutes later, Dr. Guthrie stopped in to

discuss the side effects I had experienced. They weren't anything completely out of the ordinary, but she was concerned over my being so dehydrated and not eating due to the nausea.

"I am going to have Margaret give you another anti-nausea drug today in the IV drip. I would also like to prescribe Marinol for you to take for three to four days after. It will help keep the nausea away and will increase your appetite."

"How does it do that?"

"It's an FDA-approved synthetic byproduct of cannabis, also known as marijuana. A few of my patients have had great success with it."

I raised a curious eyebrow. "Do I smoke it? I've never smoked anything before."

"No. It is a pill that you will swallow. You need to be careful of the dosage, as it can make you feel a bit loopy." She smiled at this warning. I assumed she must have had an issue with another patient taking a few too many.

"Noted."

"Agreed. I'll monitor the intake of them like I do the other meds," Noah interjected.

"Great. Well, I think we're done here. I'll have Margaret call in these prescriptions so that they are ready for you to pick up on your way home."

"That would be wonderful," Noah and I said in unison. We were not about to have a repeat of two weeks ago.

As promised, Margaret loaded me up with four different meds before treatment started and my prescriptions were ready when we stopped by the pharmacy on our way home.

With the bottle of small orange sphere-shaped pills ready for me, I ate a light dinner of soup and crackers. I wasn't going to risk getting sick, so I popped one right away. *Yeah, this was going to be fun!*

I made it through the first night without throwing up, which was huge. However, as Dr. Guthrie warned, I was feeling pretty loopy. The Marinol definitely made me feel like I was tripping, but at least my appetite was back. *Find the positives... always the positives!*

After two days, I cut back on all of the nausea meds and the fog started to lift. I had felt like I was in the Twilight Zone and honestly didn't remember much of what went on for the last few days.

This treatment was much better, and while I still felt knock-down tired, I was feeling more like myself, which was good because Noah had to fly out on Tuesday night for a briefing in Chicago on Wednesday. He would be back late Wednesday night.

I wasn't comfortable with being home alone the entire time, so on Tuesday night, Bobbie Jo brought dinner and stayed the night. We gossiped and I fell asleep by nine o'clock. I definitely was not the life of party.

By Friday I was happy to be part of the active living again. I was looking through the stack of cards that arrived in the mail when an appointment alert went off on my phone.

Notification: *Fill appointment with Dr. Forrester @ 2:30 p.m.*

Whoops! I forgot I had made an appointment for my first fill today. I looked at the clock, and it was only ten o'clock, but I wasn't sure if I should drive yet after the Marinol. The warnings were very specific to not drive, and I knew Noah had meetings all day.

Bobbie Jo said to ask if I needed anything, so I

gave her a call.

"I get to meet Dr. McHottie? Fuck yeah, I'll take you! Be ready to go at two," she squealed before hanging up.

I finished my bagel and strolled up to the bathroom to take a quick shower. My hair was starting to shed on my pillow this morning, and I figured it was only a matter of time before it was all gone. A few larger clumps were hitting the shower floor as I was rinsing.

The one thing that I wasn't going to cry over was losing my hair.

As I stepped out of the shower, I looked in the mirror and noticed patches were missing here and there, with no rhyme or reason.

Well crap. I wasn't prepared for that.

Grabbing my hair towel, I started to rub the remaining hair dry while debating what to do. *Should I shave it all off, or just put on a hat and ignore it until it all fell out on its own?* I continued to move the towel around on my head and stopped when I noticed something odd.

I looked down at the towel in my hands, and it was covered in dark brown hair. I peered back up at myself in the mirror and realized that I had pretty much rubbed most of the leftover hair off of my head with the towel.

Was it possible to rub off your hair? Yes, apparently it was. Okay. I could do this.

I wasn't going to cry; in fact, I was going to make the best of it. Reaching for another towel from the linen closet, I finished wiping my head clean. A small pinkish-colored birthmark toward the top of my head on the right side caught my attention. It had a slight heart shape to it and made me smile; it was a secret underneath that I would have never known about.

Maybe this journey was about discovery, and this was the subtle way of telling me to look for positive signs.

I spent a little extra time doing my makeup today since I wasn't sure if I was just going to embrace the "bald is beautiful" look or try a scarf or hat.

Today was going to be a good day. I pulled on a pair of jeans and a soft cashmere cardigan, and the fact that I was seeing Dr. Forrester didn't hurt. He was handsome and had always been so caring toward me.

I attempted to wrap a scarf around my head, but it looked like a turban gone wrong, and I only had a few baseball hats, and they looked funny. Bobbie Jo would definitely agree to a hat shopping spree after my appointment, so I would just go au naturel for today. *Bald is beautiful!*

When the doorbell rang, I took a deep breath and opened the door.

"Well, look at you, all shiny and new! God, your head is perfectly shaped, and you look kinda hot," she said with a clever little smirk on her face.

"You're just saying that to make me feel better."

"Hell no, I'm not. You look beautiful. Are you okay with it being gone?"

"Yeah, I actually am. I knew it was going to happen, and today was the day. I'm good, really." I shrugged as I grabbed my purse, which contained a scarf . . . just in case I wasn't as ready as I thought. "Let's go see the good doctor, and then you're taking me hat shopping. I need something to keep this noggin warm come January."

"Shopping is my specialty." She looped her arm in mine and led me out to her car, which was still running. "I turned on the ass warmer just for you."

We were seated in Dr. Forrester's waiting room and Bobbie Jo was touching up her lipstick. "Is he single?" she asked me like we were sitting at the bar.

"Um. No. I don't think so." *Was he?* "Well, I guess I don't actually know," I whispered, hoping nobody else heard her question. I had never noticed a wedding ring, but then again, I had never really looked for one.

"Well, we need to find out."

"Bobbie Jo, don't you dare ask him in front of me. He is my doctor, not some guy I'm trying to set you up with. Please behave yourself." *What the hell was I thinking when I called her?* She could tell I was getting a bit worked up.

"Calm down. I won't do anything to embarrass you. You know my bark is worse than my bite. I'm just trying to keep you in a good mood." She patted my leg. "Don't worry, sizzle tits—I'll behave."

Elizabeth called my name, and Bobbie Jo followed me to the treatment room.

I had never been in this room before. It was definitely more clinical. White tiled floor, an exam table, and a few pieces of equipment tucked back by the sink and counter. There was a silver tray sitting close to the table with a large looking syringe, a bunch of tubing, and a bag of fluid.

I quickly looked away, as I didn't need or want to see that. Elizabeth stepped out so I could slip on the little pink gown, open in the front, as usual.

There was a knock on the door, and Dr. Forrester stepped into the room with Elizabeth in tow.

"Good afternoon, Victoria. It's great to see you again. I love the new look—you wear it well." He smiled, referring to my now-bald appearance as he shook my hand. "How is chemo going?"

"It's nice to be back, and this last treatment was much better." I rubbed my head feeling a bit self-conscious for the first time. "My hair just all fell out this morning, so this is my debut."

"It looks great. Did you know you had a little heart-shaped birthmark on your head?" *He noticed the birthmark.*

I smiled in response. "No clue."

"It's very unique." He looked over at Bobbie Jo, who was actually speechless. "Hi, I'm Dr. Forrester. And you are?"

The words struggled to leave her mouth as she held out her hand to him. "I'm Bobbie Jo. One of the best friends and chauffeurs."

"It's nice to meet you. Victoria mentioned that a few friends might be coming with her to appointments in her husband's absence. Thanks for bringing her today; that's really nice."

I didn't even know it was possible, but Bobbie Jo actually started to blush. Clearing my throat drew their attention back to me, and I smiled at them both.

"So, are you ready for your first expander fill?" he asked as he walked over to the sink to wash up and slip on a pair of blue medical gloves.

"Yes, I think so." I took a deep breath as I reclined back on the partially propped-up table.

"Great." He stepped forward and helped me lie back. "Let's get started. I'm going to find the ports using this magnetic guide and mark where we can do the injection."

I opened my gown, and he held some kind of contraption over my "lady lumps"; I watched as the little magnetic pointer moved around and he found the spot he needed. He pulled out his trusty purple Sharpie and marked me with an *X* like on a treasure map.

He repeated the process on the other side and

pulled the silver tray closer. I noticed him picking up the syringe and filling it with fluid through a tube attached to the saline bag. He moved to my side and wiped my chest with an alcohol swab.

"You are going to feel a bit of pressure, but just breathe through it. Are you ready?"

I nodded. "As ready as I'm going to be."

I looked over to Bobbie Jo so I could avoid seeing the needle I knew he was preparing to stick in me. Her eyes grew big, and when she shifted them over to my anxious ones, she smiled supportively.

I felt a slight pressure and then it released.

"Okay, I'm in. I'm going to start with twenty-five cc's, and we'll see how you're feeling."

He started pushing down on the syringe. "How are you doing?"

"So far, so good."

"I'm about to hit twenty-five . . . do you want to continue to fifty?"

"Sure." I honestly didn't know, but I wasn't feeling anything that uncomfortable yet. Plus, the faster I could get the fills done, the faster I would get rid of the expanders.

He continued pressing on the syringe. "Still feeling okay?"

"Yes. Should I be feeling something painful?" I questioned, not sure if something was wrong.

"No, not at all. I can inject up to one hundred cc's if you're comfortable with it, but you need to tell me your limits. Some women have a difficult time with twenty-five. Everyone is different."

"Okay. Let's keep going then," I said. He nodded and continued.

"We are at seventy-five; do you want me to keep going?"

"Sure—go big or go home." I smiled, feeling triumphant and proud of myself.

"All done with the left side," he said as he slowly pulled out the needle and placed a round Band-Aid over the spot where the needle had been. I looked down. *WOW . . . I had a boob!*

I started giggling. "That is crazy. It's like insta-boob. Bobbie Jo, you have to see this."

She walked over to see my now-filled left boob and my still deflated right one. "Oh my god. That is fantastic. I wanna take a picture," she said as she fumbled for her phone.

"Oh, no you don't!" I objected. "My boobs, or lack thereof, will not be shared on any kind of social media, and they most definitely will not be stored in your phone. Give that to me right now!" I ordered, sticking my hand out.

She backed away slowly with her hands up in the air, surrendering. "Okay, okay. I won't take pictures. Settle your tits. Or rather, fill her tits, good doctor." She winked at me, and Dr. Forrester just shook his head and tried to hide his smile.

Kill. Me. Now.

He filled the right side to one hundred as well and fixed me up with another Band-Aid to match. After he removed his gloves and washed his hands, he returned to help me sit up.

A few moments after I sat up, I suddenly felt dizzy and started to sway. He quickly noticed and grasped my shoulders to help me lie back down.

Bobbie Jo was on her feet right next to me in seconds. "You okay?" she asked.

"I think I just sat up too fast and got dizzy. I'll be fine."

Dr. Forrester muttered something to Elizabeth, and she was back a minute later with a can of ginger ale and a straw.

"Take a sip of this." He held the straw toward my lips, and I took a sip. "Your body has been through a lot lately, and your blood sugar might be a bit low. You probably need to get something to eat."

"I haven't had anything since breakfast. I guess I need to eat a bit more. Can I try sitting up again?"

"Sure, but let's take it slow this time." Bobbie Jo gripped my right arm and Dr. Forrester gripped my left as they helped me sit upright. Neither of them released their hold on me until I confirmed that I wasn't dizzy anymore.

"Take as long as you need to get up and moving. Go slow and get something to eat. You can take some ibuprofen and apply heat to your chest to help with any discomfort from the fill. It's normal to feel sore and tight for a couple of days. If you're feeling up to it, let's do this again in two weeks. I would prefer to alternate weeks with chemo at this time."

I nodded in understanding. "Okay. I'll schedule for the Friday after Christmas."

"Great. It was nice to meet you, Bobbie Jo, and Victoria, take care of yourself. Call if you have any concerns. I'm on call this week should you need anything . . . anything at all."

"I will, Dr. Forrester. Thank you, and thanks for the ginger ale, Elizabeth," I said as I lifted the can in a "cheers" motion as they left the room.

"Damn. He is fine," Bobbie Jo purred next to

me. "Did you feel the sexual tension? It radiates off of him. There is no way he is married, and if you ask me, I'd say he was flirting with you."

"WHAT?! No. Way!" I said in shock as I pulled off the gown and put on my sweater, trying to ignore the sudden soreness in my chest. "What would give you that impression? He's my doctor, and I'm married." I grabbed my purse and walked out the door with Bobbie Jo hot on my tail.

"Open your eyes, sweetheart," she said in a sassy, singsong voice.

I walked with her to the car since I refused to wait for her to pick me up like Noah would've insisted. I was turning into an angry bear and needed to eat.

We drove to the mall next door and parked in the lot by PF Chang's, Cheesecake Factory, and Rojo's. I let my stomach decide, and Cheesecake Factory won by a landslide. Before we got out of the car, I grabbed the scarf I had slipped into my purse and proceeded to wrap it around my head. I was fine with the "bald is beautiful" look at the doctor's office, but I wasn't quite ready for it in a public restaurant.

"Looks fabulous," Bobbie Jo said encouragingly

as we walked into the restaurant. Sitting on one of the upper levels along the back wall provided me with a perfect view of the cheesecake display. My mouth instantly started watering.

"Can I start with dessert? I can't think of a better way to boost my blood sugar levels," I joked. Well, not really.

"You can order whatever the hell you want. I don't judge," Bobbie Jo said as she studied the cocktail menu. "I'm thinking Sex on the Beach or maybe just a Blow Job." She snickered. "I might as well be getting it somewhere."

"Why must your cocktails revolve around sex too?" I asked as I drooled over the cheesecake menu. "And since when have you had a dry streak?"

"Well, when you call it a *cock-tail*, it makes me think about sex, and I haven't had any in five days."

"I guess that is a drought in your world." I just shook my head. "I'm going to head up to the display and take a peek; I can't decide by looking at the menu. I need to see what my options are."

"Go for it! I think you've earned at least two pieces. One for each of your newly filled tits. Go show those ladies off—stick your chest out loud and proud." She waved her hand to dismiss me.

I couldn't help the snort that escaped as I started to slide out of the booth and looked up at the display case. There was a couple sharing a passionate kiss. The man ran his hands through the woman's beautiful thick hair, which made me reach for mine, only to find nothing but a bald head under a scarf.

I felt my phone buzz and looked down to see a text message from Noah.

> *Hey, I'm just leaving a meeting at the Cheesecake Factory.*
> *What kind of cheesecake would you like?*
> *I'm coming home early. Let me know. Noah.*

I looked around the restaurant for him but couldn't find him anywhere. My eyes drifted back toward the display and to the couple that had been kissing earlier. They weren't kissing anymore. As recognition hit me, my phone fell out of my hand and clattered onto the table.

Bobbie Jo was quick to pick it up. "Victoria?" Bobbie Jo said as she guided me back down into the booth, the look on her face etched with concern. "Is everything okay?"

I said nothing and stared at my phone in her hand, encouraging her to look at the message.

After she read the text on my phone, she looked up at me with a smile and started to look around. When her eyes landed at the cheesecake display, I watched as the smile on her face morphed into a sneer.

Noah was standing at the counter, but he most definitely wasn't there on business like he said. What I never in a million years would have expected was Stacey hanging on his arm, pointing at the various flavors of cheesecake like a cozy couple.

I felt my blood start to boil and was positive that was what the Red Devil would have felt like if it had exploded in my veins. It burned.

Bobbie Jo frantically typed on the screen of my phone and handed it back to me. She nodded to me to read it. I looked down at the screen.

Why don't you ask Stacey what flavor she recommends?

"All you have to do is hit *Send*, Victoria." Bobbie Jo nodded when I looked back up at her. "Do it."

I was in a panic and not thinking clearly as I did as I was told and hit *Send*.

My hands were trembling, my heart was pounding, and I was sure that I was about to have a stroke when the sound confirming that the message had been sent chimed.

Undo. Undo. Undo! I screamed silently inside my head as I looked over and saw Noah reach for his phone in his pocket, watching as he pulled it out and read the message.

His head instantly snapped up to attention, and I saw the color drain from his face from the other side of the room. I watched, in what felt like slow motion, as he pulled away from Stacey's hold and turned his body to search the restaurant.

It took several seconds before his eyes swept past our booth. I had hoped he didn't recognize me with my scarf-covered head, but his eyes quickly shot back, pinning me in my spot. I couldn't describe the look on his face as he made his move and started to walk around the partition toward our table. He seemed possessed.

Stacey looked stunned by his sudden departure. Her eyes followed where he was headed, and she spotted me as easily as if a spotlight had been shining on our table. I'd like to think it was a look of surprise on her face, but it wasn't. The bitch had the nerve to look smug.

The fight-or-flight instinct took over, and I

stood quickly, pulling Bobbie Jo with me as we hurried out of the booth. I started walking in the opposite direction of Noah as I discovered my escape route.

I heard him call out, "Victoria, wait!" as a woman with a baby stood to block his path toward me. He tried to move around her, but the baby was screaming and the mom wasn't about to let him through. I've never been so thankful for a screaming child in all my life. *Thank you.*

I kept moving. There was no way in hell I was going to slow down. I had my chance to escape and took it as we ducked out the door. I took off running, leaving Bobbie Jo in the dust.

The need to throw up hit me hard, and it forced me to stop running. I made it to the corner of the parking lot before the violent heaves began.

Bobbie Jo caught up to me and started rubbing my back to calm me. "Come on, babe, let's get you home."

"No. I'm not going home," I blubbered between breaths, tearing the scarf off of my head. "He will expect me to be there and . . . I can't . . . I just can't. How could he do this to me? How could he do this now?" I sobbed.

"Honey, you need to calm down." She wiped my tears with her hands. "You're staying with me tonight."

"Just get me out of here. I don't want him to find me. I can't deal with this."

"My car is just over there," she said as she nodded two rows over and grabbed my hand to lead me there.

I swear she thought we were in a chase scene from a movie as her tires squealed when we backed out of the parking spot. She looked in the rearview mirror and gunned it.

I didn't look. I closed my eyes and found comfort in knowing that whatever was behind us was now gone. I was gone. My perfect life was gone. I was left with nothing. I was nothing.

Chapter Fourteen

I AM NOTHING

I woke up on Saturday morning with a start and opened my eyes to take in my surroundings. The nightmare I had in my sleep left me unsettled. As I looked around the room, it dawned on me: it wasn't a fucking nightmare. It was real. Very real.

Still wearing my jeans and cashmere sweater, I was curled up on Bobbie Jo's bed. My chest hurt, but it wasn't from the expander fill. It was from the hole that had been carved into my heart the day before.

After crawling out of bed and stumbling to the bathroom, I decided to take stock of what was left of me.

I looked like shit.

I felt like shit.

And, at this point, I really didn't give a shit.

I stripped out of my clothes and turned on the

shower to warm up. Digging through Bobbie Jo's cabinets, I found a spare toothbrush to scrub away the retched breath that was still present from yesterday. The steam from the shower took over me as I stood under the water until it ran cold. Ice cold.

I dug through Bobbie Jo's dresser and pulled on a T-shirt and pajama pants before making my way to the kitchen. I heard her voice ringing out in anger.

"No, asshole. I'm not listening anymore." She paused. "Don't even try it. You're not welcome here, and if, and I truly mean *if*, she wants to talk to you, she will contact you directly. Don't try to go through me, Jen, or Dana to get to her. She is fighting for her life, and you just skewered her heart and put it over the fire. You deserve to burn in hell for what you've done to her, you bastard!" I heard a phone slam against the wall and break into pieces.

"Morning," I said sheepishly.

"Good morning," she said as she turned toward the doorway and saw me standing there. "I owe you a new phone. Sorry."

"I would have done the same thing. Thank you for taking that call for me. I'm not ready to face that."

"What are friends for?" she asked as she pulled away from the counter. "What can I get you for breakfast?"

"Nothing. Not hungry."

"I'm sure you aren't, but you need to keep your strength up. You haven't eaten since yesterday morning, and there is no way you're going down on my watch." She pushed out a stool for me at the counter. "Waffles or pancakes?"

"Fine. Pancakes. No syrup."

She started moving around like a master chef to make breakfast. "So, do you want to talk about it?"

"Not really, I don't know what to say." I let out a heavy sigh as my chest constricted. "Up until a few days ago, everything seemed fine. Well, as fine as they could be, all things considered."

"What do you mean 'up until a few days ago'? Did you know something was going on?"

"No. But something happened the other night, and my brain got the best of me and I assumed it was paranoia or from the meds. I guess I was wrong." I shrugged. "How could I have not seen this?"

"This isn't something you should be looking for. Jesus Christ, Victoria, you're fighting for your life, and he is out dipping the wick with another woman. Who the hell does that?" She was livid, and I was afraid for the pancakes because she was wielding the spatula like a butcher knife.

"Noah. My. Noah." God I was appalled with myself for letting him do this to me. I wasn't going to let him get away with this. "What the hell do I do? How do I talk to him—and what do I even say? Do I even have the energy to try?"

"Give it time. Let it fester in his mind. Let him feel like shit because he damn well deserves it. You don't owe him anything until you're ready. You need time to think about what you want. Do you want to fight for your marriage?"

"Why the hell do I have to always be the one fighting for something? I'm fighting cancer. I'm fighting off nausea. I'm fighting for my life. And now . . . now I need to decide if I want to fight for my goddamn marriage. 'For better or worse, in sickness and in health.' Guess he doesn't recall saying those words in front of my family and our friends."

I was angry and exhausted and I felt like I was in the midst of a drug-induced nightmare. "I'm tired of fighting. I'm not doing it. If he wants this marriage, he can fight." I started to cry. "He fucked up. Not me. I'm not fighting for shit because as far as I'm concerned, he's not worth fighting for at this moment. And right now you're burning my goddamn pancakes because of him!"

"Oh shit." She jumped as she saw smoke billowing off of the griddle. "So, how do you feel about going out for breakfast?"

Thursday arrived the same way the last several days had, in Bobbie Jo's bed. My phone had been out of commission since last Saturday, but Bobbie Jo's home phone continued to ring off the hook with Noah's number showing up hourly.

He called from his mobile, home, and office, but I never answered. I knew I couldn't avoid him forever, but the thought of him showing up for my third chemo session, which was scheduled for the next day, was weighing on me.

Bobbie Jo had called my parents and filled them in on what had happened. They never asked me for the complete story. "We love you. We're here for you. Call us if you need anything," ran on a constant loop when I finally worked up the nerve to call them last night.

They were hurting too. Noah had vowed to take care of me, and my parents took those vows very seriously. I would bet my life that my dad had "spoken" with Noah, and I could guarantee that my father had the last word.

I had crashed at Bobbie Jo's house since last Friday, so I felt she deserved some space. She hadn't signed up for a roommate, let alone one with more drama than a country song, so it was time to give her some privacy. So I arranged to stay with my parents for a few days, and they would watch over me after chemo.

Thankfully, Jen and Bobbie Jo both agreed to go with me to my chemo appointment. There wouldn't be any changes to the treatment plan from last time, so I had a good idea of what to expect. It was time to start facing the reality of my life, and spending time with my parents would definitely help.

I had been living in Bobbie Jo's clothes for almost a week and needed to go home to pack a bag for the next few days. The idea of going there alone stressed me out, so I called Jen to go with me. We planned to go during the day, knowing that Noah would be at the office.

As we pulled up in the driveway, I took a moment to look at my house. My home. The home we bought together and built a life together in. We hadn't talked a lot about having a family, and after my cancer diagnosis, we both knew the chances of that happening were extremely low. Cancer changed everything.

We headed for the bedroom right away. I pulled out two large suitcases from the back of the closet and started packing my clothes. Jen was in the bedroom pulling all of my lingerie and smaller items out of the dresser and putting them into another smaller suitcase. Once the bags were packed, we hit the bathroom for my toiletries and makeup.

When I stepped back out into our bedroom, I saw the corner of a shopping bag sticking out from under my side of the bed. It was the leather briefcase I had bought Noah for Christmas at the Coach store. I had his initials imprinted into the leather. It was perfect for him.

I looked at my watch and was impressed by the fact that we packed it all in less than an hour. Jen had started carrying the bags out to her car, and I yelled out to her I would be right down. I opened the drawer in my bedside table and found a piece of stationary and a pen.

> *Noah,*
>
> *I stopped by to pick up some of my things. I'll be spending the week with my parents after tomorrow's chemo session. The girls are going with me, so you don't have to disrupt your day to be there. I've had time to think about what I saw, and I know we need to talk. I hope you have had time to think as well. Please don't try to call me. I'll call you next week when I'm ready and the fog starts to lift.*
>
> *I hope you will respect my wishes. This is not easy for me.*
>
> *Victoria*

Jen was standing quietly in the doorway, watching me. "You done?" She nodded to the note.

"Yeah, I'm done."

I put the note on the top of the shopping bag on the end of the bed. It was the same spot where I found the chocolate cake only a few weeks ago. I walked down the stairs and out the front door and did not look back.

Considering my life had been flipped upside down in the last week, chemo wasn't actually half bad this time around. It was thanks to the company I had brought with. Bobbie Jo and Jen were a two-woman show and had several of the nurses laughing and hanging around a little longer than usual.

Noah definitely wasn't fun at chemo; it was a somber event for us. These two had other plans. They brought party hats and Mardi Gras beads to share with all of the patients undergoing treatment while we were there.

It was hard not to smile as we played "truth, dare, double dare, promise, or repeat" like we were teenagers. They also informed me that they were sleeping over at my parents', even though they knew I would be a foggy, doped-up mess.

Personally, I think they wanted to see me messed up because I was always the responsible one who never drank too much. They claimed they wanted to be there to help and take me back to the hospital the next day for my white-count booster shot. I didn't argue because they always had my best interest in mind.

We arrived at my parents and we all changed into our pajamas for the evening.

Bobbie Jo and Jen were jabbering away while they blew up air mattresses in my childhood bedroom. A cozy and cramped night was in store for the three of us. I was starting to feel the buzzing in my head and get the burning flushed feeling in my face. It was time to start the Gatorade and water cleanse to flush the Red Devil out of my system as fast as possible.

"Ladies, if you don't mind, I'm going to check out of this conversation," I said as I curled up in my bed. "Thank you for coming with me to support me today and staying the night. I love you both more than you will ever know, but I'm done. Good night."

"Good night, beautiful, and sweet dreams," they said before slipping out of my bedroom and down the hall to the kitchen where my parents were preparing dinner. I could hear them talking as I drifted to sleep and a few other times when I woke up to go to the bathroom.

Unbeknownst to me, my chemo schedule couldn't have worked out any better, as I was still in my chemo fog on Christmas Day.

My parents did their best to try and make it special by inviting people over. People came and went all day and made small talk. I felt bad for them because they didn't know what to say. Hell... I didn't know what to say.

Shortly after dinner, I excused myself, claiming to be exhausted, and went to bed. It was a lie; emotionally, I was dead.

I couldn't sleep. Instead, I stared at the ceiling, trying not to think about Noah and failing miserably.

His parents were out of the country for the holidays, so I knew he wasn't back in Chicago. I wondered what he was doing, and I even worried about him. To my surprise, Noah honored my request not to contact me, and now I lay there regretting it. I missed my husband.

The last few days after Christmas were good. I kept myself occupied by helping my mom put away the decorations. She was just as sick of them as I was this year. The chemo fog had passed, and I was starting to think about my expander fill appointment the next day.

It had been thirteen miserable days since I last saw Noah... with *her*... and I knew it was time to talk. I needed to talk. He wasn't going to call, so I knew I needed to do it and I was not looking forward to it. I pulled out the new mobile phone Bobbie Jo had bought me for Christmas and dialed his number. My heart was beating louder than a bass drum.

"Hello?" Noah answered immediately.

"Hi. It's me, Victoria," I said, sounding nervous and unsure of myself. I felt like a stranger.

"I know. I recognized the number. How was chemo?"

"Good. I followed the same regimen as last time, and it seems to be working."

"That's great."

The awkward chitchat needed to stop. I couldn't pretend that things were fine and dandy anymore. "We need to talk, and I'd prefer to do it in person."

"I agree. When and where?"

"Do I need to call Whitney to make an appointment?" I said sarcastically, even though I meant it.

"Stop it." He sounded annoyed. *Good,* I thought to myself before he continued, "Are you free this evening, or would tomorrow work?"

"I have my second expander fill tomorrow afternoon at three-thirty, but I can make any other time work tomorrow."

"When did you have your first fill?"

"Right before I saw you at the Cheesecake Factory. Bobbie Jo took me to get something to eat because I almost passed out during the procedure. I was going to go look at the cheesecake display when I suddenly lost my appetite."

"No need to bring it to that level. I thought we could have a civilized conversation like adults," he remarked snidely.

"Excuse me? I'm pretty sure my level isn't as low as yours," I huffed in exasperation. "What time would you like to meet tomorrow? From the sound of your voice, I'm pretty sure it will be short and not-so-sweet."

"It should be fairly quick."

"I don't understand how this could happen to us. How could you do this?" I asked, trying to hold on to every shred of dignity I had left... which wasn't much.

"We'll talk tomorrow," he answered brusquely.

My emotions were all over the charts—anger, sadness, fear, and insecurity. However, anger won out, and after his nonchalant brush-off that we'd talk tomorrow, I was ready to explode.

"Are you willing to fight for me? Because honestly, Noah, I don't have the energy to fight for us on my own. I've got enough on my plate right now, and fighting for our marriage was not on my radar. I had no idea it was damaged."

"I'm getting another call. I'll meet you at the house at one o'clock sharp. Good-bye." Click.

Well, that was a fucking success.

I arrived at our house at twelve forty-five and was sitting in the living room when I heard the front door open and Noah walked in. He put his keys in his jacket pocket instead of tossing them in the bowl on the entry table like he normally did. As pissed off as I was, I still found him handsome, and I loved him. I didn't like him at the moment, but I would always love him. That was probably my biggest mistake.

Tugging to loosen his tie, he spotted me and began walking my way. I sat on the sofa wearing leggings and an athletic jacket. He had yet to see me bald, so I made it a point to not cover my head. Maybe the shock of it would make him feel something? Anything. By his rigid body language and emotionless expression, I knew he wasn't here to comfort me. He wasn't here to beg me for forgiveness. I was pretty sure I was going to regret coming alone after Jen offered to be here for support. I told her no, again, because I was a big girl and could handle this on my own.

"Thanks for meeting me," he said as he tossed a manila file on the coffee table and took a seat in the chair across from me. When he looked at me, I could see shame and pity in his eyes. The question was: were they for me or because of me? "You look tired. When did you lose your hair?"

"Two weeks ago. It was a big day for me. I lost my hair, had my first expander fill, and saw my husband passionately kissing and embracing another woman. So, the fact that I look tired isn't news to me." I tried to sound controlled, but I was shaking like an earthquake on the inside.

"I'm sorry," he said, actually sounding like he meant it. "I never meant for you to find out like you did."

I froze. *Did I hear him right?* He "never meant for me to find out like I did." My brain was slowly processing, but the ability to speak escaped me. Sitting in silence, I gathered my thoughts, which was a challenge because my brain was still foggy from chemo and the ability to express how I was feeling was hampered.

"Let me get this straight—you didn't want me to find out 'like I did'? Does that mean that you meant for me to find out eventually?" I fought back the bile that was rising in my throat.

"Yes, eventually. Stacey and I have been seeing each other for over a year. She helped me see that I wasn't happy in our marriage and hadn't been for a while. The sex with you was great and we still had fun, but we weren't moving forward. We were stuck in the same pattern. I wanted to start a family, and you were just getting your firm off the ground and kept insisting that the timing was bad. I guess you could say we were roommates with perks."

His words were like a slap across my face. Is that really how he felt? Is that really what we were... roommates?

"I'm sorry, but are you telling me we were simply 'friends with benefits' during our *marriage*? Because that is what it sounds like." My god, I couldn't make sense of anything; I shouldn't have been here alone.

"I guess I never thought of it that way, but, yes, that's a good way of looking at the last few years. I love you, but I'm not *in* love with you anymore. Our relationship was comfortable and stable. But I want more. I need to *be* in love, and Stacey is that love for me. I was planning to tell you after New York, but then you found the lump, and well . . . I couldn't find the right time after that."

"But NOW is the right time?" I couldn't contain my anger. "I put college on hold for you. For your dreams—which I thought I was a part of. How the hell could you do this to me? How the hell can you just brush off our marriage like it was something to pass the time? And especially now when I'm in the midst of battling cancer!"

"No, now was not the right time. I didn't mean for you to see us. The plan was to wait a few more months until you were done with treatment and on the road to recovery. I tried to be a good husband and be supportive, but I just can't handle it. I'm not the right man for you."

"You had it planned?"

"Yes. I had it planned out, but cancer kind of put a little detour in my plans."

"Wait—did you just say that cancer put a little detour in *your* plans?" He just looked at me with a blank expression, one he mastered in law school no less, as I continued, "Cancer has fucking *ruined my life*, and I'm sorry if it 'put a little detour in your plans.' When did you become such an asshole? Are you telling me the last few times we made love meant nothing? Because the night we shared with the chocolate cake was pretty damn incredible."

"It was incredible. I knew it would be the last time we would be together sexually, and I wanted it to be special for you. It was all about you."

"Well, isn't that fucking kind of you! I suppose I should thank you for the farewell fuck?" I was livid and felt every muscle in my body vibrate with rage for the first time. "Everything that has happened since New York has all been an act? Correct?"

"Yes, I'd say that's a fair analysis. I intended to do a few special things in New York. I wanted it to be a happy and memorable trip for you, but when you told me you found the lump, everything changed."

"Then why did you take me on the trip to Chicago? I don't understand why you would do that if you were going to leave me. That trip was special and ultimately devastating. When you told me how strong I was on the Ledge, it held more than one meaning, didn't it?"

He nodded.

"The fact that I now know you pretended to love me on that trip makes me sick. You have tainted one of the most special moments of my life. And then when Dr. Freeman called to tell me I had cancer, you *comforted* me—you held me and made me feel safe. It disgusts me to find out that the last few months have been a complete lie. Any happy or special memories are now dead."

Tears of anger started flooding my eyes. "All that remains is a dark empty hole in my soul that was left by a man who I thought loved me. You're a fucking spineless bastard."

"Victoria, I'm not the cold-hearted villain you're making me out to be right now."

"Like hell you're not," I hissed back at him, venom in my voice.

"Look, I know you're angry and surprised at what I've admitted to you. But I've been honest with you today; I haven't said anything that wasn't the truth. I do care about you, and I tried to be there for you, but I can't do it anymore."

I couldn't listen to him any longer. "What's in the file, Noah? No, actually I take that back—let me guess." I calmly reached for the file, knowing what it was. "You already wrote up divorce papers. Am I right?" The bitterness was evident in my voice.

"You would be correct."

A laugh escaped my mouth, and it was a sickening sound. "Care to give me the highlights?"

"The mortgage has been paid in full, and the house is now solely in your name. Your Mercedes has also been paid off, and I've set up a very generous monthly stipend for you until you can reestablish your career or get remarried, whichever occurs first. I'll continue to cover your health insurance and medical expenses until your treatment is complete and you're financially secure enough to take over the policy premiums or qualify for a policy on your own."

I was dumbstruck. He had it written up and had it ready for my signature on the black line.

The house was mine and paid in full. My car was paid in full, and financially, I would be fine. But I didn't have my husband or a marriage anymore. I could give a rat's ass about the money; I was more upset at the loss of the person I loved who didn't love me anymore. It tore my heart out that he turned this into a business transaction.

I found my voice, knowing I would regret asking

the question now burning in my mind. "I guess this means you weren't planning on fighting for me . . . for us?"

"No. It wouldn't get us anywhere at this point, and you already told me that you wouldn't be fighting for it either. You were very clear in that statement."

He moved toward the edge of the chair and rested his elbows on his knees, folding his hands in front of him. "I took it upon myself to get everything drawn up so you could move on and not have this hanging over you. You have enough going on right now. I tried to provide everything so you don't have to worry about anything financially until you're back on your feet. It was the least I could do."

"How thoughtful." I wanted to spit the words out at him, but I couldn't as much as I tried. I was exhausted, mentally and physically. "What if I changed my mind and wanted to fight for us?"

"It's too late. I can't. I made up my mind and already moved my stuff out."

I paused and looked around. Everything seemed in place; however, upon further inspection, I did notice a few things had been moved around and others were missing, including the bowl that used to be on the entry table. My heart completely broke. He didn't want me anymore. My ability to fight was gone.

"I moved out earlier this last week. I'm renting an apartment downtown near the firm. Stacey left her husband after the New York trip and has already moved in with me." He sat upright and tried to appear sincere. "I'm happy, and I hope that someday you will be happy too. I don't expect you to forgive me for what I've done, but I do care about you."

"Fuck you!" I spat back, anger boiling over at what he just said. "You don't care. What I just learned is that you are shallow and self-serving, and you know what? Stacey couldn't be more perfect for you. Get out of *my* house." I stood abruptly and pointed at the door. "Now."

"The papers . . ."

"The papers? Is that all you have to say?" I shook as I stood before him.

He stepped toward me like he wanted to give me a hug, but I stepped to the side. "Don't," I warned. "You don't have the right to comfort me anymore."

I moved on shaky legs to the foyer and opened the front door, showing him the way out. "I wasn't worth the fight, so you aren't worth a proper good-bye. You aren't the man I married; you're a fucking stranger, and I can't look at you any longer without wanting to vomit. You just threw me away like trash. I'm your wife. Your fucking wife, and all you're worried about is the goddamn papers. You'll get your papers, just not today. Close the door behind you when you leave."

I turned and walked to the kitchen for a glass of water. With a trembling hand, I lifted it to my lips and listened for the door to shut. When it did, a loud shuddering breath escaped my mouth, one I had apparently been holding. Startling myself, I dropped the glass at my feet, causing it to shatter into a million little pieces. Just like me.

Chapter Fifteen
I AM BROKEN

"Victoria, are you okay?" I heard feet hit the landing at the bottom of the stairs, and my head snapped up to see Jen rushing toward me.

"What are you doing here?" I sobbed as my body began to tremble harder.

"I didn't want you to be alone after he left. I saw movers moving his stuff out of the house a few days ago, so I was pretty sure he would be the one leaving and not you. I parked down the block and have been sitting in your bedroom listening. I heard everything. I'm sorry." She sounded uncertain as to how I would receive her confession.

I didn't know what to say.

She moved closer and extended her hand to me. "Let's get you away from this broken glass."

I took it and carefully stepped around the shards of glass sparkling in the sunshine.

She guided me to the sofa and turned on the TV before handing me the remote. "I want you to sit while I clean up the glass and get you something to eat. We need to leave for your appointment with Dr. Forrester in a little bit, and I will not have you close to passing out on me like you were with Bobbie Jo. Find something to watch to keep your mind busy."

A short time later, Jen placed a bowl of soup in front of me with some French bread for dipping. "I found your mom's soup in the freezer... I hope that's okay?"

"It's fine." But I couldn't bring myself to lift the spoon. I had no appetite and placed it on the coffee table. Jen noticed the file sitting next to it and quickly moved it out of view.

"Eat," she ordered.

"I'm not hungry."

"At least take a sip. Your body needs it even though your mind says it doesn't." She picked up the bowl and fed me a spoonful like I was a toddler.

I was completely numb and needed confirmation of what I thought had just happened. "Did that really just happen?"

"Yes, I'm afraid it did."

"What do I do?" My brain was such a mess, and

I had no clue what I should be doing. Should I be sad? Should I be angry? Should I be relieved?

"You take a deep breath and you keep moving forward. One day at a time. Just like you've been doing since the beginning of November."

"What's the point of moving forward? I feel empty. Unwanted. Damaged. Forever broken. Who wants that? Nobody. He made up his mind, and we both know that his decisions are always final. It's over. End of story."

"You are needed, perfect, and strong. Anyone who knows you loves you. Noah didn't make you; *you* made you. And you're better than that. Don't let him make you feel less. Power and money do funny things to people who aren't strong enough to be themselves. They give into wants and forget about needs."

"Who wants a boobless bald woman?" I mocked. "I mean look at me. This is not sexy or appealing. Dating is at least two years out if I have any hope of dating at all. By then I'll be thirty-four years old with fake boobs covered in scars and a high likelihood of not being able to have children. What man in his right mind would want that?"

"The right one."

"Why are we even talking about this? My husband just walked out the door and isn't coming back. I'm left fighting for my life alone. But because of his chivalry, I'll be taken care of financially, so why should I complain? This is all kinds of fucked up, and I feel like I'm in some sick dream. I can't do this!"

"You can and you will. I'm not going to sit here and watch you give up. That is *not* you Victoria, and you damn well know it! These last two weeks have been devastating; I'm not going to dispute that. However, you have options, and you're not pulling this 'I don't care, nobody loves me, I'll just shrivel up and die' bullshit with me."

I tried to cut her off, but she shoved her hand in my face. She literally gave me "the hand," and I gave her the finger in return. It didn't faze her.

"You're stuck with me and I expect you to hate me for many things I've already said and will say. Brutal honesty is what you will always get from me and you know it. I will not allow you to wallow in pity for days on end, and I know for a fact your parents won't either. We love you and care about you. We will not let you fall down and not get up." She looked at the clock on the mantel. "You have one hour until I drag your ass to your doctor's appointment, which you are not canceling. You need to keep moving forward. You are not allowed to put your treatment and reconstruction on hold because of him. He's not fucking worth it."

When I tried to argue she stopped me. "Buck up, babe . . . you've got some serious ass to kick." And with that, Jen walked out of the room.

I sat in silence. My husband had just served me with divorce papers out of nowhere, my best friend just told me how it is, and now I was going to the doctor for an expander fill like any normal person would do.

What. The. Fuck. Let me repeat that. *WHAT! THE! FUCK!*

―※―

True to her word, Jen dragged me to my appointment with Dr. Forrester, even though I looked like absolute shit. "Do you want me to go back with you?" she asked.

"No." I was still pissed off and needed a break from her hovering. Even when I went to the bathroom before leaving the house, she stood outside the door waiting for me. She was concerned—I get that—but I could do without the constant shadow.

"Victoria, we're ready for you," I heard Elizabeth cheerfully greet me. It was nice to see her smiling face. She didn't know that my life had completely imploded just two short hours ago. Everything was the way it should be . . . for a breast cancer patient, that is.

"How are things going?"

"Fine," I lied.

"How was the pain after the first fill?"

"It wasn't bad. I didn't really feel much after it." This was technically true. I honestly hadn't felt much of anything after my heart had been massacred two weeks ago. I chose to keep that little fact to myself.

"I'm happy to hear that. Some women have a really hard time with the fill process, I'm glad you aren't one of them. Keep it up!" She handed me the robe to change into before stepping out to get Dr. Forrester. "We'll be in shortly; he is just finishing up with another patient."

I changed into the robe and sat on the exam table looking down at my hands, specifically at my wedding ring. I had lost weight during chemo, and I had noticed it was sliding around on my finger all the time. It slipped off of my finger easily, and I was mesmerized by it sitting in the palm of my right hand when Dr. Forrester and Elizabeth came in.

He noticed what I was doing. "Is everything all right?"

I quickly slipped it back on my finger. "Yes, everything is fine. I just noticed that I've lost some weight, and it slipped right off my finger. Guess I should get it resized or just take it off." Yeah, that would be a great excuse. I took it off because I lost weight.

"It's probably not a bad idea to take it off—you wouldn't want anything to happen to it." He nodded at my hand.

"You're probably right." I slipped it back off and put it in the pocket of my jeans. "Better," I said.

"Elizabeth told me you did well after your first fill."

"Yeah, I think so; I just had some tightness. Nothing that raised a flag that something was wrong." Which was the truth . . . I honestly didn't notice a damn thing.

"Let's stick with the same game plan this week." Maybe the discomfort would be noticeable this time, and it would take my mind off of my shitty life for a few days.

"Okay. One-hundred cc's again?"

"Yes."

"Okay." He helped me lie back down on the table before he started prepping. "Did you come alone today? I was expecting Noah or your friend again."

"One of my other friends, Jen, drove me, but she stayed back in the waiting room. She doesn't do medical stuff." I fibbed again, but he would never know.

"Understood. We'll wait a few minutes with you after to make sure you don't get dizzy like last time," he said as he started to locate the ports on my expanders and marked each spot with an X when he found them. Elizabeth was helping him with the bag of saline this time.

I sat quietly during the quick and fairly painless procedure. Other than the pressure, I was okay and could handle the discomfort. Hell, it felt better than the piercing pain in my heart. He helped me sit up slowly. "How was that?"

"It was fine." I could handle the physical pain of life, just not the emotional part right now. I was doing this alone. Alone.

My eyes started to water with that realization, but as much as I tried to hold them back, it was useless. I wiped them away with the back of my hand just as Dr. Forrester turned back toward me while drying his hands on a paper towel.

"Did we do too much today?" he asked with a concerned voice. He had again asked me every twenty-five cc's if we were good, and I had confirmed yes each time. "Elizabeth, why don't you go and get Victoria a ginger ale?"

"Sure thing—I'll be right back." She disappeared out the door, and Dr. Forrester turned back toward me, waiting for my answer.

"No. It was fine, really." I sniffled as he handed me a tissue. "It has just been a rough couple of weeks since I saw you last. I'll be okay."

"Anything I can do?" he asked as he rolled a stool over and sat down facing me just a few feet away.

"Not really. Life has just thrown me a few surprises I wasn't expecting and my emotions are a little out of control. I didn't mean for you to see me tearing up. This isn't the time or the place."

"Sure it is. Reconstruction is a very emotional

process, and many women struggle with it. You aren't the first patient to cry in my office and won't be the last. I don't take it personally. It's part of the journey."

"The journey?" I pondered that for a moment. "You have always called it a journey. Why is that?"

"Because that's what this is. A battle sounds like you're going to war, and death is a higher probability in war. A journey will bring you many highs and lows, and while some journeys end well, some don't. What you experience along the way can have a positive effect on the outcome. Good or bad."

There was a knock on the door, and Elizabeth popped in with a can of ginger ale. "Thank you, Elizabeth. I'm going to be a few more minutes with Victoria. Please let my next patient know I am running a few minutes behind."

She nodded her head in acknowledgment. "Take care, Victoria. I'll see you in two weeks."

After the door closed, he shifted on the stool and rested his hands on his knees. "I lost someone special to breast cancer five years ago. Her outlook was always positive, even though the odds were against her. It made an immense impact on my life. She was at peace with her choices, and before she passed, she reflected on the amazing parts of her journey, not the low points. She never called it a battle, and now I understand why."

"That's beautiful," I said, with fresh tears in my eyes. "Thank you for sharing that with me. She sounds like she was an amazing woman."

"Yeah, my mom was amazing." He smiled affectionately.

"Noah left me."

As soon as I realized what I just blurted out, I instantly felt the heat rise on my face. Embarrassed about what I had just declared to my doctor, I looked down and began fidgeting with my hands. He wasn't a therapist who was used to this; he was a plastic surgeon. *My* plastic surgeon. This wasn't good.

Dr. Forrester quickly shifted on his stool and almost lost his balance. "I'm sorry, can you repeat that?"

"Noah served me with divorce papers two hours ago." I stated it clearly this time but kept my head down. "I saw him with another woman after I left your office. He was planning to leave me before I was diagnosed with cancer. But then he decided to stick with me until I was done with treatment…

until I caught him two weeks ago." I was like a fucking fountain, just spewing everything out to this poor man. He didn't need—or want—to hear this, and I needed to shut up. God, I felt like a complete fool.

The room was silent. Uncomfortably silent, until I looked up and was met with Dr. Forrester's brown eyes, which were full of unease. "Victoria, I'm terribly sorry."

"I am too." It was all I could say.

"Your news surprises me immensely. Why are you even here today?"

"Jen wouldn't let me cancel my appointment. She said I needed to keep moving forward and couldn't let him be the reason I stopped," I said as my shoulders slumped and I moved my arms around my middle to protect myself.

"She sounds like a good friend," he said as he stood and held a hand to help me stand. "I don't think you're going to pass out on me now. Why don't you change and I'll meet you outside when you're ready."

"Okay."

After I changed, I stepped out of the room, and Dr. Forrester was standing in the hall like he had said he would. He handed me a card. "I need you to schedule your next appointment with my partner, Dr. Anne McGuire."

"Umm, okay," I said with confusion. *Did I do something wrong?*

"I'll be out of the office that week, and I want you to stay on schedule with your fills," he said in explanation.

"Oh. Okay, thank you." I tucked the card into my purse. "I'm sorry for what happened. I shouldn't have done that; it was inappropriate of me."

"It's not a problem, Victoria, don't worry about it. I'm glad you felt comfortable enough to talk to someone about it."

Not really sure how to respond, I just smiled and said, "Thank you."

I stopped to see Elizabeth to schedule my appointment with Dr. McGuire, and my nerves must have been showing because she was quick to strike up a conversation. Her bubbly personality was so encouraging. She set my mind at ease by telling me a little bit about Dr. McGuire and gave me a hug before I walked out to the waiting area.

Jen was flipping through a magazine when I appeared. "I'm ready to go."

She nodded. "Lead the way."

As Jen turned the corner down my street, my heart started to speed up. When my house came into view, it went into overdrive. The driveway wasn't empty.

Dana's car . . . check.

Bobbie Jo's car . . . check.

My parents' car . . . check.

"What the hell, Jen? Did you call in back-up?"

"It wasn't me. I can't take credit for this one." She laughed, letting a snort slip out.

"I don't find this funny or entertaining in the least. It has been a shitty day, and the last thing I need is to answer to all of them. I don't need their pity." The dam broke. "I can't face them. Please keep driving."

She did as I asked and drove to one of our favorite spots from when we were younger.

"Do you have a hat and gloves with you?" she asked as she parked the car.

I nodded and put them on before stepping out of the car. She pulled a blanket out of the back of her car, and we started walking toward the band shell at Lake Harriet. Winter in Minnesota was usually cold, but this year, it was unseasonably warm for December. The sun was turning the sky a burnt orange color as it started to set.

We found a bench facing the lake and sat in silence as we watched people out for their after work run. The sound of their feet hitting the path was the only sound.

"What do you need me to do?" Jen finally broke the silence. "It's you and me against the world, just like in high school. I'm guessing your parents called the girls and asked them to be there when we got home. I'm sorry. I don't know why they would think that was a good idea."

"I'm sure my mom is freaking out since they're leaving for Gulf Shores in a few days and now this happened. She didn't want to go in the first place, and my dad called me to talk her into it. I told her everything would be fine and that Noah would be there with me every step of the way." I sighed heavily. "He's not going to be there now, and I'm sure she's refusing to go. If I had to guess, my dad set this up to talk with my friends about taking turns being with me so I'm not alone. That's the only way my mom will go."

"You think he would do that?"

"Yeah, I'm positive. He thinks it will be good for her to spend time with their friends away from here. All of their friends are south for the winter, and she has nothing to do other than worry about me. Quite honestly, I don't want her here now; she is going to suffocate me if she stays. Maybe ditching them wasn't a good idea," I said as I started to move to get up.

"Wait." She stopped me by placing her hand on my shoulder. "We came here to talk. You need someone who understands you and is on your side with a level head right now. Lucky for you, I was in the house and heard everything, so you don't need to repeat it. That is the last thing you need to do right now. And as shocking as this may sound, it's me." She gave a half smile. "Tell me what you want me to do, and I'll do it."

"I don't want pity from anyone; I have an abundance of it for myself right now. I don't want to have to tell everyone what happened. I want people to keep going about their business like they have. I had planned for you and Bobbie Jo to go with me to a few chemo appointments when Noah was supposed to be traveling anyway. So that will stay the same. I can bring myself to my appointments with Dr. Forrester, since I won't be all drugged up. I'll need help when it comes time for surgery, but otherwise, I can do this."

"Yes, you can. I knew you would find your inner strength." She nudged my elbow with hers. "You're going to have good days and bad days." She stopped for a moment to consider her words. "We should get going. I need to stop at my house to pack a bag, and we need to pick up your things at your parents'. I'm moving in as your roommate while your parents are gone."

"Jen, I'm more than capable of taking care of myself. You don't need to put your life on hold."

"I'm not. I'm doing this for you so your parents will know you have someone there if you need it. They will see that you're capable of doing this. I'll stay with you as long as you want me to. It'll be like old times."

I was stunned by her offer. "You would really do that? You'd stay with me?"

"Hell yes!" She smiled. "We can relive our twenties, but you can experience them for the first time without having a gatekeeper in the way. It's time to get your party on."

"Slow down. My schedule is booked with doctors currently, plus I'm not much fun. My idea of a fun night is a bath and bed by nine. I'm not really in a party mood, and if I ever get there again, it will be after I've finished my cancer journey, when I look like a woman. Not when I'm bald and breastless."

"Ha! I like that . . . 'the bald and the breastless'. You're like a fucking soap opera!" She giggled. "And what's with the 'cancer journey' comment? Where did that come from all of a sudden?"

"Dr. Forrester said it to me today. He gave me some perspective that I needed to hear, and . . . I may have slipped up and told him that Noah left me today." I uttered the last part under my breath.

"You did what?" she shrieked in disbelief.

"It slipped out. I don't know how, but it just did. He had just told me that he lost his mom to breast cancer, and it felt so personal and I just blurted it out. I would have told him eventually, just not today."

Talking about it with Jen made me regret what I did. Feeling like a complete idiot, I began berating myself in my head. *Could this day get any worse?*

"What did he say? Did he seem uncomfortable?"

"No, he didn't seem uncomfortable, and he was very understanding. But it felt a bit weird when I left. He handed me the card of his partner and asked me to schedule my next appointment with her. I felt like I had overstepped my bounds, but he explained that he wouldn't be in the office that day and wanted me to stay on schedule with my appointments."

"Well then, you have nothing to worry about. Let's get this show on the road. It's time to move back into your house and kick everyone out. I'll bring the ice cream!" Jen said as she gathered the blanket from our laps and started toward the car.

I was a mess when we got home and needed some time to myself. Jen shooed me upstairs and instructed everyone to sit and wait. She wasn't going to let them go paparazzi on me at this moment. After drawing me a bath, she told me to take my time and try to relax a bit.

A breakdown wasn't in the cards; it would only make things worse.

When I finally appeared downstairs, there was no questioning the fact that Jen told everyone what went down with Noah. Not a single one of them asked me what happened, and I couldn't have been more relieved.

After two more hours of appeasing everyone, we

kicked them all out and sent my parents packing for Gulf Shores five days later.

It had been two weeks since Jen moved in with me.

My final Red Devil chemo treatment went well, and I rang in the New Year in a Marinol-induced stupor. It was magnificent. Four rounds of paclitaxel were left to complete before I was done with chemo, but putting the first phase behind me was a huge feat. I made it through . . . somehow.

The light at the end of the tunnel was coming into view, but I still had the reconstruction ahead of me. Not that I ever wanted to wish time away, but I was ready to move on and make this year a good one since the last year had burst into flames.

I had spent a few days avoiding the file folder Noah had left before finally opening it a week later. What he offered was generous, but it didn't make me feel any better. I hadn't heard from him since the day he walked out and didn't expect to at this point. He'd moved on. Maybe I needed to do the same. *But how?*

Today I was scheduled to meet Dr. McGuire for my third expander fill. I was anxious about meeting a new doctor. Jen agreed to take me again and said she would stay in the waiting area like last time.

When I broke down and admitted to her why I didn't let her come back during my last appointment, she jumped down my throat and insisted on coming back for the insta-boob procedure. She was pissed that she wouldn't get to meet Dr. McHottie after what Bobbie Jo must have said about him, but she'd get over it.

While we were waiting, we were discussing a few ideas. I had to update the house, also known as Operation "No More Noah," when there was a soft tap on the door.

A tall and slender woman with dark brown, almost black, hair and sparkling blue eyes walked in. "Good afternoon, Victoria. I'm Dr. McGuire. It's a pleasure to meet you," she said with the most beautiful smile. She was stunning and married. The ring on her left finger probably cost more than my Mercedes SUV.

"And you are?" she said as she turned toward Jen with her hand outstretched.

"I'm Jen, one of her friends. She asked me to come back with her; I hope that isn't a problem."

"No, it's nice to see friends supporting each

other." She sat down on the stool in the corner. "Dr. Forrester filled me in on your case, and I just want to review a few things with you before we start."

"Sure. I'm fine with that," I answered, wondering why we were reviewing my chart because as far as I knew, I would only be seeing her today and then go back to him.

She did the cliffs-notes review of my chart, from surgery through my last fill. She asked how I was doing physically with chemo and if I had any concerns with the plan Dr. Forrester had laid out. I didn't have any questions, and honestly, now that Noah wasn't a factor, I felt more at ease with everything. It didn't feel like a race to get it done for anyone but myself.

During the insta-boob procedure, as Bobbie Jo had named it, Jen was laughing. "That was quite possibly every small-chested woman's dream. To have your boobs grow in a matter of minutes. And by every small-chested woman . . . I mean me."

Dr. McGuire started laughing too. "Well, if you ever want something done, I'm sure between myself and Dr. Forrester, we could make it happen, but sadly, it won't be as easy as an injection." She stepped back and nodded to me. "Go ahead and sit up, Victoria."

I sat up slowly and admired my chest. To be truthful, my chest actually looked like a male body builders' pectoral muscles: hard, round, and up too high. Frankly, they weren't very attractive, but they belonged to me, and I was proud of them... for now.

"How are you feeling?" Dr. McGuire asked after she washed up. "Any dizziness or lightheaded feelings?"

"Not this time. I learned my lesson."

"Well, I'm impressed! Not many women can handle one hundred cc's at a time. It's very rare."

"I just want to get it done, and if I can handle the discomfort, I might as well," I admitted. "So should I go ahead and schedule my next appointment for two weeks out with Dr. Forrester?"

"Yes, stay on the same schedule if you can handle it with chemo. You're doing great. It was a pleasure working with you, and I hope to see you again." She shook both my hand and Jen's before leaving.

Jen went out to the waiting room while I stopped by the scheduling desk to make my next appointment.

"I'm sorry, but Dr. Forrester doesn't have anything available that day. I can get you in with Dr. McGuire again if that would work? She has a few late afternoon openings."

"Does Dr. Forrester have anything available the day before by chance?"

She checked and the answer was the same. "Nothing available that day either."

"Thanks for checking." I sighed. "I'll go ahead and book the Friday appointment with Dr. McGuire in two weeks."

I was disappointed with not being able to schedule with Dr. Forrester. Everything in my life was changing, and I worried that I had done something wrong. He probably didn't want to make me uncomfortable by telling me he couldn't see me as a patient anymore, so he just casually moved me over to Dr. McGuire.

I sulked as I walked out to the waiting room.

"Turn that frown upside-down, cupcake. What happened?"

"Nothing," I said as the elevator doors shut. We rode down in silence, and it continued until we got into the confines of the car.

"What happened back there? You were fine

when we walked out of the treatment room, and when you returned from scheduling your next appointment, you looked as though your puppy died. Spill it!"

"I wasn't able to schedule my next appointment with Dr. Forrester; he was booked both Thursday and Friday." I looked out the window and continued, "I feel like I overstepped doctor-patient boundaries, and he doesn't want to make me feel bad by telling me he can't be my doctor anymore."

"That is the most absurd thing I've ever heard. This isn't high school. He's a highly sought after and successful plastic surgeon and his schedule was full. It's not because of you. You don't honestly think that . . . do you?"

I looked over at Jen, feeling like a pathetic mess. "Just take me home, please."

She didn't say another word and started driving toward home.

Chapter Sixteen

I AM INVINCIBLE

A week later, I was preparing for my next chemo session and the introduction of a new regimen of drugs. I was told these appointments would be longer, but the side effects were much easier to contend with. It was a compromise.

The best news of all was that I would be able to discontinue the shot the day after chemo, which was a royal pain ... everywhere! I was officially halfway through treatment, and I had to believe that things would start looking up again. They had to.

Dana was in town and volunteered to go with me today for my treatment. She hadn't had the privilege of going with me yet and seemed a bit nervous. I knew this was outside of her comfort zone, so it meant the world to me that she was making the effort.

We got settled into the treatment room, and I

opted for the bed today so Dana could have the comfy imposter recliner for our few hour stay. Once the drip was started, we broke into the snacks.

"So, how are things going?" Dana asked before shoving a handful of Old Dutch puff corn in her mouth.

"Each day is getting better. I can't complain." Well, I could, but I was tired of always whining. It was wearing me down.

"I've been getting bits and pieces from the girls while I've been traveling. Have you spoken to Noah again?"

Just the sound of his name made my skin crawl. "No. I haven't seen or spoken with him, and I don't plan to. My dad's attorney is looking over the divorce papers Noah had written up. He thinks it's actually a very good settlement and is suggesting that I accept it. He was rather astounded by what Noah was offering. I attribute it to guilt."

"Guilt?" she questioned before shoving a pita chip in her mouth.

"Yes, we all agree that Noah feels guilty about leaving me in my 'current condition,' and that this is his way of making it okay . . . in his mind anyway. It's completely fucked up, if you ask me."

I still couldn't believe this was my life. My marriage was a sham for the last year, especially the last several months. While I was busy climbing my way out of hell after each round of chemo, he was busy earning a first-class ticket to a VIP table there.

"Completely. So you're done?"

"I am. He wasn't willing to fight for us, so why should I bother? I'm hurt and I feel abandoned. If he doesn't love me anymore—and he doesn't—I'm not going to force him to try to work it out because he will only end up hating me more." I took a sip of my Gatorade. "What disturbs me is how easily I have accepted it. I was so angry when we talked, but the last few weeks haven't been that bad. He was always working, and when he was around, we were either having sex or he was in the study working. Is it wrong that I'm not fighting to save my marriage after so many years?"

"Yes and no. You were so wrapped up in Noah's world—he was your everything. I don't think you were ever his, and that's the difference. Subconsciously, I think you knew his career came first and you were second to that. However, I don't think you ever imagined that you were third behind another woman."

She stood up and walked over to sit on the edge of the bed with me. "Is this okay?" she asked, seeming concerned about being on the bed next to me.

"Totally okay." I moved over and patted the spot beside me so she could recline next to me.

"I know you loved him, Victoria, I truly do. But I feel that it was a premature love and that he wasn't the 'forever' man for you. I think deep down you felt it too."

"Hmm," I said as I considered what she said. I never really stopped to look at it like that. She was right. My love for Noah was young love, and we were both wrapped up in each other and getting through school. When it came time to grow up and be adults, we started to drift apart and go our separate ways. We *were* like roommates with benefits, as Noah had said. She was right. How did I not see this?

"My 'forever' man, huh? The sex was great. We got along well. We had fun, but we never really talked about a future. Our life was always scheduled and businesslike after college. I just can't believe that he actually cheated on me. That's what hurts the most. It's not the loss of him . . . it's *how* I lost him, and to that bitch. That hurts."

I continued, "In the beginning, our marriage was about paying the bills, studying, and going out on the rare occasion we could afford it. But after his success, everything changed, and we only really went out for business dinners and when we traveled together. How did my marriage turn into a business arrangement?"

"It just did. I don't think anyone plans for it. I only wish it wouldn't have come crashing down like it did and when it did. I'm shocked at how cruel he was to you. Does that man have no empathy?" she asked in disgust.

"His job has hardened him over the years, and I'd like to say I was surprised with how he handled it, but looking back on it, honestly, I'm not. The fruit doesn't fall far from the tree; he's just like his parents. Cold-hearted." I shook my head remembering their comment when we told them we were getting married. "Do you know his parents sent us a note after we got married that said we were irresponsible and would regret our decision?"

"You're kidding me!"

"Nope, and surprisingly, they were right." I actually smirked at this because I'd despised them for saying it at the time. "I'm sure they won't be smiling when they meet Stacey either."

Dana let out a laugh and offered me a monster brownie loaded with caramel and dark chocolate chunks.

I took a huge bite just as Dana added, "They're in for a ride with her and her broomstick. Payback is a bitch."

※

I woke the next morning to a commotion downstairs. Looking at the clock, I saw it was already eleven, so I pulled myself up and out of bed to investigate what was going on.

As soon as my feet hit the floor, all was quiet. It was almost like the devil was thinking, *Oh shit, she's up*, and ran for cover.

"Hello?" I called out when I opened my bedroom door.

There was no answer, so I proceeded down the stairs slowly. While this chemo treatment didn't hit me as hard, I was still wiped out, but felt like I could function. *Bonus.*

As I made it to the bottom step, the smell of coconut and tangerine hit my senses and woke me up. The smell of the tropics was always a favorite.

I walked into the kitchen and noticed a plate of fresh tropical fruits, croissants, and several types of juices in crystal decanters, with a note sitting on the breakfast bar.

Good morning Victoria,

Please sit down and enjoy your breakfast. We have a relaxing day in store for you, and you don't even have to leave the house. We are bringing the tropics to you.

XO Dana, Jen, and Bobbie Jo

Just then, I heard the sounds of waves fill the speakers in the house. It was a soothing sound on its own, and then the soft sound of steel drums started to echo throughout the house.

I grabbed a croissant, some mango slices, and a glass of pineapple juice before sitting down at the kitchen table. A silver bucket of bright colored gerbera daisies sat in the middle. I ate in silence, enjoying the peace, but I had a sneaking notion that I wasn't alone.

I finished my breakfast and heard a soft and unfamiliar female voice call my name from the foyer.

When I turned the corner, there was a petite

young woman dressed in black yoga pants and a soft green polo-style shirt. Her blonde hair was pulled back into a ponytail and she had a friendly smile.

"Good morning, Victoria. My name is Kim, and I'm here to give you a massage. I'm set up in the study and would like to begin your ninety-minute massage as soon as you're ready. You have a few other appointments scheduled today."

I'm sure the surprised look on my face was pretty damn funny alongside my appearance. Here I stood in the foyer wearing a pair of Caribbean blue plaid boxers and a pink T-shirt, and I was as bald as the day I was born, not to mention my mouth was hanging open.

The girls had arranged for a spa day in my house the day after chemo. My emotions started to bubble to the surface as I thought about how thoughtful they were and how much I needed this.

"Thank you," I sniffled as I smiled at Kim. "Let me step into the bathroom first, and then I'll be in."

She nodded with a smile. "Take your time," she said and disappeared back down the hallway.

When I arrived a few minutes later, the study was warm and the muted natural light streaming through the window was perfect. I noticed the massage table set up off to the side and more soft music playing.

"Come in," Kim said as she pulled back the top blanket on the table. "I'm going to step out so you can change. Undress as much as you're comfortable with and lie down on the table, face up." I nodded, and she stepped out of the room.

The massage table was heated, and I melted into it the moment I laid down.

Kim's hands felt magical as she massaged out every ounce of stress that was knotted throughout my body. I had finally let my body relax for the first time in months, but as she neared the point where I would need to roll over, I got nervous. The thought of lying on my front worried me, since I hadn't laid on it since before surgery.

"Let me help you roll over. I have a few bolsters that I will place under your shoulders and tummy that will help keep the pressure off your chest."

Relief washed over me as she got me situated. The bolsters made all the difference, and the next forty-five minutes passed by far too fast. I was beyond relaxed and was sure it would take a crane to get me off of the table.

"Take your time getting up. It was a pleasure to

work with you. I hope you enjoy the rest of your day." And with that, she disappeared.

A short time later, I peeled my body from the table and threw on my boxers and T-shirt. When I stepped out of the room, I found a path of hot pink and white rose petals leading upstairs. *Strange.*

The path led me through my bedroom and into the candlelit bathroom, where a warm bubble bath was waiting. I quickly tossed my clothes on the floor and sunk in. Once the water turned cool, I reached for a towel and heard a knock at the door.

"Yes?" I called out.

Dana poked her head in. "Hello, sweetheart. How are you feeling?"

"Like a limp noodle, thank you."

"You bet. I've laid out some pajamas for you to put on when you're ready. The girls and I will be downstairs waiting. Take your time." She gave me a wink before leaving the bathroom.

Lying on my bed was a hot pink Victoria's Secret pajama set and a pair of soft pink sandal slippers that were beaded and had a pink ribbon across the top. I smiled to myself. The name was correct, but I didn't have any secrets. Not anymore.

I arrived downstairs to Dana, Jen, and Bobbie Jo

all in the same pajama set, just different colors.

"There she is, looking relaxed and as beautiful as ever," Bobbie Jo said as she walked over to me with a tropical drink. "Don't worry. It's a mango smoothie, no alcohol. We wouldn't want to mess with your already drugged-up body by getting you drunk too."

Dana and Jen were both sitting on the floor of the living room. It was covered in blankets and pillows with a low table set in the middle with seashells, tropical flowers, and white sand. They brought paradise to me, and I didn't even have to leave my house. It was just what the doctor ordered.

"Pick a spot and sit your ass down," Bobbie Jo said as she led me to the two open spots on the floor.

I plopped down next to Dana, who had a sneaky smile covering her beautiful face. Tropical music began playing in the background, but it wasn't the soothing music from earlier. It was reggae music; Bob Marley was singing "Three Little Birds," when I heard the sound of a male voice.

"Are you ladies ready for the first course?"

I whipped my head around to see a man standing in my living room with nothing but a sexy smirk and pair of board shorts on. *Gulp*. He had spiky light brown hair, blazing green eyes, and his body was . . . I had no words. The boy was gorgeous.

"Yes, we are," Jen said, trying to suppress her shit-eating grin.

"Who the hell is that?" I asked after he stepped out of the room. I was suddenly feeling hot and bothered.

"That, my dear, is one of our cabana boys," Dana said with a devilish twinkle in her eye. "Wait until you see the other two."

"Oh. My. God," was all that I could say before Cabana Boy Number One appeared with a tray of tapas.

"Here you are, ladies. Can I get you anything else?"

"No," I said quickly, as I could see the wheels in Bobbie Jo's head kick into high gear. "We'll let you know when we are ready for the next course."

"Very well. Enjoy." He smiled before turning to leave. All four of us focused on his tight ass as it sauntered out of the room.

"What the fuck did you do that for?" Bobbie Jo sulked. "I wanted to see if he would lie down on the table so we could eat off of him. Nice job ruining all my fun."

Rolling my eyes, I filled my plate, as I was surprisingly hungry after the last few hours of relaxation.

Cabana Boy Number One returned a short time later with Cabana Boy Number Two, who had a similar look, but with dark black hair and a deeper tan. I swear they must have picked them up at Hollister. They cleared our plates and refilled our drinks before disappearing again.

I was pretty sure I was the only one with the nonalcoholic version, but I wasn't going to tempt fate by drinking. Someone had to stay sober, even though I was still highly medicated.

We made it through dinner, barely, without seeing Cabana Boy Number Three. My guess was he was the chef and we wouldn't be ogling over him. Oh well, the other two were easy on the eyes, and I definitely wasn't complaining. Hot barely dressed men were in my house . . . life was good.

Cabana Boy Number Two stepped toward me and offered me his hand. "Dessert will be served in the dining room."

Taking his hand, he helped me up, and the ladies were right behind me. The dining room was dim, but I could see candles flickering as we got closer.

Holy mother of all that is right in this world... thank you!

The dining room table was loaded with cupcakes, cookies, brownies, cheesecake, and other sticky, gooey treats. The crowning glory, however, was the platter they were served on... Cabana Boy Number Three.

Number Three was lying on my dining room table in a pair of snug swim shorts. He had shaggy blonde surfer-style hair, baby blue eyes, and lips that were made to suck on.

"Dig in ladies," Bobbie Jo said while assessing the situation. "I'll take the leftovers when you're done."

"I'll lick up the crumbs," Jen chimed in while wetting her lips.

I quickly grabbed a few sweet treats from an arm, ab, chest, and thigh before looking up at the sexy smirk on the man who surprisingly didn't have a tent in his shorts. Scratch that, there was suddenly a little movement in the area and I wasn't the only one to notice. Actually, upon further inspection, there was nothing "little" about it. I quickly turned on my heel and headed back to the living room...

and noticed that nobody else followed.

When I arrived back in the living room, the other two cabana boys were straightening up the pillows on the floor.

"How are you doing?" Number Two asked as he helped me sit back down.

"I'm good, thanks." I put my plate down and looked back up at him. "Can I ask you a question?"

"You sure can," he said as he sat down next to me. Number One followed suit and sat on the other side of the table.

"How the hell did you get roped into doing this?"

"One of your friends called in a favor from a friend of ours, and here we are," he said with a laugh. "He warned us about Bobbie Jo, but said it would be good fun, and he was right."

Number One chimed in, "You ladies are quite entertaining, and we couldn't help but overhear your dinner conversations." He was blushing. "I can only imagine what would happen if you were all out on the town."

"Next time we go out, we'll invite you to join us," Jen said as she took a seat next to Number One. I assumed Dana and Bobbie Jo were still drooling over the dessert table and hopefully not licking or sucking on him.

"Definitely give us a call when you do. You would be a lot of fun to party with," Number Two commented.

"I agree. The six of you would have a blast," I said between bites of my brownie.

"Six of us? What about you?" Jen asked with a look of confusion on her face.

"You'll have to wait a few months before I'm ready for a night on the town, and you ladies shouldn't have to wait that long. Go out and have fun, but I expect all the juicy details."

The three of them started laughing as Dana, Bobbie Jo, and Number Three entered the room.

He was surprisingly cleaned up and sat between Dana and Bobbie Jo with a naughty smirk on his face. I didn't want to know what put that look there, but the girls both looked like the cat that swallowed the canary.

Oh. God. *Swallowed the canary?* The image was forever etched in my mind now. I may need to bleach my eyes.

Over the next few hours, the seven of us laughed. The guys even helped clean everything up.

It was only eight o'clock, but I was exhausted. "I think I'm going to head up to bed. It has been a wonderful and relaxing day, but my pillow needs some head and my sheets need some ass." I smiled before continuing, "You ladies behave yourselves. Boys, make sure you cover *it* up."

I heard them all gasp as I turned toward the doorway to leave; a pillow flew by my head as I left the room.

"Good night," I hollered back, trying to contain my laugh.

Chapter Seventeen
I AM GOOD

The next week went by without incident, and I was heading to the doctor for my next expander fill. Bobbie Jo and Jen insisted on driving me, but I wanted my independence back and refused both of them. This last round of chemo was so much better than the last four rounds, I felt almost human again . . . almost.

I stopped at my attorney's office on the way to my appointment so I could sign the divorce papers. Noah hadn't reached out to me after our meeting, and there was nothing left to discuss; his mind was made up. There was no point in trying; it would have only made me feel shittier about myself. Our past was just that . . . the past. It was time to move on.

I signed the papers on my terms and not out of pressure from him. He had everything set up for me, and I was told that we would need to wait for the judge to sign the papers for it to be final. The emotional wounds were still deep, but I didn't have the energy to drag myself back down. I tucked everything that had to do with Noah in the far dark corner of my brain and walked away. Chapter closed.

Dr. McGuire was ready for me when I arrived, and before my butt could touch the seat in the waiting room, I was called back. She was still the ever chipper and lovely doctor from our last appointment, and she seemed genuinely happy to see me again.

"How are you feeling today? I have to say you look a little more relaxed."

"I'm feeling good. My friends planned something special for me, and it was just what I needed to pick me up. It has been a rough few months, but I'm getting closer to the finish line. I can see it in the distance."

"That's great. I know it's been a long road, and you've done an amazing job. I'm happy to see you smiling a genuine smile."

"Thank you," I said as I laid back against the table so she could begin the expander fill.

I did really like her, but I missed seeing Dr. Forrester. He had a calming effect about him that made me feel comfortable. Not that Dr. McGuire didn't, but there was something about a male doctor that made me feel safe.

"Well, it looks like we only need to do two more fills before you're expanded to where I want you to be," she said as she helped me sit up.

"Really? This is going faster than I thought it would." I pulled my gown closed.

"It will take about six weeks after your last fill before we can replace the expanders with permanent implants." She flipped through my file. "Did you still want to go with the silicone?"

"Yes. They felt more natural, and these expanders hurt like hell. Sorry, I just want something soft in my chest," I answered flatly. She didn't pick up on my disappointed tone.

"I think you will be very happy with your choice," she said as she closed my file and stood to leave. "I'll be scheduling your surgery before you know it."

"That's great, thank you."

Once she left, I changed and started assessing my chemo and expander fill dates to occupy my mind. I was upset about the change in my doctor that was, apparently, made for me. Grabbing my purse, I stepped out into the hallway.

"Hi, Victoria," a deep, familiar voice said. I looked up to find Dr. Forrester leaning against the wall in the hallway. He was wearing a dark suit with a blue tie and had his arms folded across his chest. What caught my attention most of all was the smile on his face. It was a friendly and relaxed smile, which stunned me completely.

"Dr. Forrester," I said in surprise. "I didn't think you were in the office today. I tried to get an appointment with you but was told you were out."

"I'm sorry—my schedule has been a bit hectic lately," he said as he stood up and walked toward me. "I'm glad I caught you. Do you have a few minutes to talk privately?"

I swallowed hard. I already knew what he wanted to talk about. He wasn't going to be my doctor anymore because I put him in an awkward position. "Yes, I have time."

"Great," he said. "Follow me."

I followed him down the hall to his office feeling like a high school student making the walk of shame to the principal's office. My heart rate was through the roof and my palms were cold and sweaty.

As I stepped into his office, my eyes were immediately drawn to a beautiful mahogany desk that was set in front of a row of windows. Two wingback chairs sat in front of it.

Off to the side was a sitting area. It was more inviting with a beautiful Persian rug, a small love seat, and two overstuffed chairs set around a beautiful glass table. Two Tiffany-style lamps completed the look, giving off a warm, comforting glow.

I looked back when I heard him shut the door, and he held his hand out, guiding me to take a seat in the sitting area. I moved to one of the club-style chairs and took a seat. I would have preferred to do this with a desk between us because it would feel more like business; this felt more personal, and I felt vulnerable.

"So, what do you think of Dr. McGuire?" he asked in a direct but casual way.

My stomach was in knots. "She's very nice."

"That she is... I'm glad you like her. She's also an excellent surgeon." He paused and I nodded to him to continue because I knew what was coming next. "I've asked her to take over your care going forward."

It took everything I had to hold back the tears that were threatening my eyes. "I understand," I said as I shifted in my chair to stand, but he placed his hand on my knee, telling me that I wasn't excused.

"No, I don't think you do understand," he said with genuineness in his voice. "I would like to explain."

I took a deep breath as the tears I had so desperately tried to hold back began to trickle onto my cheeks.

Dr. Forrester reached for a box of tissues and handed it to me. "It's going to be okay. I promise. Why don't you take a few minutes to collect yourself? I'm going to step out to get you a glass of water."

When I heard the door click shut, I let out the breath I had apparently been holding. Here I sat, a grown woman, crying in the office of my doctor who transferred my care to another because of my big mouth. It wasn't possible to feel like a bigger fool. I'd lost my husband and now my doctor. One more strike, and I was out. You couldn't make this shit up.

I needed to get out of there as fast as I could. I looked around for a secret door to escape out of, but it wasn't there. Whatever he had to say, I would just agree to it so I could get out of there. I was tired of feeling like a failure. I dried my eyes and focused on calming my breathing before he came back.

"Here you go," he said as he placed the glass of water in my hand and sat back down.

I plastered a fake smile on my face before I looked up at him. "Thank you."

"You're welcome. I'm worried about you."

"Don't be. I'll be okay. I know I put you in an uncomfortable position. It was inappropriate of me to tell you my personal problems, and I'm fine with seeing Dr. McGuire going forward. I'm sorry if I crossed the line. It wasn't my intention."

"You did no such thing, and you have nothing to be sorry for. I'm the one who needs to apologize for how I've acted since then. I needed time to figure out how to handle this situation appropriately." He took the water from me and placed it on the table before shifting his body so he was sitting on the edge of his chair turned toward me.

"Victoria, Dr. McGuire has agreed to take on your case as a favor to me. My reason for wanting you to change doctors is a selfish one and not because of anything you have said or done."

My eyes started to fill again, and I looked away to try and stop them, but it was no use. I gave up trying to hold them back and was positive I would become dehydrated just from the tears I had shed these last few weeks.

"Please don't cry," he said as he moved to crouch down in front of me. "Look at me."

It took everything I could to look at him. When I finally managed to, I didn't recognize the man kneeling in front of me. The confident doctor I had come to know wasn't there; instead he seemed nervous and uncertain. "Victoria, I cannot be your doctor anymore for professional and legal reasons."

"Stop," I sobbed. "I can't listen to this anymore. I just signed divorce papers two hours ago, and the last thing I need are more legal issues. Please, just stop, I . . ."

Dr. Forrester put his hand over my mouth, and my eyes grew to the size of saucers in surprise.

"Victoria, I cannot be your doctor because I'm

attracted to you. I want to explore my options with you and get to know you personally."

The room was silent. He was now communicating with me through his eyes, and the realization of what he said finally hit me.

"I'm sorry, can you repeat that?" I whispered.

"I would like to get to know you better and ask you out on a date. When you're ready to date of course," he said clearly; however, I could still sense a hint of nervousness in his voice. "I've never been in this position with a patient. I've been attracted to you from the moment I met you. I shamelessly called you personally to check in and purposely spent extra time with you during your visits because there was something about you that made me feel something I've never felt before. I knew it was wrong because you were married, but I couldn't get you out of my mind."

He looked down at my hands, which were now fidgeting in my lap, and reached over to pull them into his own. The warmth of his touch comforted me as he continued, "When you told me Noah had left you at our last appointment, it really threw me, and I needed time to think. There were steps I needed to take professionally if I wanted to clear the way to see you on a personal level, that is, if you were truly available . . . and you just confirmed it."

"Pinch me."

Dr. Forrester looked surprised. "I'm sorry, what?"

"Pinch me. This can't be real, I must be dreaming."

"I will not pinch you," he said, as he let go of my hands and moved back to his chair. "You're not dreaming. I would like to take you out for coffee after you've had time to process what I've just told you. I need to be sure that you're okay with my decision to turn your care over to Dr. McGuire and not just because I decided it for you. That was presumptuous of me. I made note in your chart that I would be referring you to her care after our last visit four weeks ago."

"You did?"

"Yes, I did. Victoria, I'm serious. I want to get to know you, and I want you to get to know me. Meeting for coffee would allow us a chance to talk outside of this office and see if this is something we both want to pursue, if and when you're ready. Would you be willing to meet me for coffee?"

I wasn't prepared for what he just dropped on

my lap. It was a shock to my system, and while a part of me wanted to scream *yes* right then and there, I couldn't. "I need to think about it. I honestly don't believe this is happening. I need to figure out where my head is at and if I'm ready to date someone. This is all so new to me, and it's overwhelming."

"I appreciate your honesty and don't want to pressure you into something you aren't ready for." He reached for a business card on the table and wrote on it. "I put my mobile number on the back of the card for you. Call me if you want to meet. No rush."

I took the card and put it in my purse before moving to stand. "Thank you for being candid with me and sharing your feelings. I know it wasn't easy for you, and I admire that. I'll be in touch."

"I look forward to hearing from you, Victoria." He stood and held out his hand for me to make my way to the door.

I wasn't sure what the proper etiquette was in this situation, so I put my hand out to shake his. He took my hand, raised it to his mouth, and placed a soft kiss on it. "Have a good afternoon, Victoria." I felt a shiver run down my spine and felt my cheeks flush.

"You too, Dr. Forrester."

"Blake." He released my hand and opened the door for me like a gentleman. "Please call me Blake."

I started to step out the door and looked back over my shoulder before I was completely in the hallway. "Thank you, Blake. We'll talk soon." I smiled and nervously walked out of his office, trying to focus on not falling.

When I got home, I felt giddy and needed to talk to someone. Jen was at a work function so I called Bobbie Jo instead. I wanted to explode over the phone to her, but instead asked her to pick up Chinese and come over.

Thirty minutes later, she pushed her way through my front door. "What the hell is going on? I haven't heard you that frantic in months. Is everything okay?"

"Yes. Everything is good. I just needed to talk to somebody about what happened at the doctor's office today. I need your honest advice, and if there is one thing I know about you, it's that you're honest—sometimes too honest." I rolled my eyes.

"I saw that," she said as she put the bag down on the counter and pulled out the containers and chopsticks. "Plates or containers?"

"Containers."

She sat down next to me at the breakfast bar. "Okay, spill it."

"I had my appointment with Dr. McGuire today, and when I was leaving, Dr. Forrester was waiting for me in the hallway."

She choked on a noodle. "He was waiting for you in what sense? Like he was upset with you, or like he wanted to pin you to the wall and make you his?"

"Would you stop?" I shook my head. "He wanted to talk to me in private to discuss moving my case to Dr. McGuire permanently. He isn't going to be my surgeon anymore." I dug into my container of pot stickers and made her sweat it out, like I did.

"What the fuck? He dumped you as a patient because of what happened? Jen told me how you lost it the last time you saw him. What an asshole."

"Easy, tiger." I laughed at her protectiveness of me. "Before you start chastising him, there's more... He asked me to meet him for coffee to talk."

The room was silent for the second time today, and I looked over at Bobbie Jo. Her mouth was hanging open, and her eyes were bugging out of her head. "Dr. McHottie wants to do the McNaughty with you! Damn girl."

"No! I'm not jumping in the sack with the man," I said before I told her the story about how he needed to make sure Dr. McGuire would take my case before he could pursue talking with me. It would be inappropriate for a doctor to ask out a patient. "He wants to meet over coffee."

"Open your eyes. If you think he just wants coffee, you're blind. He wants you. What doctor would go through all of that if he just wanted coffee?"

I was so confused. "Isn't it too early for me to consider coffee with a man? I'm in the middle of cancer treatment, and I've only been separated for a month and just signed the divorce papers this morning. Isn't it too soon?"

"Hell no! You signed the papers. Noah is off in Slutville, and Dr. McHottie is clearly interested in you; there are no rules on meeting for coffee. Seriously, nothing stopped Noah from fucking someone while he was still married."

My quick intake of breath caught her attention.

"Oh shit, I'm sorry, Victoria. I didn't mean to

say it like that." She quietly cursed herself out. "I just wanted to make the point that this life is yours to live and do with what you want. Nobody makes the rules but you, and as long as you aren't hurting anyone with your decision, why are you worried? We aren't going to judge you. How could we? We haven't walked a step in your shoes, and if you want to meet Dr. Forrester for coffee, you should. Nobody is stopping you but yourself."

"Blake. His name is Blake. He told me after he kissed my hand good-bye."

"Why are you hesitating? The signs are all there. What harm is coffee going to do? What are you afraid of?"

"I'm afraid of getting in over my head and having feelings for him only to have my heart crushed again. Noah stomped on my heart so quickly, and I'm not sure I have fully recovered, even though I know it was over long ago," I admitted as I put down my chopsticks and pushed the container away. "He's a successful and attractive doctor who can have any woman he wants. Why would he want me?"

"That's something you need to ask him."

I sat quietly, trying to process my conversations

with Blake and Bobbie Jo and how I truly felt. I was excited about the prospect of seeing him again, but I was afraid of getting my hopes up and eventually having everything come crashing down on me. Was now even the right time? I was just barely halfway through treatment, and I still had a long road ahead with the reconstruction and healing.

I couldn't put myself in a situation that could potentially hurt me more. I excused myself from the kitchen and grabbed my phone before disappearing into the study.

My hands were trembling as I reached for the business card in my purse and dialed the number written on the back of it. It began ringing and after the third ring, I assumed it would go to voice mail. Typically, most people answer by the second ring. I was wrong.

"Hello?"

The End

Acknowledgments

On September 21, 2013, I messaged a friend with a crazy idea to write a book about a woman with breast cancer. I wasn't expecting her to challenge me to write 1,500 words that night, but she did, and I wrote them. They were crap, but they were the beginning of a story. This story. A story that quickly grew to 100,000 words before my eyes. I wrote at night, while my kids were at dance. I wrote on the weekends, when I should've been cleaning. I wrote in my head in the middle of the night, and grabbed a post-it note to write it down. I made the decision to split it into two books because I wasn't close to being done, and I didn't want to rush Victoria's story.

Here I sit, one year from when it all started, and I'm hitting the publish button. It was just an idea and a challenge. I'm not one to turn down a challenge.

This wouldn't be possible without a bunch of amazing people. I wrote down the name of everyone who helped me so I wouldn't forget . . . however, I forgot where I put this list. It's in a special place, of that I'm sure, and I'm sorry if I left anyone out. It was not intentional, and according to my oncologist, I can still claim chemo-brain!

Jack and my little crazies, thank you for your love, support, encouragement, and excitement for me in this journey. I have the best husband, daughters, co-survivors, cheerleaders, and housekeepers a woman could ask for! I love you all to the moon and back . . .

Beth, you are the reason this book was written. If it wasn't for your challenge, I wouldn't be writing this acknowledgment. You gave me the courage to pour my heart out onto paper, and tell a story that will hopefully make a difference in the life of *a* woman. Just one woman. That was my goal from the start. Thank you for your love, support, kindness, feedback, and your sense of humor. You said you were going to "ride my ass, until I hit publish," and that you did! You are a blessing in every sense of the word . . .

Bobbie Jo and **Whitney**, my "Costa Rica Hotties". The two of you have been by my side from those first horribly written words, and you continued to read until the end. You were there for me when I began to question myself and my ability to write. I couldn't have arrived to this day without your constructive criticism and numerous brainstorming sessions. I love you both for all you have done, and most of all for your friendship. I'd be lost without you two . . .

Cara, you have been my sanity for the last few months. Your calming voice, willingness to help, and ability to make me smile will never be forgotten. We jumped into this "world" together and I couldn't have asked for a better friend along the way. I see lots of cookies, cocktails and the spa in our future . . .

Amanda Krause, my hero. Fate was on my side when I found you. I was so nervous when I emailed the first ten pages to you, just to see if you were interested. When you responded the next day that you were, I cried. You took my baby and you worked your magic. When the document came back with a few thousand noted revisions, I spent twelve hours going through each and every one of them one-by-one. While it was a tedious process, I can't thank you enough for your expertise and attention to detail. I look forward to working with you again on book two . . .

Jen, **MJ**, **Rose**, and **Valerie**, between the four of you, my horribly written first words morphed into something actually readable. Your comments and corrections were paramount to the final product. Thank you for taking the time to read my book in draft form, and for giving me your unconditional love and support through it all! I lucked out by gaining some pretty fabulous friends in the process . . .

Ginny, **Jen (#2)**, **Kara**, **Keshia**, **Kizzy**, **Shannon**, **Stacy**, **and Teri**, where do I start? This amazing group of ladies made up my beta readers. Some are old friends, and some are new. One is a sonographer (thank you for the technical linguistics), three are authors, and one is even my daughters' dance teacher. Your feedback, positive and not-so-positive, was pivotal in helping me write scenes that made sense to a wide range of readers. Thank you from the bottom of my heart for reading and sharing your thoughts . . .

Beth (#2), **Candace**, **Dana**, **Danielle**, **Jenny**, **Jennifer**, **Kristin**, **Lauren**, **Renee**, **Tammy**, **Tina**, **and Vi**, friendship knows no bounds. Each of you have been an important part of this journey. Some of you have read snippets of my book and provided feedback. Some of you have provided professional guidance in writing and design. And, some of you were by my side when I fought my own battle with breast cancer. The one thing you all have in common is your ability to make me smile and bring me joy. You have made a positive impact on my life, and you all hold a special place in my heart . . .

Random fact: I have a lot of Jen, Jennys and Jennifers in my life!

Last, but not least, **thank you to the readers.** Thank you for taking a chance on me by reading my debut novel. I hope you enjoyed reading it and much as I enjoyed writing it. My ultimate goal in writing this story was to bring awareness to breast cancer. I encourage you to pay attention to your body and perform monthly breast self-exams. *While this is a fictional story, the reality of breast cancer, and what it's capable of doing, is not.*

Beneath You're Beautiful, book two in the Beneath Series, is tentatively scheduled for release on March 24, 2015. I can't wait to share the conclusion to Victoria's story with you!

Did you enjoy *Beneath It All*? If so, please feel free to leave a review on Goodreads and retailers.
goodreads.com/book/show/22602764-beneath-it-all

About the Author

Happily married and the mother of two, Tori Madison, is active in the world of philanthropy and finds joy in making a difference in lives of others. She is an avid reader, lover of life and a breast cancer survivor. Currently residing with her family in Minnesota, she can often be found at Caribou Coffee or at the dance studio with her kids. With a well-known weakness for dark chocolate with sea salt and cheesecake, she also has a fondness for chips and fresh salsa.

Writing a book was never on her radar. After a challenge from a friend to write 1,500 words the story came to life and a new opportunity to make a difference was born.

Beneath It All is her debut novel.

Contact Tori

Email:
authortorimadison@gmail.com

Facebook:
www.facebook.com/ToriMadisonAuthor

Twitter:
twitter.com/authortorimadis

Pinterest:
www.pinterest.com/authortorimadis

Goodreads:
goodreads.com/author/show/8342405.Tori_Madison

Made in the USA
Charleston, SC
01 December 2015